SEAL of HONOR

Iron Tide Brotherhood
Book One

Jessica Ashley

B.A.D. PUBLISHING CO
believing in the power of reading

Iron Tide Brotherhood
Chronological
Reading Order

While the books in the Iron Tide Brotherhood series are written in a way that you *can* read in any order, I do recommend you read in this order to avoid any possible spoilers.

Happy reading!

1. SEAL of Honor
2. SEAL of Bravery
3. *Coming soon*
4. *Coming soon*
5. *Coming soon*

SEAL of Honor
Iron Tide Brotherhood Book 1
By Jessica Ashley
Copyright © 2025. All rights reserved.

Scripture used in this novel comes from HOLY BIBLE, New Living Translation®, NLT®.
Used by permission. All rights reserved worldwide.

Edited by The Editing Soprano
Proofread by Love Kissed Books, LLC
Proofread by Dawn Y.
Cover Design by Covers by Christian

SEAL of Honor

She disappeared on their wedding day. Now she's back, and someone wants her dead.

Zane Knox is a man who doesn't exist. The former Navy SEAL has spent years buried in the shadows, forced into off-books missions for a government agency that doesn't technically exist. He doesn't do it because he wants to...he does it because, if he refuses, the secrets he carries will send him to prison.

He's made peace with living as a ghost. Until the woman who left him at the altar shows up on his boat, battered and begging for medical supplies.

Tessa Lane doesn't know who is after her or why, only that nowhere is safe. She no longer believes in God, in love, or the vows she nearly made to Zane. But when the past collides with a deadly present, she has no choice but to trust the one man she swore she'd never face again.

Protecting her may be Zane's mission, but restoring Tessa's faith—and rekindling the love he never gave up on—is a fight he refuses to lose.

Even if it costs him everything.

Explosive action. Unfinished business. And a second chance worth dying for.

Authors Note

This one was a rough one to write.

Not because of the story itself, but because I spent most of the time stuck in doubt mode where every word I wrote felt wrong. Nothing felt like it hit the feeling I was going for.

For the first time, I had to push an editing date back multiple times because I just couldn't move past it. But after a lot of prayers, some tears, and moments of absolute frustration, SEAL of Honor was finally finished.

Now, I love this story. The characters, the faith, the fight. Every word of it. But I was so afraid that it was only one-sided. That the rest of the story wouldn't resonate the way I wanted it to.

When I sent it off to the editor, I was sure that she was going to write back and tell me that I needed to start over.

That I missed the mark and it was time to return to square one.

I was *so sure* of it that I even hesitated to open up her email when she finally did send it back.

When I finally decided I couldn't hide from it forever and opened it, instead of what I'd feared, she'd written: "I'm confident that the reason you struggled so mightily is that you are doing Kingdom work."

Kingdom work.

Those two words hit me square in the chest, and I just sat there, staring at them, tears in my eyes. Because Kingdom work is exactly what I wanted to do.

When I made the switch to writing Christian Romance, I knew that I wanted to tell stories that would not only bring glory to God but hopefully help point people to Him. To the love He offers and the hope we have in Jesus Christ.

But there was still a part of me that was nervous about how it would be received. After all, I come from a side of the book world where mentioning your faith is the fastest way to end up cancelled. (*Which is INSANE, of course*.)

The further I've gotten into this journey, though, the more I've prayed for boldness in my faith. For strength and courage, and the words to speak the truth, no matter what circumstance I'm faced with.

I think of Stephen in Acts, and how he refused to speak anything but the truth, even though he was stoned to death for it.

I think of Paul and how he spoke of love and hope even as he sat behind prison bars.

I think of the apostles, who continued to speak the truth even as they were imprisoned, tortured, and killed for it.

They all showed boldness in the face of a world determined to drown out their voices.

I definitely can't help but draw parallels to the world we're living in today, where speaking the truth can lead to losing one's life.

Still, I pray for that kind of courage.

For the kind of boldness that inspires.

That defends.

That spreads the Good News about Jesus and the hope that comes from believing in Him.

I mean, it is literally THE BEST news. We are ALL sinners. Each and every one of us. And that sin separates us from God. But because of Jesus Christ, the Son of God, we can be reborn. Because of His sacrifice, we can spend an eternity of peace in The Kingdom.

In SEAL of Honor, Zane boldly proclaims his faith to Tessa, despite the doubt she carries. I believe we all will cross paths with a Tessa at some point in our lives, and I pray that we are all granted the same boldness to defend our faith and to point others to Jesus so they might also find the salvation He grants us.

As we move forward, let us all pray for boldness and for hearts that always speak out of love. Even in moments where we are faced with hate.

Choose love.

Choose Him.

Choose forgiveness. For others…and yourself.

And with every single book I write, I pray that I am doing Kingdom Work. That I am being a light amidst a world of darkness.

Every story I write has a verse that leads as its inspiration, as the focal point of the faith journey. For SEAL of Honor, that verse is Ephesians 2:8-10: "God saved you by His grace when you believed. And you can't take credit for this; it is a gift from God. Salvation is not a reward for the good things we have done, so none of us can boast about it. For we are God's masterpiece. He has created us anew in Christ Jesus, so we can do the good things He planned for us long ago."

Our salvation is His gift to us.

Let's go out and tell the world about it so that they can find the peace that comes with knowing Him, too.

-Love always,

Jessica

A meaty fist slams into my face, and pain radiates through my jaw, spreading up into my head and down my neck. It's a dull pain, not sharp or stinging anymore, thanks to the dozens of times I was hit before I lost count.

I spit blood to the side and grin up at the man standing above me. His face is shielded by a mask, but I can *feel* the anger radiating off of him. "Hey now, that one didn't hurt as bad. Are you going soft on me, Killer?" I ask, doing my best to keep my tone level.

It's not fear that has me wavering. No, I ran out of fear a long time ago. This is pure exhaustion, dehydration, and the fact that I haven't eaten anything in at least twenty-four hours.

Then again, if he keeps this up, I'll likely never eat anything solid again.

The man rears his fist back again—

"Wait! I'll talk!" Sawyer Maddox, a member of my team, calls out from across the room. Like me and the other captured member of my team, Ryker Granger, his hands and feet are bound to a metal chair. He's sitting at the edge of the blacked-out basement, his face bloodied and swollen just like the rest of ours.

Though Killer here has definitely taken a liking to messing up my face over theirs.

"Keep your mouth closed," Ryker growls. He's the largest of all of us, built like an actual tank and currently being held to his chair with chains since he managed to snap the ropes they'd bound him with the first time.

If he weren't on my side? *Then* I might be slightly intimidated. But scared? Nah. Because I know I have God with me, and with Him at my side, what should I fear?

Death can do nothing to me since I put my faith in Jesus Christ.

"No," Sawyer snaps. "You might be okay with them using Cap's face as a punching bag, but I'm not, okay?" He feigns tortured emotion and closes his eyes.

I grin because I know what's coming. I've seen Sawyer stare down the barrel of a rifle with a smile on his face. There's no way he'll bow down now.

But they don't know that. And the nature of the game? Delay until the cavalry shows up.

"Talk," the man wearing my blood like a glove orders, his finger pointed directly at Sawyer.

"Okay." Sawyer takes a deep breath. "It was me," he says. "I'm the one who took your sister out last night. Listen, I know we stayed out late, but it was all honorable. You have my word. I didn't even—" Sawyer's words are cut off when Killer charges across the small room and slams his fist into his face.

"I told you to keep your mouth closed," Ryker says, chuckling.

Sawyer laughs and spits his blood onto the concrete floor. "Yeah, but then I would have missed out on that sweet little love tap." I'm pretty sure he winks, but with one eye completely swollen shut, it's also possible he was just blinking.

"Look, how about a little quid pro quo?" I ask. "You answer my questions, and I'll answer yours."

"Do you think that's how this works?" Killer snarls and turns back toward me. Reaching down into his boot, he straightens and withdraws a blade nearly as long as my forearm.

Okay, maybe things are getting a *bit* more heated now.

Lord, please be with us here in this room. If it is Your will, please let us walk out of this. Amen. As I pray, peace washes over me. Death doesn't scare me. It never has. Maybe that's why I'm as good at this as I am? Because I know that, no matter what happens to me here, I'm going somewhere better.

Both Sawyer and Ryker have gone completely silent,

their serious gazes trained intently on the man in front of me. So far, he's the only one in this room, though I know there are plenty more above ground. We saw them firsthand when we infiltrated this place, looking for the missing teenage daughter of a French diplomat yesterday.

Unfortunately, the intel we were given was flawed, and there were far more guns within the walls than we anticipated. Hence, the whole being tied to a chair thing. It's also what's kept the cavalry so long. Dealing with that many opposing forces takes planning and precision.

The man closes the distance between us and presses the cold blade against my cheek. "How about I start removing things and we see just how brave you are then?" he questions, dragging the blade up toward my ear.

Come on, Demo. Bring the rain.

Even as I think the thought, a roaring explosion rocks the very ground we're sitting on. Overhead, the ceiling opens, and rubble rains down on top of us. Chunks of the ceiling slam into me, and pain radiates through my head.

But it can't steal the joy in my heart because this is about to be nice and wrapped up in a tight little bow.

My attacker leaps backward, and I use his momentary distraction to lean down and slice the ropes at my ankles, utilizing the handy blade I'd managed to keep hidden in the hem of my sleeve. I'd managed to cut my arms free at least an hour ago, which made taking those hits even more difficult. But making a move before I knew it was clear upstairs could have led to my taking something a lot more permanent than a punch.

I kick the knife away from him and flip him over, pressing my knee to his back as dust fills my lungs.

I cover my mouth and nose with one arm and cough, hoping to get as much of it out as I can while the air continues to clear.

"You guys miss me?" Garrison Holt calls down with a sly smile on his face, a detonator in his hand.

"Took you long enough," Sawyer calls back as he stands and stretches.

"Sorry, Cowboy and I had our hands full up here. You guys couldn't have handled at least a few of them for us?" he jokes as he tosses a ladder down into the pit. "How long did it take you to break through those ropes?" he asks.

"Not long," Sawyer calls out. "Less time than Tank here—" He turns toward Ryker, who is still sitting in his chair, chains around him. "Oh, sorry, big guy. Forgot you were in chains."

"You let Sawyer beat you, Tank?" Garrison asks.

"Hardly. They just caught me first."

"That's because you used your brute strength to break out while Cap and I used sleuthing skills." Sawyer continues to work on Ryker's bindings, so I shift my attention back to the man pinned beneath me.

"Where is the girl, Killer?" I demand, grabbing a handful of his hair with one hand and pressing my own blade against his throat. I won't actually kill him—not when the active threat is over—but he doesn't know that.

Besides, there are plenty of ways to make someone talk without threatening their life.

"You'll never make it out of here alive," he growls.

"You seriously underestimate our resourcefulness," Sawyer calls out.

Ryker eats up the ground between where he'd been chained and where I'm kneeling, so I straighten and flip the guy over onto his back. I remove Killer's mask, revealing a glorified sorority boy in *way* over his head. Apparently, the government is recruiting straight out of college these days.

"If you don't tell me, I'm going to let Tank here treat you like a chew toy," I warn him.

In pure Ryker fashion, he growls, and Sorority Boy's eyes widen almost comically.

"She's upstairs. Top floor," he sings like a canary. *Beautiful.*

"Great. Demo, care to do the honors?"

"Absolutely."

"Smile," I say as I hold his face up in front of mine so Garrison can snap a photo. Then, I throw him to the side. "Stay, and be a good boy. We have someone coming to collect you. If you run, we'll find you. We love playing hide and seek. Don't we, Tank?"

"My favorite," he replies, then rears back and slams his fist into Sorority Boy's face. He falls back, unconscious, and Ryker turns toward the ladder. "Just making sure he doesn't run," he adds when I shake my head at him.

Ryker is the first up the ladder, then Sawyer, then me. As I reach the top, Garrison pulls up the ladder. Rubble blocked the only door in or out, so without the ladder, he'll have an interesting time trying to escape.

There are at least half a dozen men on the ground, scattered throughout what used to be a foyer. Given the bullet holes in the glass and the blood spatter on the floor, I know this was Cowboy's doing. Considering how fast he is, he likely took the last one down before any of them even realized what was going on.

The death makes my stomach churn, but sometimes there is no other way. And in this war? It's us or them. With a teenage girl added to the death toll should we fail.

Reaching down onto the floor, I lift a discarded weapon, then check it for ammunition. Since they relieved us of our weapons when they grabbed us, both Sawyer and Ryker do the same as I, arming themselves with whatever they can find.

"You know there was a door," Sawyer tells Garrison. "You didn't have to blow a hole in the place."

Garrison shrugs. "It would have taken too long to find it. Besides, then I wouldn't have had the amazing entrance I got."

"Yeah, well, let's hope they didn't hear the explosion and kill the girl." I start toward the stairs. "Cowboy, do you read?" I ask through the earpiece our lovely hosts didn't check for when they searched us. Lungs still burning from the rubble, I cough. As is protocol, we'd gone radio silent the moment the three of us were abducted.

"Loud and clear, Cap," Weston Hayes, my oldest friend, replies. After the last few hours, his smooth southern drawl is a welcome sound. I'm far from being the rank of Captain—especially since I technically no longer serve in the Navy—but it's a nickname that's been with me for nearly a decade. "Things are quiet out here. I took out the two guards at the top of the stairs. You should be clear going up, but I can't get a visual on the girl. All the windows are closed up."

His tone is strained, and I know it's because this mission is hitting close to home. It's that way for all of us, but for a guy who lost his younger sister at the same age this girl is, he's struggling. I only hope this has a happier ending than the tragic story that ripped apart what remained of his family after his dad abandoned them.

"We'll get to her. Everything else clear?"

"Crystal," he replies.

"Great." I turn to survey my team. Even dirtied and bloodied, there's no other group of men I would count on to have my back. They're the best of the best. And I'm lucky to serve beside them. "Let's go find this girl and get her home."

"On you, Cap," Sawyer says as he raises his weapon at the ready.

With a final nod, I turn and raise my weapon then head

for the stairs. Cowboy was right, and both men at the top of the stairs are down, their eyes frozen open, pulses nonexistent.

God, please let her be alive.

Please don't let us be too late.

I pause by the door and hold up a fist for my team to pause, too. Pressing my ear to the door to listen for any sounds, I gently close one hand around the handle and try to turn it. The door's locked, and I hear nothing on the other side.

If she were dead, they wouldn't have kept the door locked.

Either she's in there alone—or she's not. But my hope that we'll find her alive grows.

Adrenaline pumping through my veins, I shove the anger down to keep a clear head. Details matter in moments like this. Emotions will blur already distorted lines.

Glancing back at my team, I motion for Ryker to come around. He offers me a slight nod, and I raise my weapon all the way, training the barrel on the door. Ryker raises a heavy boot and slams it into the door.

It splinters, and we move in as one.

It takes less than a heartbeat to get inside, but that heartbeat feels like it takes hours when I see a silver blade pressed to the throat of a trembling teenage girl. Her blue eyes are wide and terrified, her cheeks dirty, trails of tears cutting through the grime.

The man behind her glares at me, dark eyes darting

back and forth between me and the rest of my team. He's sizing us up. Trying to decide if he has a chance. Given that he used to be one of us, he likely knows he doesn't.

"Come on, Martin, you know the only way you're walking out of this is if you let her go," I warn, my weapon trained on him and the girl since I can't get a clear shot through her, considering the coward is using her as a shield.

"You're on the wrong side," he snaps.

"You've got that backward, Bud," Sawyer comments. "Good guys don't kidnap terrified teenage girls. No matter the circumstances. I always knew you were a loose cannon."

"Please," she whimpers, the word barely audible with her thick accent and the terror in her tone. "Let me go."

"Shut up!" Martin yells, pulling her tighter against him. She cries out, and a bead of crimson drips down the side of her throat where the bite of the blade got her.

I glance at Sawyer. Then Ryker. Then one final look in Garrison's direction.

Their gazes say the same thing I'm thinking: Martin is going to kill her as soon as he comes to the understanding that he's not leaving here a free man. He knows he's going down, and he'll take her with him just to cause as much damage as he can.

Something I can't allow.

"It's going to be okay," I tell the girl. "Okay?"

Her eyes widen, but she takes a deep breath.

I squeeze the trigger.

The gunshot is deafening in this small room, and the girl screams in pain as the bullet rips through the meat of her shoulder and slams into her abductor. Martin releases her and stumbles backward. Both Ryker and Sawyer move in on him while I rush for the girl.

Garrison is already getting his med kit ready to go while I lay my weapon aside and apply pressure.

"I'm sorry," I tell her. "I had no choice."

"I-I know," she whimpers. Tears stream down her face. "My dad. I want my dad. Can I go home now?" she sobs.

"Absolutely," I reply.

"Got the quick clot," Garrison says.

"She okay?" Cowboy asks through my coms.

"Yeah. Bullet wound to the shoulder. Make the call."

"They're already on their way," he replies. "I'm coming in."

I tear a larger hole in her shirt so I can access her shoulder, then flush it with saline. She cries out and squirms, but Garrison takes her hand in his.

"Squeeze, okay?" he tells her. "You're doing so good. So brave."

Moving as fast as I can to ensure she doesn't bleed out, I fill the wound with gauze, packing it as tightly as I can. I hate that I caused her pain. But a bullet to the shoulder, with a clean exit, is a lot better than what Martin would have done.

Cowboy comes rushing in right as I'm finished with the front of her injury.

His hazel eyes narrow on her, nostrils flaring in anger when he gets a look at the guy Ryker is currently detaining.

"You guys have no idea what you just did! You kicked a hornet's nest! They'll make you disappear, and you'll never see the light of day again!" Martin yells. He's always been a loose cannon, but I never would have pictured him taking the terrorist route.

I ignore his threats, focusing only on the girl. "I'm going to gently roll you to your side, okay? So I can get the exit wound."

She nods.

Blood pools beneath her, slower now that I've got one part of the injury packed. Gently, I roll her over, feeling terrible when she hisses in pain.

"She's losing consciousness," Garrison warns.

"Shock. Stay with us, Charlotte," I say urgently as I pack her exit wound. "Wrap." I reach out a hand, and Cowboy slams a wrap into it. Placing the end on her entry wound, I wrap her shoulder as best I can, given the awkward location.

Injury packed and wrapped, I gently lay her back, then stand and turn my attention to the guy who'd been holding her. His familiar face is one I'd honestly hoped to never see again.

"Martin Shaw." I shake my head. "You've got that backward on the hornet's nest. You should have left the girl alone."

"This isn't over," Martin warns again, a sadistic smile on his face. "You have no idea what you just stepped in."

"That's what they all say," I reply as the door opens and four men wearing black tactical uniforms rush in, weapons drawn. When they see that we've got it covered, they lower them, and two rip Martin from the ground.

He's rushed out of the room, and two medics load the unconscious teen onto a stretcher, then carry her out. As they're leaving the room, our handler, Brenda Leroy, strolls in wearing black slacks, tall heels, and a black suit jacket. Her dark hair is slicked down, so shiny I can practically see my reflection.

Her red lips are flattened in a tight, disapproving line. "A lot of bodies out there, Knox," she says. "You get a little trigger-happy?"

"Actually, that was me," Cowboy replies, tone sharp as a razor. "And there was no way to get to the girl without dropping them. You vastly underestimated the firepower here. That, or you just decided not to clue us in."

Her disapproving look isn't unfamiliar. "You know that I am only as good as the intel I get. I was unaware of the number of people Shaw managed to get on his side. Apparently, the corruption ran deeper than we thought."

"He claims we kicked a hornet's nest," I tell her. "My guess is this is only the tip of that iceberg." Crossing both arms, I glare back at her.

We've known Brenda for years. Ever since our last official op as Navy SEALs six years ago went sideways and she offered us off-books contracts or prison cells.

Obviously, there wasn't much of a choice there.

"Who shot the girl?"

"I did," I say, earning an arched brow. "It was that, or Shaw was going to kill her."

"We'll get his bullet hole patched up and find out who he's working for. Until then, lie low. This isn't going to be a fun one to explain."

"Feel free to cut us loose," Cowboy replies coldly.

"You're cut loose when I say you are," she snaps. "And I'm not done with you just yet."

"Prison's looking pretty good these days," Sawyer comments dryly.

"Given that you just put a bullet hole in the daughter of a French diplomat, I wouldn't rule it out just yet," Brenda replies. "Now, go before I have to include your names in my paperwork. I'll be in touch with your next assignment," she adds as I pass by.

I don't miss the irritated glance she throws my way right before she starts barking orders at the men who'd come in to start cleaning up the mess.

Tomorrow, there will be no evidence of anything that happened here.

They'll destroy this place, creating a new black site somewhere else unlisted to replace it. The *only* reason we haven't fought our way out from beneath her thumb is because we do good work. My team and I hunt rogue government agents and military operators.

We bring them to justice before too much damage can be done.

And today, we saved the life of an innocent seventeen-year-old.

So, despite the way Brenda makes my skin crawl, I'll keep pushing forward until the day she becomes a rogue agent in need of justice that I will *happily* deliver.

Chapter 2

Tessa

Pain radiates through my right leg, spreading fire through my veins, but I keep moving. Each step is agony, but if I stop, I'm not sure I'll be able to start moving again. With dawn coming soon, I have to make sure I'm out of sight.

My foot catches on something, and I cry out as I fall forward, my hands scraping against the pavement. Tears burn in my eyes, and I crawl into the nearest alley and out of view. With a building at my back and one a couple of yards to my front, I'm completely shielded in the darkness.

I whimper, hands trembling as I check the bandage on my thigh. It's saturated with blood. Given what I know about injuries, which is all self-taught, I don't have long before the blood loss becomes a major issue. Truthfully, I'm not even sure how I'm still alive as it is.

Keep moving.

The two words are deafening in my mind, so I use the building at my back to push myself up to standing. Doing what I can to keep weight off of my injured leg, I take one deep breath before pushing forward.

Sweat beads on my skin despite the chill in the air.

The small-town street is silent tonight, aside from the chirping of bugs in the air, but every single noise has my already-racing heart rate spiking.

Did he follow me?

Can he hear my hammering heart?

Can he sense my fear?

No. This is a man. Not a monster from a horror film. The sobering reminder does little to ease my terror, seeing as the worst monsters I've ever known have been little more than men.

As I draw in ragged breaths, I study every shadow, waiting for a hooded figure to emerge and finish me off. Wouldn't that be ironic? I fled this place to save my life, only to lose it here eighteen years later.

Different man. Same outcome.

With that sobering thought, I continue forward, crossing the street in the shadow between the streetlamps.

To my left, ocean waves crash against the shoreline. The scent of saltwater clings to the air around me. It should be welcoming. Familiar. But all it does is send shards of pain through my still broken heart.

Focus. I need supplies. Not that I'll know what to do with them. Breaks, bruises, and cuts? Those, I can handle.

But a stab wound? This is a first—even for me.

I guess it's a good thing I know how to sew. Because that may be my only hope here. So long as I can remain conscious through the pain.

I continue limping forward, looking left and right for any sign that someone is out and about. In this small town, someone is bound to recognize me. It's only a matter of time. My only chance is to get out of sight before the sun comes up. Then I can hide until dark.

If I make it that long.

Tomorrow night, I'll make my way to that broken-down trailer on the other side of town. That place is practically condemned and has been sitting vacant since my dad died two years ago. Unless the state's taken control of it in my absence.

Breathe, Tessa. One problem at a time.

With any luck, my old first-aid supplies will still be hidden beneath the loose baseboard in my room. The very idea of setting foot back in that place makes my skin crawl and my stomach churn, but there really isn't much of a choice.

Going to a doctor is out of the question. They'll have to report the injury, and the last thing I need is anyone in this town knowing I'm back. Especially since I have no idea who attacked me or if they're still looking to finish the job.

What if they're monitoring police scanners?

Time to heal.

Time to think.

That's what I need.

Since it's nearly two in the morning, I have about three hours before the bakery opens and people start moving around.

Three hours to make my escape or find a place to hide.

Sweat continues to slick my skin, matting my hair, as the pain becomes nearly unbearable. My vision wavers, and I reach out to steady myself against a light pole.

I'm not going to make it far. I may not know much about stab wounds, but I know the amount of blood saturating my leg is hitting dangerous levels. And if I pass out here—I shudder. I can't think about what will happen if I pass out on the street.

Get it together, Tessa. I can do this. I was in worse shape when I left this place nearly two decades ago.

Most places in this tiny town never had a need for security cameras, but there's no telling what's changed in the last eighteen years. Because that's exactly how long it's been since I walked the streets of Stormwatch Landing, South Carolina.

When I'd come for my dad's funeral two years ago, I steered clear of town and hid in the trees of the cemetery so no one would notice me. I'd been successful then, so here's hoping that luck will carry forward.

The paved sidewalk running between the buildings on Main Street and the coastline hasn't changed much, aside from some fresh plants placed strategically on either side of the walkway.

A few new benches here and there, but aside from that, everything is pretty close to the same. As soon as I can, I step off onto the grass so I hopefully don't leave a blood trail on the pavement. In this small town, that would be front-page fodder.

My leg begins to throb even worse as the adrenaline wanes.

I stumble forward and catch myself on the back of a bench.

Supplies.

I need supplies.

Something to stop the bleeding and possibly some thread and a needle, or even some glue to close it up. *But where?*

Everywhere is closed, and the *last* thing I need is to get arrested for breaking and entering. I can see the headlines now: LOCAL DRUNK'S RUNAWAY BRIDE DAUGHTER RETURNS AS A THIEF.

I groan.

Why did it seem like such a good idea to come back?

Because I had nowhere else to go.

As I'm stepping off Main Street and coming up on the marina, a familiar boat catches my eye. Its sails are down, and the green striping along the side is slightly faded—but unmistakable.

As is the faded *The Tessa* painted on the bow of the ship.

My heart leaps at the sight of my name. I would have

thought he'd have painted over it. Renamed it something else.

Something better.

Don't think on it too much. He probably just got busy. Shoving the past back where it belongs, I change course and head straight for the marina.

Supplies.

A cautious planner, he always had a first aid kit on board. Here's hoping, like the town, that didn't change. I can find the supplies, tend to my leg, then slip out before anyone ever notices that I crawled back to this place.

With renewed strength, thanks to my plan, I continue forward until I hit the dock. My shoes thud against the boards as I limp my way toward the boat, all the while glancing behind me to make sure I'm not being followed.

As soon as I climb aboard, I head straight for the door that will lead me into the cabin. I know this place like the back of my hand because nearly *every* good memory I have of this town happened here. On this boat. With *him.*

I pull open the door, and his scent hits me. Salt and teak. *Home.* Because it smells like him. Tears blur my vision for reasons other than the pain now, and emotion sears the inside of my throat.

There hasn't been a day that's gone by when I haven't thought of him.

My vision wavers again, a sobering reminder that, if I don't stop focusing on the past, I won't have a present, so I fumble around for a light switch I know I can't use for long without drawing attention. But trying to find supplies in the dark, on a boat I haven't been on in nearly two decades, seems improbable.

Supplies. Maybe a little rest. Then I'll be gone before he knows I was here. Maybe the holding tank even has water in it so I can take a quick hot shower.

Man, wouldn't that be lucky?

I continue toward the right, running my hands over the walls.

But when the cool steel of a gun barrel presses against the back of my head, I freeze in place, dread coiling in my stomach like a deadly snake ready to strike.

No way. There is no way they found me here. Not this fast.

Light floods the room when a lamp is flipped on. I blink rapidly as my vision adjusts to the assault.

"Tessa?"

My heart flutters at the recognition even as my stomach plummets to the floor. *No. Of all the people to run into, why did it have to be him?*

Right as I turn toward him, the floor gives way, and the room tilts. Or, maybe it just feels that way because everything goes dark.

"Stay with me, please!" that familiar voice orders.

If only I could tell him that I never wanted to leave in the first place.

A thin line of sunlight draws me out of sleep, but the peaceful feeling ends there. As soon as I've crawled out of the dark nightmares, pain assaults me. There's not a single inch of my body that doesn't ache, and my left leg might as well be on fire.

The steady beeping of machines claims my focus next, and the all-too-familiar sound brings a wave of nausea over me. *No. No. Did he find me? Will he find me?* My heart begins to pound, but I keep my eyes closed tightly.

Like someone trying to avoid a bear attack, I play dead —or rather, unconscious.

"Tessa, you're safe." The deep voice is comforting and familiar, but it brings an onslaught of emotions even more powerful than the fear.

Zane.

My eyes flutter open, and I look up at him. He's standing over me in faded jeans, a worn sweatshirt with the word NAVY across the front, and a tattered South Carolina baseball cap pulled low over his sun-kissed hair.

Oh, Zane. His face is glorious torment and sweet rescue all at once.

He's here.

Where is here?

"Hey there, sweetheart! You're awake!" A woman in blue scrubs with kittens all over them comes breezing over toward the bedside. "How are you feeling?" Her expression grows more worried the longer it takes me to respond.

"Throat dry," I choke out.

"I'll get water." Zane turns to leave, and I want to beg him to stay. The moment he's out of sight, my heart begins to pound again.

What if he doesn't come back?

What if he does?

"Easy, sweetie. Zane's not going anywhere." She smiles softly. "Do you remember me?" She runs her hand over my forehead in a way that brings suppressed memories to the surface with the force of a tidal wave.

Her black hair is threaded with silver, but her soft brown eyes still hold the same kindness as the woman who spent far too many years helping me with broken bones or injuries that required more than a Band-Aid.

"I do. Hi, Nurse Rose."

She smiles kindly, then finishes checking my vitals. "Hi, sweetie. Listen, we have you checked in under a different name, okay? Zane wasn't too sure what was going on, so he convinced Leopold to—"

"Leopold? As in Officer Alan Leopold?" *No. This is bad.* I try to sit up, but whatever pain medicine they gave me has my vision swimming.

"Honey, relax. You're safe here."

"No. I can't—the cops. If they're looking for me, they'll find out—"

"Who will find out?" Rose asks, her brow furrowing.

Zane breezes in, and I freeze in my bed. He sets a plastic cup on the bedside tray, then shoves both hands into his pockets.

"I'm going to go update your chart," Rose says. She squeezes my arm gently. "You're *safe* here, Tessa. You always have been." With one final smile, she turns and leaves the room, cracking the door behind her.

"Are you feeling okay?" Zane asks.

"I need to leave."

His jaw tightens. "You can't go yet. You haven't been released yet."

Our gazes hold, his green eyes having been burned into my memory since the moment I first saw him. I know them better than I know my own. And as usual, his expression nearly strips away every wall I've built over the last eighteen years.

I never thought I'd see him again.

I never dared to even *hope* to see him again.

But here I am, sitting here in a hospital gown, mere feet away from the only man I've ever loved.

CHAPTER 3

ZANE

Eighteen years.

It's been eighteen years since I last laid eyes on Tessa Lane. She hasn't changed much—her hair has a bit more copper threaded through the dark strands, and there's a scar on her temple that wasn't there before. But her eyes—those gorgeous, coffee-colored eyes—are still the same.

Haunted.

Full of fire.

I've dreamt of this day. Of seeing her again.

Because, for the last eighteen years, I've thought she was dead. The fact that she's not is barely comprehensible. As much as I want to celebrate the fact that the woman I've loved since we were kids is standing here with a pulse, now there's another question that needs to be answered: Where has she been?

"Who hurt you?" I ask, trying my best to keep my tone level when all I want to do is pull her into my arms and praise God that she's alive. That she's safe.

That the woman I love didn't die the day she disappeared. That her father didn't murder her in cold blood and hide her body in a place where no one could find it. Her disappearance has been the root of nearly every nightmare I've had since the day she vanished.

It's been my biggest failure. Even considering the one six years ago that ended with me nearly spending the rest of my life in an off-books prison.

Now she's here, and I can't help but feel a bit betrayed even though I don't know the whole story.

Did she choose to leave without a word?

Did someone abduct her?

Is that why she's hurt now? Did she escape and come back?

"It doesn't matter," she says. "But I need to leave. It's not safe."

"You are absolutely safe." The idea that she'd be anything but with me here is ridiculous. I'd die before I let anything happen to her. Time may have made me a tad more cynical, but that will never change. "Did you escape someone? Are they coming for you?"

I'll hunt them down for you.

I'll bring them to justice.

I'll make you safe.

"Look, I know you were attacked. You had a stab

wound in your upper thigh that needed stitches, as well as a bruise on your cheekbone and defensive wounds on your hands." I reach back and drag the chair I spent all night in closer to the bed before sitting down in it. "I just want to help, Tessa."

Because I'm desperate, I reach for her hand, but she rips it back and crosses her arms, closing her eyes and looking away from me.

"You *can* help me," she says, "by letting me go."

"Do you really think I can do that? It's been eighteen years, Tessa. I've been searching for you. Everyone thought you were dead." That last word is vile poison on my tongue, but it's the truth I've been living with for far longer than I ever thought possible.

Losing her the first time nearly killed me.

I don't know that I'll survive the second time around.

"Clearly I'm not dead," she says, keeping her gaze averted. "So you can stop looking and move on."

So. Many. Walls. Every one of them thicker than concrete. It was like that in the beginning, too. She'd been terrified of letting anyone close enough to get through, but I'd finally convinced her I wasn't going anywhere.

And I didn't—ever.

"What took you away from me?"

Now she turns to me, eyes shimmering with unshed tears. "I did, okay? I walked away from you because I decided that we weren't a good fit. I just didn't know how to tell you that. But now you know."

Lie. Tessa's tell has always been her bottom lip. Whenever she's lying, it quivers ever so slightly. "That's not the whole truth." Still, the words are razor blades in my heart because, just like I know she's lying, I can tell that part of it is the truth.

The question is…which part?

That she chose to leave? Or that it was because she knew we weren't a good fit?

"If that were true, you couldn't be bothered to call me? Leave a note? We were supposed to be getting married, Tessa."

"I'm well aware."

"Then why did you leave?"

She flinches at the anger in my words, and I push up from the chair to get some distance. After walking toward the only window in the hospital room, I stare out at the bright ocean.

"I told you," she says, voice all but a whisper. "We weren't a good fit."

"That's a lie, and you know it." I remove my baseball cap and set it aside to run both hands through my hair. Afterward, I replace it on top of my head and take a deep breath. "Look, the why isn't important right now. Who attacked you?" *Focus on the problem at hand. Then we can deal with everything else.*

"I don't know."

"You don't know, or you won't tell me? I know it's not your dad, given he's six feet under, so who else would hurt you, Tessa? A boyfriend? Husband?" The words are foul as I speak them, but without much else to go on, it's the likeliest answer.

Her gaze turns furious. "Because anyone I'd be in a relationship with would be abusive, too? Poor Tessa Lane can't seem to settle down with someone decent." The hurt is there, plain as day, and I can't help but wonder who put that idea in her head. That just because her dad was abusive, that was the only future in the cards for her.

"I wasn't trying to imply anything," I snap, my own frustration cutting through the joy of seeing her again. "But those are the most likely scenarios, and I'm just trying to help."

She's quiet for a moment. "I'm not in a relationship at this time."

The relief I feel is unwelcome. "Then tell me who hurt you."

"I don't know," she repeats. "And asking me over and over again isn't going to get you a different answer. I didn't see him."

"But you know it was a *him*. Do you know if someone sent him?" If it wasn't a domestic violence situation that landed her here, and she's afraid of someone finding her, it means she's likely being targeted.

What has she gotten herself into? What has she been through since the last time I saw her?

"Why are you asking me? You're my doctor, right? Isn't it the cop's job to question me?"

There's no mocking in her tone. No insult. But the occupation she speaks of is nothing but remnants of a future I gave up on long ago. A dream that existed before my life was shattered by what I thought was her death.

"I'm not a doctor."

Her eyes widen. "But you are."

"No," I reply. "I'm not."

She continues staring at me for a moment. "A cop then? Is that why you're asking me questions?"

I take a deep breath. "Look, all you need to know is that I know how to handle difficult situations. It's kind of what I do now. So if you're honest with me, I might be able to help you. In order to do that, though, I need to assess the current threat."

She's quiet for a few moments. *Am I finally getting through to her?*

"You're not a cop," she finally says.

"No."

"And you're not my doctor."

"No."

Her gaze locks on mine, and in this quiet moment, the tension between us becomes nearly unbearable. Finally, she shifts her attention from me toward the door. "Then I want you gone."

The words are a dagger to my already wounded heart. "What?"

"I want you gone. You heard me. Leave, Zane. I don't

want to see you." The words are laced with agony, and her bottom lip quivers, but she refuses to look at me.

"You don't mean that."

"Yes, I do. Nurse Rose!" she yells.

Is she serious?

The door opens, and Rose walks in, a curious expression on her face. "What is it, sweetie? Do you need something?"

"Yes. Him gone."

Rose looks from Tessa to me, then back to Tessa, clearly confused as well. "Zane? Are you sure? Honey, Zane is the one who brought you here."

"I understand." Tessa refuses to look at me. "But yes, I'm sure that I want him gone, and I don't want him to come back." Her voice breaks, and her bottom lip quivers, but she maintains the statement.

Rose turns to me, her expression sympathetic. "I'm sorry, Zane, but—"

"I get it." Reaching down, I grab my Bible and head toward the door. I pause before leaving, though, and turn to face Tessa, who is still refusing to look at me. "They know how to get a hold of me if you need me, Tessa."

"I don't. I never did." She closes her eyes, and a tear slips free. "Leave, Zane."

Even though it kills me, I do as she asks and leave the room. Rose closes the door behind me.

"Are you okay?"

"No," I say. There's no point in trying to hide it. Rose has been a family friend for as long as I can remember. She'd been there when my world fell apart after Tessa disappeared. "I know you can't tell me much, but will you make sure she stays safe? She's acting like someone might be coming after her."

"Of course, sweetie. She's safe here. I'll make the call to Leopold."

"Thanks."

She squeezes my arm. "Keep your head up, Zane. We don't know where she's been or what she's been through. Give her some time to open up."

"Yeah."

"I walked away from you because I decided that we weren't a good fit."

Tessa's words echo in my mind, but they are mismatched to the woman I knew before. Our relationship may not have been perfect, but there was never a doubt in my mind that we were meant for each other.

I was hers, and she was mine. Always and forever—that's what had been before us.

Honestly, I don't even believe what she's saying now. Rose is absolutely right—there *is* more to this story. But if Tessa isn't willing to see me, how will I ever find out?

***

"That ought to do it," I say with a half-hearted smile as I finish placing the final book on the new bookshelf I built for my mom. It covers an entire wall in the living room of her single-bedroom duplex and is already completely full. "But I think you need another shelf."

She laughs as she carries two coffee mugs over and offers me one. "I think it looks perfect."

"Have you actually read all of these?" I question as I take a seat on her couch.

"Most of them." She sits down in her favorite armchair.

The duplex is much smaller than the home I grew up in, but seven years ago, she sold it and downsized. Doing so gave her the chance to pay cash for this place, then rent the other side out for profit. She'd also insisted on giving my sister, Anastasia, and me the rest of the money to split. I hadn't needed it, so I used my half to invest in Anastasia's coffee shop.

While there are plenty of days I miss standing in the same living room my dad once did, I know that Mom was happy to have a fresh start. The two-story, four-bedroom house was just too big for her once my sister and I moved out.

"What's on your mind?" she questions, pulling my thoughts back to the present.

"Huh?"

"You're a million miles away."

"What makes you think that?"

My mom's hazel gaze narrows on my face. "Because you get the same look your father did when something was weighing on him. What is it?"

How much do I tell her?

She'd grieved Tessa, too, and telling either her or Anastasia that Tessa bailed on me is just not something I want to do right now. Not when I haven't even finished processing it yet. Though, even with Leopold keeping Tessa's name out of any official reports, it's only a matter of time before word gets around.

Someone will tell someone, and then my mom will be wondering why I didn't tell her first. Anastasia will never let me hear the end of it.

So, I remove my baseball cap and run a hand through my hair.

"Oh, this *is* serious," my mom jokes. "When the baseball cap comes off, I know to brace myself."

"I found Tessa." It's the first time I've spoken those words out loud. When I'd gotten to the hospital with her in my arms, everything had been little more than a blur of movement where I hadn't even had the chance to fully comprehend what was happening.

When I turn to my mom and see the tortured expression on her face, I know it's because she's worried I'm about to say that I found Tessa's body. That what we always feared was the truth.

"What?" Her voice is barely above a whisper. Face pale, she stares back at me with wide eyes. "Is she—"

"She's alive. I guess it's more accurate to say she found me. Sorry, should have led with that." Leaning back against the couch, I toy with the bill of my hat. "She showed up on the boat last night, injured. She's at the hospital now."

My mom shoots up from her chair. "Then we need to go. Now. Is she okay? Where has she been? Why did you wait all this time to tell me? The books could have waited!"

And here's the part that will break her heart. "She kicked me out of her hospital room. She doesn't want to see me."

Linda Knox's gaze narrows on me again. "I don't believe that for a second."

"Call Rose, then. She was there. Saw the whole thing." The bite in my words is directed at the wrong person, so I take a deep breath to calm myself. "It's fine, Mom. Tessa doesn't want me there, so I won't be there. It's as simple as that."

My mom continues to study me. "Zane Knox, I have never known you to give up. Not once."

"I didn't give up. She kicked me out."

"Who knows what that poor girl has been through?"

Woman now, I want to correct her. The girl Tessa had been is long gone, just like the boy I'd been has left, too. Life changed us. Molded us into two strangers.

"She's family. And we need to be there for her," my mother insists.

"I tried. The worst thing I can do right now is force my company on her. She needs to heal, and if I need to stay away for that, then that's exactly what I'll do."

"We weren't a good fit." That's what she told me.

Whether I believe it to be the truth or not, I have to respect her wishes. I loved her once, and that love is worth at least that much still.

"Fair enough." Mom offers me an understanding smile, but instead of taking her seat again, she crosses over to grab her purse and keys from the counter.

"Where are you going?"

"She kicked you out of her room, Zane. Not me. I'm going to go see our girl. I'll let you know what happens."

Fear that Tessa will break my mom's heart washes over me, and I lunge to my feet to try to stop her. "Mom, that's not a good—"

"I know she may not be the same person she was, but I am. And I won't let her lie there alone. She has no one else. So, I'm going to be there."

"Mom—"

"Sweetie, I'm not letting this go. Now, you'd better go and make sure Anastasia knows so that your sister doesn't hear it from someone else. She deserves to know, too."

Knowing I've lost this battle, I nod. "I'll lock up on my way out."

"Good." She crosses over and reaches up to pull me down for a hug. After planting a kiss on my cheek, Mom strolls out of her house, joy lacing every step.

Will Tessa welcome her?

Or will she also turn her back on the woman who tried to save her more than once?

CHAPTER 4

TESSA

I never thought I'd be standing in front of this trailer *again, but here I am. It looms before me, the chipped siding and sunken porch evidence that the man living inside couldn't be bothered to care whether the place lives or dies.*

Just like he can't be bothered to care whether his only daughter does the same.

This is a bad idea. *The thought has been the only thing on my mind since he called me two hours ago. Stomach in knots, I'm too afraid to take that next step.*

Forgiveness. *I'm supposed to forgive, right? Isn't that what we're called to do as Christians? And if he wants to make amends, then I should be open to that, right? My stomach churns, and a voice in my head keeps telling me to turn around.*

To leave.

Forgiveness. *I can do that. I take a step forward, then another, until I'm climbing up the creaking porch steps and raising my fist to knock on the door. Before I do, though, it opens, and my dad is standing on the other side, a smile on his face. It looks out of place, though, forced, and I can't help but wonder if he's not as nervous as I am.*

He glances around me. "Are you alone?"

"Yes. *This doesn't have anything to do with Zane, so I thought it best if we spoke alone."* And he wouldn't have let me come. *Forgiveness or not, there is so much bad blood between my dad and Zane that I can't trust the two men not to kill each other.*

"I couldn't agree more. Come in, come in." *He ushers me inside, but I remain near the door even as he closes it.* "Would you like some water?"

The stench that I attributed to this place is milder tonight, though I imagine that's due to the candles burning. Candles. My dad never had candles. He never cared what this place smelled like. Probably because he was always too drunk to notice.

"No, thank you."

"Of course." *My dad's hands remain at his sides, and I keep my attention on them even though I meet his gaze. A childhood of abuse has made me painfully aware of the location of those hands.*

"The place looks nice."

"Thanks. I cleaned. Amazing what you can get done when you're not drunk," *he says nervously.*

"That's really great, Dad," I say, feeling a bit of my nerves easing. Tears burn in the corners of my eyes. He's sober? That's a huge step. My dad hasn't been sober since —well—at least since I was born.

"Yeah, I thought so. You walking out was the wake-up call I needed." He grins and takes a step closer.

Run. Danger. *Those two words scream in my mind, but I remain rooted in my spot. He's changed. Sobriety is proof of that. And even if he backslides on his way out of the pit, we can work on it together.*

I can bring him to Jesus, and in doing that, we can finally be a family.

"I don't want to lose you to him," he says. "I know that you're getting married, and the idea of my only daughter walking down the aisle makes me sick." He smiles, and while his words don't entirely make sense, I know that it's likely just the nerves.

"I want you there, too, Dad. We can get through this. All I want is for you to be happy."

"Yeah?" he asks. "Is that all?"

I nod. "I want you to be a part of our lives. You're the only parent I have."

His smile widens. "That's true, isn't it? You're my only daughter, too. I guess we're all each other has." The words take on a tone that has those warning bells turning into a full-blown screeching alarm.

I retreat a step, but he takes another forward.

"I really should get some sleep, but you can—" I broke

rule number one because I let myself be so distracted that I wasn't paying attention to his fists.

I didn't even see it coming.

Pain radiates through the side of my face, and I slam into the wall, hitting it with such force that the paneling cracks beneath my body. Whimpering, I try to scramble away, but a meaty hand grips my ankle and rips me backward.

"Please, stop!"

"The alcohol was never the problem, girl. It was always you. Zane will thank me someday for saving him from a life with trash like you."

"Easy, Tessa, you're safe." Hands grip my shoulders, but I thrash away from them.

"Don't touch me!"

Somewhere nearby, there's an alarm screeching, but I pay it little attention because I *have* to get away. He's going to kill me if I don't.

"Tessa, honey, you're safe."

That voice. Soft. Feminine. Familiar. *Safe.* That last word wraps around me like a blanket, and I still long enough to brace for the next blow. When it doesn't come, I open my eyes.

The light is dim above me, and two nurses in scrubs are staring down at me, wide-eyed and afraid. When I remain still, they lift their hands from me and take a step back. The alarm dies, and a rhythmic beeping takes its place as Linda Knox steps into view. Her eyes are misty, but that same kind smile I've always attributed to her is in place.

"Mrs. Knox?" I whisper.

"I'm here, sweetie." She steps forward and reaches out to gently touch my hand. I don't withdraw from her, though I don't reach for her either.

This is Zane's mom, and after what I did—what I said to him—she'll want to leave, too.

"I'm sorry." The tears come rushing hard and fast. "I'm so sorry."

"Oh, sweetheart, you don't need to apologize for anything." She closes the distance between us now, wrapping her arms around me and pulling me against her chest. The familiar scents of lavender and vanilla fill my lungs, and I breathe her in, too relieved to be worried about what might come when Zane tells her what I said to him. What I did.

"Call us if you need us," one of the nurses says moments before the door closes softly.

"Are you okay? Do you hurt?" Linda asks as she pulls away.

I shake my head. "Just a nightmare."

Linda steps back and takes a seat in a chair right beside the bed. The same chair her son had been in before I kicked him out of the room like he was enemy number one, instead of the only person I've ever loved.

"It's so good to see you, honey," Linda says. "We've missed you."

I take a deep breath and toy with the blanket in front of me, the remnants of my nightmare still *very* much alive in my mind. "Did you talk to Zane?"

"I did. He said that you didn't want to see him."

"I don't."

"That's between the two of you," she says with a soft smile. "Though I do have to say that my son is a good man, and he wants to help. No matter what happened."

Swallowing hard, I press the button on the bed remote to raise the head of it so I can lean back without lying down. "I know that."

"Then whatever is going on between you two is for you to work out. I'm here because I love you, and because I want to make sure you're okay."

I've never really been okay. "I'll survive."

"Oh, honey, I know that." She smiles, but it fades quickly. "Do you want to talk about it?"

Because I don't trust myself to do just that if I open my mouth to respond, I shake my head. Linda Knox fought for years to get me to turn my dad in. She'd offered to let me come live with them and take care of me, and I know that, if I'd have taken her up on it, she would have done just that.

But how could I bring her into my hell?

How could I give my dad ammunition against the only family I'd really ever known? There's no doubt in my mind that he would have come after me through them. There was never any proof of it, but he burned down his ex-girl-friend's house—with her inside. Thankfully, she'd survived, but that's only because someone just so happened to be walking by when the place went up in flames.

He claimed he didn't think she was in there. I know he was lying because I heard him bragging about it to a buddy of his when they'd both been drunk one night.

What would he have done to the Knoxes if I'd have taken them up on a home? A family?

My life wasn't worth the risk to theirs.

"I completely understand," she replies softly. "So, how about you tell me something else? Something good that has nothing to do with why you're here?"

I smile, appreciating the change in subject. But that smile dies quickly when I realize that I have nothing good to tell her. I can't think of a single decent thing that's happened to me over the last eighteen years.

It's just been survival. One day after the other.

Lucky for me, the door opens, and a man wearing a white coat strolls in, a wide smile on his face. "How are you feeling?" he questions.

"When can I leave?"

His smile widens. "Right to the point, I like it." He scans the tablet in his hands, then looks back up at me. "I think you can be out of here this afternoon as long as that injury to your thigh looks all right."

"Really?"

He nods.

"Do you know where you're going to go when you leave here, sweetie?" Linda questions.

"I have a place." It's not the truth—but it's not a lie either.

"Where you'll be safe? Zane seemed worried about what happened to put you in here."

"I was mugged in another state. They won't be coming back for me. I'm fine." Once again, it's not entirely the truth, though I don't know enough to say it's a lie, either.

Linda doesn't seem too convinced, but she purses her lips in a tight smile and stands. "I'll be just outside, okay? Call out if you need me." When she passes the doctor, she reaches out and pats him gently. "How is your wife, Alex?"

"Doing good," he replies. "She's more than ready for the baby to come."

Linda laughs. "I bet. Let her know we're praying for her. I'll be bringing some cookies by tomorrow afternoon."

"She will love that. Thanks, Linda."

"Anytime."

With one final smile at me, Zane's mom leaves the room. *Alex.* I know that—"Alex Jones?" I ask.

He smiles at me. "The one and only."

Alex was a complete loner when we were in high school. He kept to himself, skipped class, and genuinely didn't seem to care about anything or anyone. How in the world did *he* become a doctor, but Zane didn't?

"I was wondering if you recognized me; I didn't want

to say anything just in case. I know your identity has been kept on the down low."

Down low. I grin at his choice of words. Sure, it's a common phrase, but no one adds quite the same inflection as Alex. "It's good to see you. You're married now?"

"With three kids and a baby on the way," he replies. "Melissa Lark. Do you remember her?"

"Oh yeah. No one could forget Lissa," I reply with a laugh. She'd been so bubbly we could sense her coming from a mile away. "She's your wife?"

He laughs. "Going on seven years," he replies. "Not a pairing I would have imagined, either, but she's my entire world. We dated while we were in college and got married shortly after med school."

"That's great, Alex. Congratulations."

"Thanks." He crosses over and sets the tablet down, then washes his hands. Seconds later, the door opens, and one of the nurses from my earlier freak-out comes in. She washes her hands and slips on gloves, then pulls some medical supplies from the cabinet. "I'm actually surprised that you and Zane never tied the knot. Is that why you left town?"

It's a punch straight to my gut.

A dagger to my heart.

"Something like that." I clear my throat. "So, you said I could get out of here?"

"As long as the injury looks okay," he clarifies as he folds the blankets to the side to reveal my bandaged thigh.

Carefully, he removes the bandages, and the nurse offers him some fresh gauze and another wrap.

"What's the verdict?" I question, already itching to be free of this place. Of the reminders of everything I left behind.

"Looks great to me." He finishes re-wrapping it, then takes off his gloves, sanitizes his hands, and turns back to me. "Give us a few to get the paperwork done. Then you'll be good to go. Officer Leopold will want to talk to you, so I'm going to give him a quick call, too, just to let him know that you're going to be released."

Dread coils in my stomach, but I keep the forced smile on my face. "Great, thanks so much. For everything."

"Not a problem at all. I'll send Linda back in."

"Actually, I think I might just rest for a few if that's okay? I'm pretty tired and want to make sure I'm wide awake by the time you're done with the paperwork."

"I completely understand. I'll let her know. See you in a bit." With a small wave, he and the nurse leave the room, closing the door behind them.

Leaning back, I rest my head against the pillow and close my eyes.

Soon I'll be discharged. Then, I can get to the old trailer and figure out what my next move will be. With no idea why someone attacked me and ransacked my apartment, I know I can't go back there. Which means it's time for a new name, new state, new home.

I've started over before, so it's not anything new, but this time feels different.

Maybe it's because I really liked my apartment in Savannah, Georgia.

Or because I'd finally gotten a job that helped me pay all the bills and still left me a little extra.

Or, more likely, it's because this time, I got a little taste of what I left behind all those years ago. Even sitting here now, I can picture him.

Sandy blonde hair.

Gorgeous green eyes.

Unwelcome attraction burns through me, and I shove it back down. I have no right to be attracted to Zane. Not after what I did to him. The sooner I leave this place, the better. I can put Stormwatch Landing—and him—behind me. This time, for good.

Chapter 5

Zane

The sun is high above me as I make my way from the marina toward Main Street. The town is relatively quiet today, but I've passed more than one friendly face. Unfortunately, I'm not feeling overly chatty at the moment, so it's been fake smiles, quick answers, and half-hearted waves.

All while my mind is on Tessa at the hospital. My mom is with her, has been most of the day. And since I haven't heard otherwise, I'm assuming she wasn't given the boot.

Tessa.

Why didn't I keep looking for her?

Why did I simply accept the idea that she was dead?

Because I never thought she'd leave me. The thought brings a fresh wave of pain over me, and I take a deep breath to bury it. That's in the past. Right now, she's injured and in a hospital bed.

Reaching up, I grip the handle on the screen door to my sister's coffee shop, then pull it open. Normally, when the scent of fresh coffee and baked goods hits my lungs, I can't help but smile.

But today, not even the promise of fresh muffins can bring a smile to my face.

Anastasia glances up from behind the counter and starts to smile. It dies on her face, though, and she comes around the counter. "Are you okay? What happened?"

"Why do you think something is wrong?" I ask, forcing a smile.

"Um, because of your face," Anastasia replies. Her eyes, the same shade as our mother's, narrow on my face. "Spill, Zane."

"I'm fine. Honestly." I glance around the room, studying the locals who are inside. While I'm sure word will get around soon enough, I'd rather it not be me who spreads it. "Can we head upstairs and talk in private?"

"Sure thing. Karly, I'm taking my break!" she calls out.

Karly peeks her face out of the back room and throws up a thumbs up, her red ponytail swinging as she does. "Hey, Zane!"

"Hey, Karly," I reply, trying my best to keep the forced smile firmly in place.

Anastasia takes off her apron and hangs it on a peg near the door, then takes my hand and pulls me up the steps toward the second floor, which also doubles as her apartment. She shuts the door behind us, and I survey the colorful space.

It's entirely my baby sister's taste.

Random patterns, bright colors, lots of natural light, plants with large green leaves—happy. Just like her.

"Want a bottle of water? Tea?"

"No, I'm okay." I take a seat on her floral couch and let out a sharp breath.

"This is bad. What is it? You're scaring me." Anastasia sits beside me, so I reach over and take her hand.

She's been my best friend our entire lives, despite the two-year age difference between us. When our dad passed, we only grew closer, and it's been that way ever since.

"I need to tell you something, but it has to stay between us. For now, at least."

"Of course." Her hazel eyes narrow on my face, her expression serious. "Come on, Zane. What's going on?"

"Tessa is alive."

Anastasia's mouth falls slack, and she stares at me, shocked. "Are you serious? How do you know? Where has she been? Is she okay?" Each rapid-fired question breaks my heart because I know the truth will break hers.

"I'm not sure where she's been. But currently, she's at the hospital. She sustained some minor injuries, but I think she'll be okay."

"Zane." Anastasia releases my hand and pushes to her feet, turning to gape at me. When Tessa disappeared, Anastasia had been right at my side, trying to help me find answers. She'd been with me while I grieved the loss, pointed me back to God when my anger got the better of me, and grounded me in the realities when I wanted to take vengeance into my own hands. "Where did you find her? Who hurt her? Is that why she went missing? Oh, poor Tessa."

"I'm not sure as to the who, and I wouldn't even say that *I* found her. I was sleeping and heard someone moving around my boat. When I went to see who it was—"

"It was Tessa?" she finishes.

"It was Tessa," I repeat. "She was bleeding from an injury on her thigh, and she had some other cuts and scrapes. Before I could ask her what happened, she passed out. So I took her to the hospital."

Anastasia leans back against the couch. "Wow. How did she end up on your boat? Did she escape somewhere and come to you for help?"

Due to her reaction to me, I'd say her coming to me on purpose was a big no. "I have no idea."

"I'm honestly surprised I haven't heard anything. Did you tell Mom?"

"Given her injuries, I asked Officer Leopold to keep her name off the record for now. He and the hospital staff have been tight-lipped about it. And yes, I told Mom. She's there with her now."

"That's good." Anastasia lets out a sharp breath. "Wow. This is a lot. Did she tell you why she left? I'm shocked you're not there now."

I take a deep breath. This is going to be the part she *really* doesn't like. "Tessa claims that she left because she simply changed her mind about marrying me. She also kicked me out of her hospital room as soon as she realized I wasn't her doctor."

Anastasia rarely gets mad. In fact, there've been plenty of moments in her life where she would have been completely validated in her anger, but she still chose kindness. However, at my repeat of Tessa's callous words, my sister's cheeks turn a deep pink, and her gaze narrows on me.

"She *changed* her mind? So instead of telling you that, she let you stand there in front of all of your family and friends? Alone? Humiliated? And now she has the audacity to show up on your boat? Nope." She starts toward the door, but I stand to block her path. "This is not going to fly, Zane!"

"Easy, Anastasia. Someone could be after her. She was pretty banged up."

"No. Sounds to me like—once again—she wrapped you up in *her* problem. You're too kind to tell her to kick rocks, but I'm not. Not after what she did to you."

"Yes," I say with the whisper of a smile on my face. "You are too kind."

She glares at me but stops just short of opening the door, then turns to face me and crosses her arms. "Fine. But the *audacity.*"

"To be fair, I don't think she counted on me being on the boat."

"It's your boat."

"Yeah, and she snuck onto it late at night. She said she was only there for supplies."

"So she was there to rob you?" Anastasia's eyes widen, and if I weren't so shaken up already, I might have laughed. "Are you *kidding* me? Why is she not in a cell, Zane? Did you tell the police? If someone did hurt her, then it seems to me the best place for her is behind bars." She crosses her arms.

"If someone is really after her, then that's the worst place for her to be. All it would take is one person being paid to get arrested, then taking her out once they're inside."

Anastasia stares at me in twisted shock. "This is insane."

"Besides, like I said, she kicked me out of her hospital room. I don't think she wants anything to do with me."

"The *audacity,*" she repeats. "She'd better stay away from you, Zane. I'm sorry she was hurt, but her abandoning you like that? No. You deserve so much better."

"I'm okay, Anastasia, honestly."

"Well, I'm not." She studies me for a moment, then shakes her head. "You're going to insist on helping her, aren't you?"

"Does it sound like she wants my help?"

"That didn't stop you before, and we both know it

won't stop you now. Come on, Zane, don't get involved in whatever this is. Let the police handle it. Whatever it is, it could be dangerous. You have no idea what she's been into."

"I know that, but I can't just leave her to die, Anastasia. If someone really is after her, I can help. Besides, I'm more likely to die on a mission. This is nothing." I smile, hoping it will ease some of the fear I see in her expression.

Her eyes fill. "Because *that* makes me feel better. If I remember correctly, Tessa spent more than a night in a jail cell when she was young. Maybe this is trouble she brought on herself by doing something she shouldn't have been doing."

She'd been arrested twice for shoplifting before she turned thirteen. It was the morning her dad came and picked her up the second time that I really *saw* her. I was at the precinct, waiting on my dad to finish work for the day, and she'd been brought out from the back.

Even though we'd been at the same elementary school, I didn't really know her. And since I got moved up to high school when I was eleven, I didn't have a chance.

Not until my gaze locked on hers when they brought her out from the back.

From that moment on, I sought her out, trying to know as much as I could about the beautiful, haunted girl who'd captured my attention as a young teenager.

Dad died a week later, so it was another two months before I saw her again.

"She'd been stealing food, and no charges were filed. She wasn't even officially booked."

Anastasia sighs. "Only because Officer Leopold is a big softie."

I chuckle. "I'm sure he'd love to know that's what you think of him."

Anastasia runs both hands over her face. "Zane, this is not good. I know that you beat yourself up for a long time over what happened to her, but you have answers now. Maybe you can let her go."

"I thought she was dead. Her dad practically confessed, even though they never found enough to charge him with anything. Anastasia, she's *alive*." For the first time since I realized it was Tessa who'd passed out in my arms, the full weight of that truth hits me square in the chest.

I'd grieved her.

Spent years trying to prove what everyone believed to be true.

And this whole time, she's been out there—alone.

Or is she alone? Did she find someone else? *"I'm not in a relationship at this time."* I hate that it brings me relief to know that.

And before I can focus on my reaction too deeply, I shove the thought aside.

Right now, I need to know exactly what happened to her so I can make sure she stays alive. Because Anastasia is right: Even if Tessa doesn't want my help, I have no intention of stopping until I have no doubt she'll be safe.

"I'm truly glad that she's alive." Anastasia reaches out and grips my arm. "But I've seen that look on your face before, Big Brother. I adored Tessa, but she definitely got you into your fair share of trouble. And it sounds like it's no different now."

The first time I was arrested, I was seventeen. Tessa had shown up with a split lip, courtesy of her dad, so I'd returned the favor and broken his nose.

Officer Leopold responded to the call a neighbor made. He'd convinced her dad not to file charges, and I'd been driven home in the back of a police cruiser.

After that, I did what I could to keep my distance from her dad, though I begged Tessa to tell the police what was happening to her. She'd refused, afraid of losing the only family she had left. Even given the toxic reality of her life, she'd remained loyal and lied to save him every single time the police even got close.

"I've got someone looking into what brought her here, so hopefully, I'll have some answers soon, okay?"

"I can't talk you out of this?"

I shake my head.

She sighs. "Then, fine. But if you get arrested again, I'm going to let you sit there awhile before I bail you out."

With a laugh, I lean forward and press a light kiss to the top of her head. "Deal." My cell rings, so I withdraw it and check the readout. When I see my mom's name, I answer with a smile. "Hey, Mom."

"She's gone," she says, her tone sharp.

"What?" My stomach sinks, a pit forming before I can even fully process what she's saying.

"Tessa. She left the hospital before they even fully discharged her."

"When?"

"Not sure. The doctor left her room about an hour ago and told me that she wanted to rest. I went down to the cafeteria to get some food, and when I came back, she was gone. I'm sorry, Zane."

"It's not your fault." I swallow hard, trying to bite back the anger. She left. Again. Thing is, this time I *know* she's alive, and I have no intention of letting her get away without first making sure she's safe.

After that, she can leave and never look back.

"Thanks for letting me know."

"Are you going to go after her?" my mom asks. "I'm really worried, Zane. She had a horrible nightmare while she was sleeping and screamed for help. Something is terribly wrong, but she wouldn't talk about it."

My gaze locks on Anastasia, who rolls her eyes. "We all know what you're going to do, Big Brother, so just go do it."

CHAPTER 6

TESSA

The world around me is silent as I move along the overgrown path that leads me up to my dad's old trailer. It's still in the exact same place, though the years have not been kind to it. The porch built along the front is sagging in most places, broken in others.

Overhead, lightning splits the sky, a warning of a coming storm that matches the way I'm feeling inside. Tense and ready to break through at any moment. *I can do this. It's just a shell.*

The single light on the top of the electrical pole casts an eerie orange glow over the place, giving it a horror movie vibe. Which, given all that happened here over the years, is more than fitting.

Two windows have been shattered. Since they were partially boarded up, I'm guessing the damage is likely from rocks the other kids in the trailer park threw. Even though our place sat a quarter mile away from everyone else, they still came out here and poked at my dad any chance they got.

Let's rile up the drunk. It was a game they played, and I was the one who paid the price.

Fresh pain tightens my chest.

I haven't stood here in a long, long time.

And the last time I saw this place, I was stumbling toward my dad's car, ready to steal it so I could put this place behind me. Which is exactly what I thought I'd done. Yet here I am. Once again, with nowhere else to go.

"You'll never be anything else, Tessa. You'll always end up back here." His words are damaging even after all these years. Like an anvil dropped on my head over and over again.

Considering that lying low here in town is no longer an option, I really should have left town once I'd gotten out of the hospital, but this is business left unfinished. I need to prove to myself that this broken shell doesn't hold any power over me. Not anymore. Maybe once I face it, the nightmares will stop, and I can finally truly move forward.

With a deep breath, I limp forward and grip the wooden banister of the porch. The rotting wood bites into my hand just enough that I know I'll probably end up with a few splinters. Unfortunately, climbing the steps without it right now just isn't an option, so I ignore the pain.

It's only fitting that the place leaves one final mark on me, anyway.

The door is unlocked, so I shove it open and remain outside as the putrid stench of stale beer and urine assaults me. There were days he'd just urinate all over himself because he was too drunk to even walk to the bathroom.

I'd given up on trying to wash the couch cushions and just started avoiding the living room at all costs.

Tears sting the corners of my eyes as panic rises in my chest.

He's not here, Tessa. He's dead. Long gone.

This place does *not* hold power over me.

With one arm over my nose and mouth, I move into the room.

There's no electricity in here anymore, so I use my free hand to retrieve the pen light I always have in my pocket. After one too many times locked in the dark, I know to always be prepared.

The thin beam shines over the stained carpet, or rather, what's left of the pieces of it that haven't been completely worn away.

The couch sags, its stained grey fabric a reminder of all the times I found him passed out on it. There were nights I'd even checked his pulse because I was sure he was dead. I hated the disappointment I'd often feel when I felt the steady thumping against my fingertips.

No, I couldn't be that lucky. He wasn't done tormenting me yet.

The recliner he spent most of his time in—when he wasn't passed out on the couch—is gone. Which is honestly surprising. Either someone stole it, it was thrown out after he died, or he got rid of it before death claimed him.

There are empty beer cans all over the dust-covered kitchen. Even a plate of rotted food still sits on a TV tray beside the couch.

I know he's gone, but as I stand here, I can all but picture him rushing toward me, fist raised, screaming because I'd done something in his eyes worthy of a beating. After angrily wiping away tears, I move down the hall and toward my bedroom.

The door is closed, so I shove it open. Since the curtains are wide open and the solar-powered light on the top of the electric post is just outside my window, there's enough light in here that I can turn the pen light off as I study the room.

Everything is the same.

The stench in here is a lot less than out there, though the air is stale, and my bed is still made from the last morning I'd stayed here. Posters are pinned to the wall, and there's a shelf of worn books I'd bought with spare quarters during one of the library's clean-out sales.

This was the place I'd rest my head, but it was never home.

Because home was never a place for me. It was always a person.

"I thought you'd come here."

As if my thoughts brought him here, a masculine voice

behind me has me lunging forward. I nearly fall over, but a large hand steadies me by gripping my forearm. Heat spreads through me at the contact, warming me from the outside in.

Zane.

He releases me, so I turn to face him, doing what I can to keep my walls firmly in place. I'd slipped out of the hospital room even before they'd given me discharge instructions because I didn't want to have to turn his mother down on the ride I knew she was about to offer me.

The Knox family has already done too much for me, and I don't deserve any of it. The last thing I want to do is add anything else to the invoice.

"I thought I told you that I didn't want to see you." My tone has lost all sting as I stand here in my childhood bedroom with the man who promised to save me from the nightmare that was my life. He was the one ray of sunshine in the otherwise pitch-black darkness I couldn't escape.

"You did."

"Then why are you here?"

He moves farther into the room, and the light from outside fully illuminates his tortured expression.

Outside, another bolt of lightning shoots across the sky seconds before booming thunder rattles the paper-thin walls.

"I haven't been in this room since two weeks after you left," he says softly.

"After?"

He nods.

There was a time when Zane would sneak over and tap on my window. I'd let him in, and he'd bring me food. We'd sit on my floor and eat together while my dad slept off the alcohol in the living room.

One night when we were eighteen, Zane fell asleep beside me on the floor. That's all it was—innocent sleeping after a night of staying up, talking about the future we both wanted to have—but my dad stormed in and threatened to kill him. That was the night I knew I had to leave. Because, while I could take the beatings, I couldn't stomach Zane getting hurt.

I still can't.

I'd been a coward, though, and stayed until he nearly killed me. Zane came to my rescue then, too, and begged me to leave this life. So, I finally did.

"I broke in while your dad was passed out so I could look for any sign of you. I knew he'd hurt you. There was no evidence, but I felt it in my gut. I wasn't sure that I'd find you alive, but I'd hoped." His gaze shifts to me. "I guess I was right."

The pain in his gaze is so fresh.

The ache in my heart has been multiplying with every second. "I guess so."

He shifts his attention away from me. "Why did you come here?"

It's a strange question, given all the others he could ask.

Why did I leave? Why did I sneak out of the hospital? Why did I kick him out of my room?

And every single one of those answers is the same. Because I loved him too much to let him see me broken. So I guess it's a good thing he avoided those. I'm sure I don't have the strength to tell him the truth, and I don't want to lie anymore.

Not to Zane. Not if I can help it.

Clearing my throat, I force my attention away from him. "I needed to prove to myself that this place is nothing."

"And?"

I limp forward and lift a dust-covered stuffed animal from the shelf. It's a white rabbit, won for me by the man standing just behind me at one of the shoreside carnivals. "There's nothing for me here." Even though I want to do the exact opposite, I toss the rabbit onto the bed.

He can't know how broken I am.

He can't see my pain.

Because I believe that, even after everything I've done to him, Zane Knox is still a man who would wrap me up in a safety blanket and protect me from the world. And with my track record, that might just cost him his life.

"Why do you do that?"

"Do what?" I turn toward him.

"Pretend you don't care at all? What did I do to make you hate me?"

You loved me more than anyone else in my life ever has.

"What makes you think I hate you?"

"The way you're acting," he replies. "You look at me as though you can't wait to be rid of me, all while I'm still reeling over the fact that you're alive."

Tears burn in the corners of my eyes as I force my gaze away from him.

Zane Knox is the only man who has ever possessed the power to break me.

My dad certainly tried; that's for sure. He broke plenty of my bones—shattered any hope I had of ever being worth something—but Zane Knox pieced me back together in such a way that, even in my darkest moments, there was a light surrounding me.

I *believed* that, as long as I had him, everything would be okay.

And then I lost him, too.

"I don't hate you," I reply. "I just don't have anything for you."

He cocks his head to the side to study me in that way he does. Like he can see straight through what I *want* him to see, and deep into all that I try to hide. "What makes you think I want something?"

"The fact that you're here," I reply coolly. "You followed me all the way out here because you're looking for any shred of the girl you knew before. She's gone. Dead and buried along with the remnants of our relationship." The words are frigid, but my voice trembles as I force myself to say what he needs to hear. Or rather, what I *need* him to hear because he's still looking at me like I was good enough for him.

I never was.

Zane doesn't respond, so I turn away from him and limp over toward the closet. Since my apartment was ransacked, I can't go back there. Which means the only clothes I own are the ones on my back. Thankfully, I still wear roughly the same size I did in high school, so my hope is that there are still some clothes here I can salvage.

"How is your pain?" It shouldn't thrill me that he cares, but it does. There was never a safer place for me than in his strong arms. Even back when we were little more than teenagers with no idea what waited for us on the other side of a marriage we were probably far too young to be considering in the first place.

But I can't focus on that now because it's dangerous territory. Like treading water in the middle of a hurricane. Outside, more thunder booms. The storm is right on the horizon now—much like the one in my heart.

"Why didn't you become a doctor?" I counter as I withdraw a pair of jeans and a baggy t-shirt. They smell terrible, so I shove them back into the closet. I might be desperate to stop looking like I walked through a muddy fan blade, but not that desperate.

Crossing to my dresser, I wait for him to answer.

Zane lets out a deep breath. "I will only answer your questions if you start answering mine."

Run, Tessa. Put distance between you two, and be done with it.

Unfortunately, curiosity has always gotten the better of me. "Fine. But we don't talk about the night I left. I won't answer a single thing about that. And I get the option of saying pass." It's a precedent that needs to be set because I can't have him knowing the truth. Not even now, all these years later.

"The same goes for me, then," he replies.

I withdraw a pair of sweats and a baggy t-shirt from my bottom drawer. Since these were somewhat closed in, the smell is subtle enough that I can deal with it. "Deal. I need to change first."

Without waiting for me to ask, he starts to turn—then hesitates. He doesn't even have to speak the words for me to know why he takes a pause.

"I won't bail, Zane." I'm honestly surprised it's the truth, but maybe that's more good that can come of my being here. I can finally close the chapter, not just on this trailer—but on Zane, too.

Without another word, he moves out into the hall and closes the door. The panic kicks in the moment that faint click registers.

Trapped.

My breathing goes ragged, and the walls begin to close in on me. How many times was I locked in this room?

Darkness overtakes the edges of my vision, and my

heart hammers so loud I can't even hear the storm brewing outside.

How many times did my father trap me in here because he was angry?

How many times did I go days without food because I was too afraid to sneak out the window to find some?

I don't even hear the door open, but then Zane is in front of me. "Breathe, Tessa." His hands go to my face, and I suck in a ragged breath, still too terrified to be bothered that he's seeing me like this. "You're safe. You can see me. I'm here. Feel my hands."

Touch. Sight. Sound. I use those senses to get a grasp on reality, but it's still not enough.

I'll never be safe. Not really. What happened in Savannah is proof of that.

"Lord, please wrap Tessa in Your arms. Please help her focus on You."

I can't even find the words to tell him I'm pretty sure God gave up on me a long, long time ago. As he continues to pray, his hands gently cupping my cheeks, my breathing begins to slow, and the walls ease up.

When I can finally see clearly, I pull away from him. A chill runs up my spine at the sudden distance, but I don't give in and lean back toward him.

Zane drops his hands.

"I'm fine. Thanks." But my tone is anything but steady.

He dips his head in a nod. It's hardly the first panic attack he's helped me out of. In fact, there was a time when *only* Zane could save me once the fear kicked in. Seems that, too, hasn't changed.

"Please leave the door open. Just step into the hall out of sight."

Zane hesitates a moment but nods and moves out into the hall.

My dusty bed creaks when I take a seat to remove my shoes. As I do, I reach beneath my mattress and withdraw the knife I kept tucked safely away. Running my fingers over my name carved in the wooden casing of the pocketknife, more tears fill my eyes.

Another thing Zane gave me.

He was the first one to ever give me a Christmas present. And this was it. Not a single night went by that I slept without it. Until I'd decided never to come back to this place. I'd forgotten it in my haste to escape, but I'd never forgotten it. Or the kindness he'd shown me.

I set it aside on the bed and kick off my shoes. As soon as they're on the floor, I take a deep breath and undo the buttons of my shorts. I lie back on the bed and start coughing when dust fills my lungs.

"Are you okay?"

"Fine," I bite out, then try to stand. With the injury on my thigh, standing on one leg to get the shorts off is going to be impossible. *Fantastic.* I tug the shorts back up over my thighs. "Actually. Can you help me?"

He moves into the space wordlessly, his muscular frame

taking up far more room than he should have. "What do you need me to do?"

"Close your eyes and help me get the shorts off my legs. The bed is dusty and—"

Zane shuts his eyes tightly and turns his face away. His large hands splay on my waist, and I suck in a breath as he quickly slides the shorts down over my hips. I grip his shoulders with both hands, giving him my weight as I lift each leg free.

Pain shoots up through my injured thigh, but as soon as I shift the weight to my uninjured leg, it becomes manageable again.

As I release his shoulder and steady myself on the dresser, Zane turns away completely. "What else?" he asks.

Everything. I shake the thought away. Needing anyone is a risk. But needing Zane? That's a trap I can't risk falling into. "I'm not sure I can hold myself steady enough to get the sweats on."

Eyes still closed, Zane holds an arm out, so I take it and guide him toward my upper arm. He holds me, gaze turned away, eyes closed, as I slip into the sweats.

"Okay, thanks. You can open your eyes."

He does, then moves out of the room again when I shrug out of my jacket. Thankfully, the injury to my thigh doesn't cause me any issues as I change my shirt and put my hair up in a ponytail. After I pull my jacket back on, I limp back to the bed to put my shoes on.

"You can come in."

Zane steps back into the room and immediately crosses to me before sinking to his knees. Without asking, he takes my shoe and slips it onto my foot.

"I can do that."

"It's easier on your leg if I do it," he replies.

He's right, but Zane Knox kneeling in front of me is too much for me to handle. Especially when he glances up at me through thick, dark eyelashes, his green gaze so bright it's nearly blinding.

"Why didn't you become a doctor?" I ask again, hoping that if we start this Twenty Questions game, we can get it over with, and I can move on.

"That depends on who you ask," he replies.

"That's not an answer."

"It's the only one you're getting right now. Is someone after you?"

"I already answered that back at the hospital. I don't know."

"That's not the whole truth." His sharp gaze is trained on my face, not missing a single flicker of emotion as it passes over my features.

"Someone tossed my apartment," I reply, because I know this questioning will get *nowhere* if one of us doesn't give in. "I found my door ajar and peeked inside to see that everything had been tossed. I ran and was jumped just outside."

"Where?"

"Savannah."

"Georgia?"

"That's the one."

He nods and crosses his arms, his powerful stance igniting an even stronger attraction within me.

Get it together, Tessa.

"Is that where you've been for the last eighteen years?" The question is a punch to my gut because it's exactly what I'd wanted to avoid. How do you tell the man you loved more than anything that you chose to leave him out of fear? That living a half-life was easier than a simple one with him?

That the pain was more familiar than the love, so you chose the former?

CHAPTER 7

ZANE

Standing here in Tessa's childhood bedroom is undoing me. Every memory I have here, from visiting her to bring her food because I knew she wasn't eating enough, to checking in just to make sure she was alive, slams into me at once.

Even the time her dad tried to kill me because I'd fallen asleep talking to her, and he'd thought we were sleeping together. It hadn't mattered that I told him I had no intention of having sex until marriage.

Something I didn't stick to when I strayed from God after losing Tessa. I've since asked His forgiveness and stuck to my new vow of celibacy, even knowing I would likely never marry. I've never felt anything for anyone else that even came close to what I felt for Tessa.

What I still feel for her even as she stands here, staring at me like I'm the enemy.

"We agreed that we wouldn't talk about it." Her walls are back up, firmly in place, and she glares at me like I betrayed her.

"We agreed not to talk about the night you left. Not about where you've been."

Tessa glares at me. "I've been all over the place. Most recently, Savannah," she says.

"Why there?"

"I like peaches."

"You hate peaches."

It was the one fruit she never liked to eat. I found out a few years after we met that the reason was because her mother always drank peach schnaps, so the smell nauseated her.

"People change," she retorts. "What do you do for a living?"

"Government work."

"Which explains nothing," she replies.

"I was in the Navy for a while. After that, I got pulled in for contract work." She doesn't have to know it was by force. Or that I've pulled a trigger more times than I can count. Always when it was mine or innocent lives on the line—though that doesn't make it any better.

Killing is still killing. There's no positive spin on it.

"The Navy?" She arches a brow. "I didn't see that coming."

I cross my arms. "You said you don't know if someone

is after you. Why would they wait outside your apartment after tossing it?"

"I have no idea. I'd just gotten a new job, and things were starting to look up."

"Where?"

"An environmental agency in Savannah. I was working as a secretary."

"How long?"

"Three months."

"What was the name of the company?" I press.

"Southeast Environmental Commission." She crosses her arms. "What made you decide not to become a doctor?"

It's the third time she's asked that question, and although I really don't want to answer it, I need her to keep answering mine. "You."

"Me?" Her eyes widen in surprise.

"When you went missing, I put everything I had into finding you. The police couldn't do much, and I was angry. Weston was headed into the Navy, so I went, too. Because I'd already done four years of college by the time I was nineteen, I went in as an officer, and the rest is history."

"But you'd always wanted to be a doctor. You were supposed to start med school after we got back from our—" She trails off, but I know what she was going to say.

When we got back from our honeymoon, we were going to move into an apartment in Charleston so I could start med school while Tessa worked on her bachelor's at the University of South Carolina.

"Things change." I clench my jaw. "Was the company in any hot water?"

"They're an environmental company," she deadpans. "So I doubt it."

"You'd be surprised." My gaze travels over her bruised cheekbone and the cuts and scrapes on her arms. "I need to know about the night you were attacked."

"Why? You're not a cop. Why does it matter?"

"It matters to me," I reply. "And if I know, then maybe I can find out if someone is actually after you or if you're going to be safe."

She closes her eyes for a moment, then takes a deep breath. "I don't see how that's possible since you're not a cop, but fine. If you really want to know, then I guess we can consider this show and tell." Her voice quivers.

She's afraid.

And that just infuriates me even more.

Unable to do anything else to get rid of this anger inside me, I clench both hands into fists and wait.

"Like I said, I went home after picking up some dinner. It was the first thing I'd eaten that wasn't out of a can in months, so I was pretty focused on it. When I saw that my door was partially open, I thought I'd just forgotten to close it. But when I looked inside and saw everything was a mess, I knew that something was wrong. I dropped the food and turned to run."

"Where were you going to go? The police?"

"No. I was going to leave and start over again. I've done it before."

When you left me. That's why I couldn't find her. Because she didn't want to be found.

"What happened next?"

"There's an alleyway between the apartment building and the restaurant beside it. I was passing by, and someone grabbed me." She crosses her arms, and her bottom lip quivers. "I didn't get a good look at him because it was dark. He hit me first, which is what sent me back onto the ground and gave me this." She gestures toward the bruise on her face.

It's all I can do to keep my head.

"That's when I realized he had a knife. I kicked him in the groin, which dropped him down, and he stabbed me. I didn't get the feeling he was trying to kill me, but I didn't want to wait around to find out. While he was down, I kicked him in the face, got up, and took off. I managed to get into my car before he could catch up to me—but barely."

"Why do you think he wasn't trying to kill you?"

"I heard someone yell, 'Don't let her get away,' from what sounded like a phone on speaker. Again, I didn't wait around to ask questions."

"He chased you?" If what she overheard on the phone wasn't enough to sway me toward a targeted attack rather than a random mugging, that would. Muggers don't want attention, so nine times out of ten, they'll bail at the first sign of trouble. If this guy actively pursued her, then he was out for something else.

"Yes. I still didn't see his face, though. Like I said, it was dark, and I was more focused on getting away."

Because I need to do something, I take my baseball cap off and run a hand through my hair. "Is your car nearby?"

She shakes her head. "It broke down right before I reached Tidewater Bay."

"How did you get here?"

"I wrapped my thigh in a sweatshirt I found in my trunk so no one would notice it; then I walked."

"You walked on your injured leg? That must have taken at least an hour."

"Two, actually. And yes. I needed a place to lie low, and this seemed like the best option. It's been so long since I was here; I figured there would be little chance anyone would find me."

"Why is that? It wouldn't be hard to trace you once they have a name."

She stares back at me for a moment, then shakes her head. "No, my turn. What *exactly* do you do for the government?"

I let out a deep breath, trying to decide how much I can tell her. "I solve problems others can't solve."

"That's not an answer."

"I can't give you much more than that," I reply honestly.

The corners of her mouth tilt in a partial grin that stirs

the feelings I'm trying *really* hard to ignore. "Why? Because then you'd have to kill me?" Her words are echoes of the action movies we'd watch together back before everything fell apart.

"Never," I repeat without hesitation. "I would never hurt you."

Even though you ripped out my heart and stomped on it, you're still safe with me.

Her smile falters. "Why do you want to help me? Why are you so interested in making sure I'm safe?"

"It's my turn," I say, not exactly wanting to get into the fact that, even after all this time, and the fact that she chose to leave me all those years ago, there's not a single thing I wouldn't do to protect her. "Why did you pick my boat? Any one of them would likely have had medical supplies on board, and mine is docked toward the end of the marina. It would have been a long, painful walk on an injured leg."

Her expression darkens, and she crosses her arms. "I knew you would have what I needed because you always made sure you had emergency supplies whenever you went out on the boat."

"It's been nearly two decades. For all you know, I could have abandoned the boat."

"You would never do that," she retorts. "Because you love it."

"We don't always get to keep the things we love."

Her gaze leaves me momentarily, but I never let mine stray from her face.

"Look, I don't know why you're so curious about what happened."

"Because someone tried to kill you."

"Key word: *tried.* I have no intention of letting them get another chance." She takes a staggered step toward the door, and I fight the urge to reach out and help her. Since I know she'll withdraw, though, I fist my hands at my sides and follow her out of the room and down the hall.

There's a massive hole in the floor that she moves around with ease. It was here the last time I was, too, only her dad had placed a piece of wood over the top of it to keep from falling when he was too drunk to pay attention.

She pauses just outside his bedroom door, takes a deep breath, then shoves it open to move inside.

I've only been in here once since he passed, but as I step through the doorway, it's as though I'm stepping back eighteen years. Everything is dust-covered, but it's the same. Right down to the dirty laundry off to one side and the empty beer bottles scattered on the floor and bed. I try not to pay any attention to the dark urine stain on the mattress or the haphazard way the blankets are strewn about. Tessa lived in this nightmare every day.

And from the way it sounds, she's still living one. It's different, sure, but still a nightmare.

Tessa walks over toward the closet and reaches up, stretching up onto the toes of her uninjured leg and feeling the shelf. Because she's going to hurt herself, I move around her and reach up with ease, retrieving the shoebox she was reaching for.

She glares at me when I hand it to her.

Moving across the room, she sets the box down on top of a nightstand, its varnish chipped and worn. Removing the lid, she takes a stack of dusty cash and a bone-handled revolver. After tucking the money into the pocket of her sweats and the gun into her jacket pocket, she abandons the box.

"I can't believe that's still there," I say honestly.

"Even dead, no one wanted anything from him," she says, tone sharp as razor blades. "People could sense the darkness in this place without ever setting foot in it. Even door-to-door salesmen weren't that desperate." Without another word, she moves out of the room, favoring her leg so much that she takes a pause in the hallway and lets out a deep breath.

"Let me help you."

Tessa stiffens, likely because she didn't realize I was standing so close—but I can't help it. Like the moon controls the tide, the hold Tessa still has on me seems unbreakable. It's always been that way. My instant connection to her has never made sense, but it's also the only thing that does.

Light fills the room as lightning strikes just outside. The thunder comes less than a second later, and it's so loud it shakes the trailer. Still, I can hear my own heart thundering above anything else.

Tessa's gaze never strays from mine. She pins me with an intensity that steals my breath. Desperate to pull her into my arms, I clench both hands into fists at my sides and try to remind myself that this woman left me at the altar.

She abandoned our future before we even had a chance at one.

The rain starts, its deafening drumming against the sides of the metal trailer drowning out even the sound of my own breathing.

But Tessa's gaze remains—so does mine.

"I don't need help," she replies, yelling so I can hear her over the storm.

The trailer shakes with the force of the wind as it picks up outside.

"No, you never did, right? Isn't that what you said back at the hospital?"

She opens her mouth to respond, her cheeks flushing with color. But a second later, that fight dies, and her expression turns defeated. "I need to leave." She continues forward, dodging the hole, so I do the same, moving in her wake.

"Do you really think they're just going to leave you alone?" I demand. "Whoever this is will find you, Tessa. You're not safe."

"Do you really think I don't know that?" she demands, whirling back on me. We're in the living room now, and the only light sneaks in through broken windows. Rain falls in sheets just outside, the wind blowing it in and saturating my shirt.

"Tessa—"

"No." She points her finger at me. "I'm sorry I got on your boat, but I didn't ask for your help. I answered your questions, and now I need to go. I need distance from this place. From—" Her gaze lands on me, and she doesn't have to finish the sentence.

"From me."

Tessa's gaze darts away before resting back on me. "Yes."

I move in closer. "And why is that? Because the idea of being near me is so appalling to you?" Anger laces my tone. *How could she say that? Why does she hate me so much?*

"Being near you—" Glass shatters, and I throw Tessa to the floor before my mind has even registered the bullets raining down on us. She screams as I cover her with my body and withdraw the pistol holstered at my waist.

Thanks to the storm, I can't even hear the weapon being fired, but with how quickly they're coming—I know it's got to be an automatic with extended magazines for minimal load time.

Adrenaline coursing through my system, I shut down my fear for Tessa and focus only on the mission. We need an exit. Now. I scan the dark trailer, searching for any way out, but see none. And as thin as these walls are? We're as good as dead if these bullets keep putting fresh holes into them.

My gaze lands on the hole in the floor.

I start moving, dragging Tessa with me as I go. I keep my body positioned over hers. Pain slices across the side of my face, but I keep moving, my hammering heart stealing focus from everything else. Warmth trickles down my cheek, but I ignore it as I push through the pain, my only focus on getting Tessa out of here.

I have to save her.

Tessa keeps crawling until we reach the hole. She slips down inside with ease, rolling to the dirt beneath the trailer.

I follow, then rip my cell phone free.

I've lost count of how many shots have been peppered into the trailer, but I'm honestly surprised it's still standing. Another booming round of thunder covers the gunshots.

Me: *Under fire. Tessa's dad's place. Bring backup.*

Shoving it back into my pocket, I look over at Tessa. It's pitch black down here, but I feel for Tessa's hand and grip it, squeezing gently in hopes of offering her some sort of hope.

Lord, we need You. Please be with us.

The ground is already muddy, thanks to the water rolling down beneath the trailer from the hill just beyond it. We crawl our way through, and I try to lead us as far back as we can go before turning on my side and facing the hole. I keep my weapon aimed at the beam of light that's barely visible.

And I wait.

The rain slows, and the bullets stop.

Once again, I scan for an exit. We have to run. The second they come in and realize we're not dead, they'll find the hole in the floor, and then we will be. The trouble is, with the rain and Tessa's injury, we won't make it far. Not in time.

Keeping my weapon trained straight ahead, I ignore the buzzing in my pocket from what is probably Ryker's response. The storm rages just beyond the trailer. Loud enough that I can't hear whether or not anyone is even walking above us.

Lord, please. Please be with us. I repeat the prayer over and over again, focusing on His promise that, no matter what happens in this life, an eternity of peace awaits afterward. He has a plan—of that I have no doubt. I just hope it's us surviving.

With the adrenaline continuing to wreak havoc on my system, I remain where I am, breathing steadily while I wait to pull the trigger. Because that's exactly what I'm going to do if I see anyone pop down that hole.

It's them or us.

And I won't let them get Tessa.

The storm picks up again, and lightning flashes just beyond the lattice surrounding the bottom of the trailer. It's everything I can do to maintain my breathing as I fight the urge to risk the precious moments it would take to check my phone and make sure it was Ryker messaging me back.

What if he didn't get the message?

CHAPTER 8

TESSA

I have never been as terrified as I am right now.

I can't even see Zane's face, but knowing he's trapped down here and using his body as a shield for mine is enough to send me into a full-blown panic attack. My life is expendable; his isn't. He has a mom and a sister who count on him. He might even have a wife and kids by now.

What will they do if something happens to him?

Me? No one will even remember me past the funeral.

No. He shouldn't be here. Why is he here?

My breathing is ragged. I try to remain quiet just in case our attacker comes in here to check whether or not we're still breathing.

All while I come to the realization that someone *really is* after me. It's not just some paranoid fear.

It was easy to pretend otherwise after the attack in the alley, but this erases each and every bit of doubt, leaving me with a single question: Why? What did I do to deserve this?

I have no enemies—that I can think of, anyway. The only one who might have an issue with me has spent the last six years in prison.

Who's coming for me now? Is this just my lot in life? To spend every moment at the mercy of violence?

The storm continues to rage on just outside our shelter, but it's nothing compared to the terror in my veins. Zane's body is between me and the hole we fell through, and thanks to the bright lightning outside and the lattice slats surrounding this trailer, I was able to see that his gun is aimed straight ahead.

Will he really pull the trigger?

"Zane!" A masculine voice calls out above the storm.

"Down here!" he yells back. "Come on, Tessa, we're safe now." He releases my hand and starts crawling forward.

But I don't move. Safe? I don't even know the meaning of the word.

My body trembles, and it has nothing to do with the cold.

Zane's hand finds mine again, and he gently tugs. "Come on, we're okay."

I can't even find the words to respond as I crawl

through the mud toward the hole. The good news is that I can't even feel the pain in my thigh, though after this, I imagine it'll be particularly sore.

Still, at least, we're alive.

We reach the hole, and large hands reach down. Zane pulls me forward, and I reach up, letting myself be pulled from the hole. The moment I'm on solid ground, a blanket comes around my shoulders.

I've never met the man in front of me. He towers over me, and his size rivals that of a linebacker. But his eyes are kind though his expression is hard.

"You okay?" he asks.

I nod, then turn as a man who has his back to me helps Zane from the hole. The moment I see his face, the icy terror returns. Crimson streaks down the side of his face, mixing with the mud from beneath the trailer. "You're bleeding!" I shove the blanket from my shoulders and start forward, but a large hand from the man behind me grips my arm.

I go completely still, freezing in place.

"Let her go," Zane orders. His voice might as well be coming from underwater, though, because all I can feel is the large hand gripping my upper arm.

Rough hands. Strong hands. Hands that hurt. Breathe, Tessa.

The man releases me, but I still don't move. My gaze is fixated on the blood smearing the right side of Zane's face.

It drips down onto the collar of his shirt, leaving a trail of red amidst the smudges of brown.

"Did you see who it was?" Zane questions.

The man with his back still to me shakes his head. "They were gone by the time we got here. Likely saw our headlights in the distance." His voice is familiar, beyond familiar really, so when he turns toward me, I shouldn't be so surprised.

Weston Hayes and Zane were best friends growing up. He has a long beard now, and his eyes are much harder than they once were, but there's no mistaking him.

"Tessa," he greets, though his tone is cold. Sharp. Unwelcoming.

Outside, the storm picks up once more. I shiver, and the blanket is placed back around my shoulders by the large man who'd grabbed my arm a few minutes ago. When I look up at him, he offers me a tight expression that is not quite a smile.

I shift my attention away from the giant at my back and focus on the man who saved my life. "Your face," I say again.

"It's just a graze," he says as he reaches up and gently touches the injury.

"I have stuff." My legs tremble as I move, the pain still just an echo in my mind, given the events we just lived through. I don't look to see if I'm being followed. I just limp into my bedroom and kneel beneath the foot of my bed. After prying the floor vent open, I reach down and grab a plastic bag.

It's covered in dust, but the first-aid stuff I'd stashed there to tend to my injuries is still there.

"Tessa."

I turn at the sound of Zane's voice. The blood on his face shatters me. I sink to the floor, my shaking legs finally giving out. No matter how hard I've tried to keep him out of this hell I live, he always gets pulled right back in.

And this time, I don't even know why.

Maybe it would have been better if that bullet had hit me. It would have ended the threat to his life and erased all pain from mine.

Zane crosses the distance and kneels in front of me. His strong hands grip either side of my face. "You're safe."

"It's not me I'm worried about! How can you not see that! You almost died!" I scream because I can't do anything else. Because, once again, I'm the target of someone else's fury.

"But I didn't. I'm okay, Tessa. And so are you."

I close my eyes and shake my head. "You're bleeding."

"This is hardly the worst thing that's happened to me," he says.

Opening my eyes, I stare into his. "And that's supposed to make me feel better?"

"Yes." He drops his hands from my face. "Police are on their way, okay?"

I nod. As much as I don't want to talk to the police, there's not much choice now. I just have to hope that they can figure out who came after me before they succeed. It's not like hiding will do me any good. They clearly know I'm here. And if they tracked me here, then they know my real identity.

Would running even help? Will anywhere ever be safe?

Officer Alan Leopold may be eighteen years older and have quite a few new strands of silver in his dark hair, but I'll never forget the man who didn't put me in handcuffs even though he had every reason to.

He gave me a chance to turn my life around.

And I wasted it.

He and Zane are standing in front of where I'm sitting on the bumper of an ambulance. They flushed and re-bandaged my thigh, and now that the adrenaline has waned, the throbbing is back with a vengeance.

"Did you get a make and model of the vehicle?" he asks Zane, who shakes his head. There's a bandage on his cheek where the bullet grazed him, and every now and again, I catch myself staring at it.

He came so close to dying.

Centimeters off and that bullet would have stolen the very beat of his heart.

A vise clenches around my own, and I let out a ragged breath. *You're both alive, Tessa. Keep it together.*

"We didn't see it. As soon as they started shooting, we took cover."

"We'll run ballistics," Leopold replies. "Whoever did this—" He turns toward the house that is now riddled with bullet holes. "This wasn't their first time."

The storm finally let up, leaving a muddy ground that's rutted with tire tracks. I'd watched the CSI team take pictures and imprints of them in hopes they could find something to help identify the person who tried to take our lives.

"No," Zane says as he turns toward the trailer. "It wasn't."

"So, I need to ask. With your job— Is it possible there's someone after you?" he asks Zane. "I don't know exactly what it is you do, but is it the type of thing that could cause something like this?" He gestures toward the trailer.

"Possibly." Zane glances at me. "But I believe it's Tessa they're after."

Officer Leopold turns toward me. "Any ideas who or why?"

I shake my head and cross my arms, debating getting up so I don't feel so small. "I was attacked outside of my apartment in Savannah, but I assumed it was a separate incident. Now, I'm not so sure. But I have no idea who or why. I haven't done anything."

"Is Savannah where you've been?" he asks. I don't miss the sharpness in his tone. He's angry that I left without a word, too. And why wouldn't he be? Given he's a cop, I bet he spent a lot of time trying to find me.

"For the last few years, yeah."

"And you don't have any enemies?"

"None that are walking free."

Zane stiffens.

"Care to elaborate?" Leopold asks.

No, I don't, because you'll have to arrest me, too. "My dad is dead."

He makes a note on his pad, then closes it and slips it into his pocket. "You're both very lucky to be alive."

Don't I know it.

"Thanks, Alan," Zane says.

"Yeah. I'll keep you updated. In the meantime, I'd like to assign a protective detail to you, Tessa."

"What? No." Old fear slices through the new threat, and I shake my head.

"No need, she'll be with me," Zane says.

"What? No I won't. I can take care of myself."

"It's me or an officer," Zane says, his tone leaving no room for arguing.

Now, I stand. "I'm thirty-six years old, Zane. I don't need a babysitter."

"And I'm not asking. Someone tried to kill you—and me by proxy. Until they find out who, it would be a reckless decision to not accept help." His gaze hardens, and I open my mouth to argue back—but then my gaze lands on his bandaged cheek.

On the dried blood crusted to his neck and the mud-covered shirt he's wearing.

"Fine."

"Which one?" Officer Leopold asks.

"Zane." As much as I need distance, I don't imagine I'll get it even if I accept the police protection. Zane will still be nearby. He's stubborn like that.

"Great. I'll keep you both posted. Are you sure neither of you wants to go to the hospital?"

"No," Zane says. "A hot shower will do some good." He shakes Officer Leopold's outstretched hand.

"Understood. I'll be in touch." He waves and turns away, leaving me standing here, frustration pushing past everything else.

"Thank you," Zane says, his tone soft.

I shift my gaze to him. "For nearly getting you killed?"

"For letting me help you."

"It doesn't sound like I had much choice."

"No," he confirms, and the corner of his mouth lifts in a partial grin. "But at least, this way, I don't have to be sneaky about it."

Weston and a giant man I now know as Ryker cross over. "We good to go?" Weston asks.

"Yeah. Thanks again," Zane says.

"Anything for you, Cap," Ryker says. He shifts his brown eyes to me. "It's good to meet you, Tessa. I'm glad you're okay."

"Thanks." I offer him a soft smile, but it dies when I see Weston's glare.

He's always been protective of Zane, and I imagine he told him why I left. It's no wonder he despises me. I certainly feel enough of that toward myself these days.

"We'll let Garrison and Sawyer know what happened," Weston says.

"Great. I'll get with you guys tomorrow, and we'll make a plan."

"Sounds good." Weston shakes his hand, then turns away from me. Ryker does the same.

"I'm just glad I parked my truck far enough away it didn't end up with a few new holes," Zane comments as he reaches for my arm.

I rip it away, though, not wanting anyone to see me as weaker than they already do.

Poor Tessa Lane. Always needing someone to watch out for her. Always needing Zane Knox to come to the rescue.

"Tessa, let me help."

"You already are." I continue limping forward, prepared to deal with the pain as I walk the half-mile to Zane's truck. He's already done so much for me, and needing even more help just isn't something I'm prepared to admit.

Tears burn in my eyes, and I clench my hands into fists.

Before I make it even out of the drive, Zane scoops me into his arms, his large strides eating up the distance between us and the truck.

I should complain, but to be honest? The feel of his arms around me is too good for me to deny. Especially when I came so close to losing him.

Tomorrow, I can work on the walls to keep him out.

But tonight? Tonight, I'm just happy he's alive.

He deposits me onto the passenger seat of his old Chevy truck, then comes around to the driver's side and climbs in without a word. As he turns on the engine and pulls away, I shift my gaze out the window at the trailer as yellow caution tape is stretched around the place where I grew up.

You know, it's funny.

I always figured this place would be a crime scene.

I just didn't think I'd be alive to see it.

***

"Tea?" Zane questions as he steps up into the galley of his boat. His hair is still wet from his shower, and the scent of eucalyptus dances in the air from his body wash. I try to ignore the thrill I feel at the fact that we smell the same since he insisted I shower first.

His cheek has a fresh bandage on it, and the blood and mud are cleansed from his skin. But even though it's covered, I can still see the wound there. A jagged cut that will likely turn into a scar.

My stomach churns. "Sure. Thanks."

He doesn't respond, just fills an electric kettle with

water and pulls down two mugs. I watch as he scoops loose tea into two tea bags and sets them into the cups. Instead of coming to the table, he remains where he is, staring at the kettle, his back to me.

What's on your mind? Are you regretting bringing me back into your life?

What does a man like Zane think about when the world around him is quiet?

"How is your cheek?" I ask, the quiet making me uncomfortable.

"It's fine."

"You got shot in the face. I hardly think that's fine."

"I got *grazed.* It's not even the worst injury I've had this year."

"You said that already."

He turns toward me and leans back against the counter. "It's the truth."

My heart rate increases as I look at him. This time, for an entirely different reason than earlier. *How does he still have this hold over me after all these years?* "Officer Leopold asked about whether or not someone was after you because of your job. Why is that? What exactly do you do?"

"I told you; I do contract work for the government."

"What kind of contract work?"

"The kind that makes enemies." He crosses his arms. "I can't—"

"Elaborate," I finish. "I get it." Running both hands

over my face, I groan. "I don't know why this keeps happening to me." Whether it's the exhaustion, near-death experience, or the fact that Zane Knox is standing less than ten feet from me, those walls I'd been desperate to put up are paper-thin.

I hear him slide into the booth across from me. "What did you hold back earlier? You said that no one walking free would want to hurt you."

"I told you. My dad is dead."

"We both know you weren't talking about him," he presses. "Come on, Tessa. I know you. I can tell when you're holding something back. If you remember, reading between the lines is a specialty of mine."

I take a deep breath, then let it out in a frustrated sigh. "There was a guy a few years ago. We went on a couple dates, and he didn't care for the pace. He showed up at my work and tried to take things too far. A man walked by and called the police."

Zane's expression turns murderous, his gaze narrowing, cheeks flushing with color. He clenches his hands into fists on top of the table, then lowers them into his lap. "What did he do?"

"Why does it matter?"

"Please tell me." The brokenness of his expression tells me that he's imagining the worst. And, to be honest, it very well could have ended up that way. Thankfully, someone overheard and interceded.

An old man I'll never forget because he threw himself

into the altercation without any thought for himself. Kind of like the guy sitting across from me. What does that say about me that I need to keep being saved? That I can't seem to scrape together even an inch of peace?

"Like I said, he was unhappy with the speed our relationship was progressing. He showed up to where I was working at a truck stop outside of Tulsa, convinced me to take my break because he wanted to talk, then tried to force himself on me. I took a few hits, then broke his nose, but that made him angrier. An old trucker was walking by, and he stepped in to help me. If he hadn't, things would have been worse." The memory is vile, but it doesn't strike the same fear in my heart that it used to. I survived.

I just keep surviving.

One of these days, that luck is going to run out.

"He's in prison?" The look of fury on Zane's face is something I've seen before. Whenever he'd find out that my dad had put hands on me again.

"He is. I pressed charges, then moved on and changed my name."

"Is that why I couldn't find you?"

"I've changed it a few times," I admit. "But, yeah. That's why." Sighing, I close my eyes. "You really don't need to be involved in this, Zane. Trouble finds me, and one of these days, I'm not going to walk away from it."

"Do you really think that will scare me away?"

"It should. I can't pay for your help. If that's what you do, I don't have any money."

Now his anger is directed at me. "I don't want money."

"Then what do you want?" The question slips out before I can filter it. But it's there now, and truthfully, I need to know what it is he wants. "I mean it when I tell you I have nothing to offer in exchange for your help."

"I'm not looking for anything other than knowing that you're safe."

"That's right. Zane Knox is everybody's hero." The sarcasm in my voice is unwarranted, but I can't stop myself.

"Stop doing that."

"Doing what?"

"Putting up walls whenever you start feeling vulnerable. I didn't tolerate it eighteen years ago, and I'm not putting up with it now. You're too good for that." He gets up and pulls the tea bags out of the still steaming water, then mixes honey and a splash of milk in each mug before carrying them over toward the table.

He sets one in front of me, the other in front of him as he slides into the booth seat again, this time opening his Bible.

My gaze remains on him as he scans the pages, his attention fully engulfed in God's word.

There was a time when we'd study the Bible together. He'd just been teaching me about God and had been helping me understand the words in red. And that's something else I left behind when I fled from this place. I haven't touched a Bible, attended a church service, or even prayed since that night.

"How have you not changed at all?" I ask, my voice barely above a whisper.

Zane's gaze lifts to mine, and my mouth goes dry. "I'm not the same man I was."

"You still read your Bible. Still carry everyone else's problems like they're your own. Seems to me you haven't changed much."

"That hasn't always been the case."

I snort. "I doubt that."

Zane smirks, and if I weren't already sitting down, I would have fallen over. The power of his smile has always made me weak at the knees, and it seems the years have only made it more so.

Gorgeous, gorgeous man. *If I stay here too long, I'll be at risk of losing more than my life.*

"You don't even know the half of it," he replies, piercing gaze pinning me.

"Then tell me."

"I think it's better if I don't."

I watch him as he goes back to reading the Bible, studying his profile in the dim overhead light. He's always been handsome. Even when we were thirteen and I barely understood what attraction was, I remember staring at him whenever we were together. Shocked that someone like him would ever be interested in me.

I mean, he came from a good family. Graduated from

high school and went to college at *fourteen.* Handsome, smart, strong, dependable—yet he claimed I was the only one who held his heart. It didn't make sense to me back then, and it still doesn't.

And now the baseball player has transformed into a rugged man with a short beard and scars mostly shielded by the ink on his arms, that attraction burning in my gut has only grown tenfold.

Though, if I'm honest, I guess he is right about being a different person than he was before. Because I never would have pictured Zane Knox with tattoos. Yet, here he sits, muscled, inked, and far too good-looking for my own good.

He glances up, and our gazes lock again.

In this breath of a moment, a million things are said even though not a single word is uttered. Clearing my throat, I shift my attention anywhere but him, choosing to focus on the bandage covering my thigh.

A future with this man was all I'd ever wanted.

We'd even planned on taking his father's boat—this very boat—around the world together afterward. An extended honeymoon where we'd sleep in, sail, and spend our evenings beneath the stars.

Peace.

Home.

That's what he'd offered me. Now I'm sitting across from him, not as his wife but as a hunted woman. A woman who nearly got him killed only a few hours ago.

"You really should let me go," I tell him. "I'll be fine on my own."

"You can barely walk." Those sharp green eyes pin me in place.

"It's not the first time I've been hurt, and it probably won't be the last." The night of my wedding, my father had snapped my ankle. I'd had to push through the pain then, and I can do it now. Though I don't elaborate on that.

His nostrils flare. Is he thinking of the time I was seventeen and he'd come home from college break to find me barely moving after walking in on my father and a random woman in our living room?

Or the year before that, when I'd been pushed down the stairs and broken my clavicle?

I shove those poisoned memories aside. They're in the past, and that man is long dead. He can't hurt me from six feet under.

That was only proven tonight when I stepped into his empty trailer.

He really is gone. The man who always seemed indestructible was destroyed by the alcohol he refused to put down.

"We'll start digging tomorrow, see if we can find out what's going on and who's after you. If there's something to be found, we'll find it," he says, confidence lacing every word. When I don't respond, he returns to reading his Bible, and I fall quiet, sipping my tea and watching him every chance I get.

I know God exists.

I know that He created us.

That He sent His Son to die for us.

What I don't know about is the grace they say He offers.

I know my sins.

The weight of them crushes down on me daily.

And if I can't forgive myself, how can I expect my Creator to forgive me?

CHAPTER 9

ZANE

After a night of tossing and turning, I called Ryker and asked him to sit on the boat to keep watch over Tessa. I'd needed room to breathe. To let my racing thoughts quiet if only for a few minutes.

The side of my face is a bit nastier than I let on last night. I've definitely had worse, but I probably should have gone in for stitches. Every movement of my mouth, whether to drink coffee, talk, or eat something, sends stinging pain through my cheek. Still, a run was my only chance to burn off some of this steam.

Bright sunshine sneaks over the horizon, bathing the world in gold as I pick up the pace, pumping my arms faster. The sand is cool beneath my bare feet as I sprint along the coastline. Sweat slicks my skin despite the chill hanging in the air, but I keep pushing on, hoping to outrun the myriads of emotions slamming into me every single time I see Tessa.

The fear in her eyes when I threw her to the floor in her dad's trailer last night.

The scream that ripped from her throat the moment the bullets started flying.

The bruising on her face that first night she'd shown up here.

Anger fuels me like a hit of adrenaline, and I run faster, sprinting until I can hardly breathe. Only then do I slow down and take a pause, giving my racing heart a break. Dropping down onto the sand, I raise my knees and rest my forehead against them.

Lord, I don't know what to do here. Why is she back? Why did she leave in the first place? Is her return part of Your plan? How can I forgive her for leaving all those years ago? How can I protect her now?

My chest tightens, but no answer comes.

So I push back to my feet, ready to run back toward my boat so I can shower and move on with my day. Before I start, though, my cell rings. I pull it out of the zipped pocket of my joggers and stare down at Tucker Hunt's name on the screen.

"Knox," I answer.

While I don't know Tucker well, I trained with his cousin, Silas, and his twin brother, Dylan. When Dylan was in trouble last year, I helped them rescue him and his now-wife, Emma. They're good people, and he has a knack for getting into places not even law enforcement can legally get into. At least, not without a body weight in red tape.

"Hey, this a good time?"

"It is if you've got answers for me," I reply, slightly out of breath as I start walking back toward town.

"You sound like you're out of breath."

"I was running. What do you have?"

"Fair enough. Okay, so your girl—"

"She's not my girl," I interrupt.

Tucker is quiet for a moment, but doesn't argue when he keeps talking. "Noted. Even though I wasn't able to find anything on that company she was working for, I did get some info on her whereabouts over the last eighteen years."

"Great. What do you have for me?"

"Tessa Lane didn't just run away; she fell off the map eighteen years ago. I'm talking *everything*. No new credit cards, no usage on her current ones or access to her debit account."

"I know all of that."

"Yes, but what I *did* manage to track down is the name she was living under. Or rather names. She changed them every five years or so."

She'd said as much. But I wanted confirmation. "How'd you do that?"

"Facial recognition software. I fed an old image of Tessa through a couple databases and got a hit. Tessa Lane is also Taylor Newport, Kate Angelo, Janice Lewis, and, most recently, Lisa Phillips."

"What could you find on them?"

"Taylor lived in Sacramento, California, and Kate lived in Dallas, Texas. They don't have anything but birth certificates and driver's licenses. No credit cards or tax documents. They both have pretty clean records, and it looks like, as Taylor, she worked at a department store, while Kate was a receptionist at a veterinary clinic."

"And Janice? Lisa?"

"Janice is where things get a bit dicey. She had that name for less time than the others because it got listed in a police report out of Tulsa, Oklahoma."

"Assault?" I ask. *Is this the same guy she spoke of before? Or someone else?*

"Well, she was working at a truck stop outside of Tulsa, and it looks like she was involved in a domestic dispute with a Jaguar Billings. I looked it up—twice. That's his birth name."

Domestic dispute. "She said something about that last night. What did the report say?"

"She was treated at the local hospital for some abrasions and a sprained wrist. He'd been attempting to sexually assault her when someone intervened."

Rage boils my blood all over again, and I have to bite it down to keep from exploding right here on the beach. "And after that?"

"Janice disappeared, and Lisa popped up in Savannah, Georgia, right after."

So she's been running since she left Stormwatch Landing. The thought of her out there alone, with no one to count on, makes my chest ache. "Anything on Lisa?"

"Not really. Lived a quiet life. Looks like she worked as a maid in a local motel a few months before she got a job as a secretary for Southeast Environmental Commission. It's an environmental agency, though—" He sighs.

"What is it?"

"I'm going to look into them further, but on the surface, things are a little too smooth."

"What do you mean?"

"I mean, a company like that? They're bound to have some kind of lawsuit going on. Most environmental companies are fighting against big corporations in an attempt to bring about change and all that. But this one is squeaky clean. It could be because they're relatively new, but I've got a nose for this, and something smells off."

Which means it likely is. "I can do some digging. Thanks."

"I'll keep looking, too."

"Be careful, Tucker. If they're behind what's happening now, they nearly killed the both of us last night."

He's quiet for a moment. "What happened?" The friendly tone from earlier is gone, replaced with a seriousness I've come to expect from the Hunts whenever someone they consider family is in danger.

I'm a lucky enough man to be on that list.

"Someone put a whole lot of new holes in the place where Tessa grew up—with us inside."

"Oh, man. I'm glad you're okay."

"Thanks. Me, too. If you want to leave this alone, I don't blame you. We've got enough to deal with."

"Nah, I don't run from a fight. You know that. I'll be careful, but I'll see what I can find." He's quiet a moment. "Look, I know you tried to find her, but don't kick yourself over it. I had to do some serious digging to find her, myself."

"Thanks for this."

"No problem. Want me to email over what I found?"

"Sure. That would be great, thanks."

"Anytime, man. Listen, if you need anything—"

"I'll reach out. Thanks, Tucker."

"No problem, Zane. Stay safe."

I end the call and pause to take a deep breath before continuing down the beach.

She was abused by her father and by a man she met afterward. Now, someone is trying to kill her.

Was changing names and living as different people really better than what I could offer her? Or is there more to that story, too?

"Hey there, Cap." Ryker sets aside his book and stands as soon as I'm on board.

"Thanks for this."

"Sure thing. I'll be working tonight, but if you need me, let me know."

"Will do, thanks." I start to walk away, then pause. "Actually, can you grab the others? Have everyone meet back here in an hour?"

He nods. "You get word on what's going on?"

"Tucker got back to me. I've got some information, but nothing concrete yet." I start toward the door, pausing just a moment and turning toward him. "Did she say anything to you?"

He shakes his head. "She's been down there ever since I got here. Aside from me briefly checking in on her just to make sure she didn't climb out of one of the windows, I haven't seen her."

"Got it. Thanks."

"No problem. See you soon, Cap."

"See ya." I turn back toward the door and grip the handle to pull it open.

Tessa is sitting at the table, a notepad in front of her. "I hope you don't mind, but I pilfered your stash of office supplies." Since her clothes were destroyed last night, she's wearing a pair of my joggers and one of my t-shirts.

They're far too big for her, but she's breathtaking. And seeing her in them ignites something in me I'm not quite ready to face. Especially not when the anger in my chest is building with every passing second.

"Has your life really been better without me?" I blurt out.

I should have prepared. Eased into it, but as the color drains from her face, I realize that approaching it any other way might have just given her time to put those walls back up.

I *need* them to come down because I desperately need to understand what it was about her new life that was so appealing compared to what I was offering.

"Excuse me?"

"You heard me." I can't sit, so I cross my arms. "What happened in Dallas, Kate? Or should I call you Janice? Taylor? Oh, I know—" I snap my fingers. "Lisa. I can't quite keep up with all the names you have." Anger laces every word, and even though I *know* I should have calmed myself before this conversation, my desire to get answers is stronger than the manners my mother ingrained in me.

I'm all over the place, but I just don't get it. I don't understand *why* she left. None of it makes any sense. After all we'd been through, all we were to each other, I'm just not buying her story that she simply changed her mind.

How could she?

I would have given her everything I could. Would have done *anything* to make her happy.

Tessa gets to her feet, using a hand on the table to steady herself. "That's none of your business."

"It is my business because you showed up on my boat with a stab wound in your thigh." I take a step closer. "It *is* my business because I nearly took a bullet for you. If you want my help, you need to be honest."

"I never said I wanted your help," she growls. "In fact, I was fairly adamant that I wanted you to leave me be."

I take a step closer even though closeness is the absolute *last* thing I need. "I thought you were dead, Tessa. Do you have any idea how many nights I sat outside your dad's trailer, waiting for any sign of you? How many times I broke in while he was passed out and wondered what would happen if I threw all of my morals aside and hurt him until he told me where you were?" I'm yelling now, the anger I've buried over the last seventy-two hours flooding to the surface.

She stares back at me, gaze hard. But her bottom lip trembles. *It's a mask. It's all a mask.*

"I told you. I changed my mind." But her voice wavers.

It breaks, and her bottom lip trembles.

"You're lying to me."

She swallows hard, and the visible walls of her expression crack. "You were better off without me. Why can't you see that?"

"He hurt you, didn't he?" I ignore her question because it's a deflection. A way to avoid feeling everything she's feeling. "Your dad," I add when I take another step closer. It's the only thing that makes any sense. The only explanation.

Tessa's eyes fill, and she takes a deep breath. "It doesn't matter."

"It matters to *me*." How can I make her see? How can I get her to understand that she was *everything* to me? That I would have given anything to know she was okay? Even if it was just that she'd changed her mind and didn't want to be with me?

The silence around us is deafening while I wait for her to speak again. Will she tell me the truth? Or will more lies spill out when she opens her mouth?

"He nearly killed me," she whispers as a single tear slips down her cheek.

A rumbling fills the air around us, and it takes me a moment to realize it's a growl coming from me. I clench my hands into fists, doing everything I can to keep my anger in check.

I knew it was him. And despite knowing that it's not an "eye for an eye", and vengeance belongs to God, I can't help but wish I could turn back time and make him feel everything she felt and more.

She lowers back down onto the seat. "He called and said he needed to talk. That he knew he'd messed up, and he wanted to make things right. That he didn't want to miss his only daughter's wedding."

"And you went."

"I was an idiot."

"You wanted him there. Even after everything." As twisted as it is, I can understand why she went. Not because I agree, but because Tessa was always loyal to the core. It didn't matter how many times his fist broke her; she always got back up, willing to forgive because "next time might be different."

"Like I said, I was an idiot," she says. "When I showed up, he wasn't drunk like I expected, and he'd even cleaned. It gave me hope. I hadn't seen my dad sober in—well, ever." She swallows hard. "I let him get close and didn't even see the fist before it hit my cheek."

The anger consumes me because I can picture it so clearly. Him, red-faced and furious, and Tessa, wide-eyed and innocent. Desperate to be loved by the man who should have loved her the most.

"I'm not entirely sure what happened after that. But when I woke up, I was covered in alcohol. He'd dumped all of what he'd had in the house out on me and stood there with a lighter in his hand."

Horror twists in my gut, and bile burns my throat. "He was going to light it?" My own voice cracks. She'd been facing the end of her life, and I was sleeping safely, dreaming of a future that would never come.

She lets out a shaky breath. "That's certainly what it looked like to me. Somehow, I managed to get away. My ankle and wrist were broken, my face was bloodied and bruised, and I later found out I had three cracked ribs."

"Tessa—" I start to take a seat, every ounce of anger I had before vanished beneath the weight of her confession, but she holds up a hand.

"I don't want your pity. I never wanted your pity." Tears stream down her cheeks, but there's fire in her eyes now, so I remain rooted in my spot, afraid that if I push, she'll shut down again.

"He told me that I would never be anything but what I was. That the alcohol would take me, too, just like it did my mother and him, and that one day you would see it and leave me. He said it was better if I just crawled into a hole and died and that he was more than happy to take matters into his own hands. Just like he should have done a long time before."

I turn away, afraid that she'll see the anger on my face and stop speaking. With both hands clenched into fists, I steady my breathing, drawing a deep breath in and letting it out slowly. If only I could rewind time and kill him before the alcohol took him.

Except that's not the outlook I should have—and I know it.

God, please take these angry thoughts from me. Please help me offer Tessa what she needs now. She's had enough anger in her life.

When I face her again, her cheeks are stained with fresh tears.

"You were the first person I wanted to call," she whispers. "The only one. But I knew what you would do if you saw me."

"I would have ripped him apart," I growl. "They would have been finding pieces of him all over the county."

"Exactly. And you would have thrown away your life for me when I'm not worth it. I never was. You should have found some perfect Christian girl and gotten married. Had perfect babies and lived your life without any of the baggage that came with me. You could have had a great life, Zane."

Her words bring a fresh wave of anger washing over me. This time, directed at her. "That's a pretty picture of *my* life you painted there, Tessa. There's only one problem: I didn't want anyone else. I wanted *you*." *I still do.* That realization hits me square in the chest. Because, even after everything that's happened, if she gave me an opening, I'd crawl over broken glass to get to her.

To get the chance to love her like she should be loved.

She closes her eyes and shakes her head. "It wasn't meant to last, Zane. I was bad for you. I am bad for you. It took nearly dying for me to see it, but I ran as soon as I did."

"You let him win," I say simply.

"What?" Her tear-filled eyes open. "How can you say that?"

"You let him tear us apart. He wanted you to be miserable, and you gave him that."

"I spared you."

"From what? Happiness?" I snap. "A chance to be married to the woman I loved more than anything?"

"From the toxicity that runs in my veins!" she screams, tears running down her cheeks. "Everywhere I turn, trouble follows. It caught up to me in Tulsa, too. I went on two dates with him, and when I wouldn't jump into bed with him, he attacked me. I attract darkness. Like some sort of twisted magnet."

"It wasn't you." I take a step closer to where she's sitting, not caring that she wants distance. "You were born into a terrible home, but you were climbing out of it. That's why your dad did what he did. Because he couldn't stand to see you happy. You weren't the root of your problem until you made yourself one."

"Happy." She all but chokes on the word.

"You gave your life to Jesus and were about to be married to someone who would *never* lay a hand on you in that way. He hated that, Tessa. He hated me because he knew you were the *only* thing standing between him and the grave. And I was going to take you away from that life. Away from the life of servitude and filth he'd forced you to live in."

"Jesus," she scoffs. "He left me, too," she whispers.

"No. He didn't." And the fact that she thinks He did only pushes my anger into overdrive.

How could she do this?

How could she throw away *everything* we built because a man not worthy of his biological title told her she was worthless?

She shakes her head and shuts her eyes tightly. "Look, I'm not trying to get a sermon from you, Zane. You wanted the truth, and now you have it. I ran because I wanted to spare you from a life with a criminal record that would derail everything you'd worked so hard for. I'm sorry for the hurt I caused you, but I did what I needed to do."

My fingers flex at my sides because *all* I want to do is

pull her into my arms and make her forget every ounce of pain she's ever felt. I want to make her *see* that Jesus never left her. That God has been right beside her from the very beginning. But even though the brokenness on her face is killing me, the sting of the truth is a bite I'm not sure I can forget.

"I'm sorry," she says softly. "I really am, Zane."

"I would have done anything to keep you here," I say softly. "Tessa, I would have done anything for you."

"I know," she replies. "And that was the problem. If you don't want to help me anymore, I understand. I can go and—"

"No. I'm still going to help you."

"Why?"

Our gazes hold, and emotion snaps between us like a live wire. *Because I am still in love with you. Because even though you shattered my heart, I'd still tear the world apart to protect you.* "Because you meant a lot to me back then, Tessa. I only ever wanted you to be happy. And now I want you safe." Before I can confess a whole lot more, I run a hand through my hair. "I need to get a shower," I say. "Then I need to make some calls."

"About what?"

"So I can start getting us some answers."

TESSA

"*I would have torn him apart.*" Zane's words have been on repeat in my mind ever since he headed down the steps to shower.

It's all I can think about.

His reaction is *exactly* why I couldn't stay. My dad was always going to be trouble for us. No matter what. Had Zane and I actually gotten married? There's not a single doubt in my mind that he would have made our lives miserable.

But, man, how I'd wanted to walk down that aisle.

When things got bad over the last eighteen years, which was more times than not, I'd imagine that I had. I'd imagine Zane lifting my veil, of him leaning forward and capturing my lips as man and wife. And for a moment— one brief, blissful moment, I'd been happy.

And then reality set in, and I'd remember that I lost everything that ever mattered to me.

My gaze drifts back to the door where Zane disappeared fifteen minutes ago. Why didn't he ever settle down?

Masculine voices outside rip my attention from the door and plunge me back into the present. My heart begins to beat faster as flashes of last night assault my mind.

Did they find us?

Are they here for me?

When the voices grow closer, my heart rate increases. I push to my feet and grab a steak knife from the drawer to the right of the stove. Heavy bootsteps thud just outside the door, and two large shadows pass by the curtained window.

I tuck myself into the corner.

Zane is down in the shower, completely unaware of what's happening up here. I could scream, could yell for help, and he'd come running. I'd rather die than have anything happen to him. So, heart in my throat, I remain as still as I can…and wait.

You can do this, Tessa. You can fight.

The door opens, and two men I don't recognize stroll in. One has a gun holstered to his hip, the other a large knife on his.

Adrenaline surges through my system, and I charge out, blade raised. The pain in my leg is barely registerable as the fight in me surges to the surface and blocks out everything else.

The one closest to me ducks, and the man behind him shoves me back and pins me against the wall as he rips the blade from my hand. "We're not here to hurt you," he says softly. His brown eyes are kind as he looks at me, and just as quickly as he disarmed me, he releases me and takes a step back.

"Speak for yourself, Demo," the man I attacked says as he straightens and brushes both hands over the front of his shirt. "She swings another blade at me, and I'll throw her overboard. I hope you can swim," he adds.

The man he called Demo chuckles softly and strolls over toward the bench seat where I'd been playing solitaire. He's just sitting down when Weston and Ryker walk in.

Four large men. All of them dwarfing the small cabin.

I stay where I am, closest to the door, my heart hammering as panic claws at my throat. Large men. Large hands. I know Weston won't hurt me. And Ryker hasn't been anything but kind, but the trauma response doesn't get it.

And my fight or flight is currently weighted *heavily* toward flight. "What is happening?" I ask, doing what I can to keep my voice steady as I consider how long it would take for me to reach the door.

Could I get out before anyone could stop me?

"Girls' night," Weston says, his southern accent lacking all humor.

"Yeah, we're going to braid each other's hair," the man I attacked quips.

The door to Zane's room opens, and he steps out wearing jeans, a dark t-shirt, and boots. His hair is wet, and the cut on the side of his face has been freshly bandaged. Just seeing him eases my panic, and my racing heart begins to slow.

He'd never let anything happen to me.

And he wouldn't keep company with people who would hurt someone.

"You guys are early," he says.

"Yeah, and your girlfriend tried to take a few inches off the top." The man I'd attacked gestures toward his hair, then the steak knife on the counter.

Zane looks from it to me, then back to him. "You should have knocked," he says simply.

"Never have before," he replies.

"I'm not here alone anymore."

The man grins.

"We're sorry that we didn't knock," the guy who'd disarmed me says with a soft smile. "It was rude, especially knowing what you've got going on."

"Thanks."

"You okay?" Zane asks.

Our gazes hold, and the same heat that was between us before sparks to life, but this time it's laced with understanding of just what happens when you light a match amidst a sea of kerosene.

Because that's what lies between us.

It's always been there; I was just too foolish to see it.

"Apparently, Zane has lost his manners. I'm Sawyer." The man who threatened to throw me overboard grins at me, though the smile doesn't reach his caramel-colored eyes. Tattoos climb up one of his arms, disappearing beneath the sleeve of his t-shirt.

"This here is Garrison. But we call him Demo," Sawyer introduces the muscled guy beside him. He's the same one who disarmed me, but he doesn't say anything in response to the introduction. Just offers me a simple nod.

"Demo?" I arch a brow.

"He likes to blow stuff up." Sawyer winks and points to Weston. "Of course, from what I hear, you already know Cowboy."

My gaze lands on Weston, who is still glaring at me. There was a time when I counted him amongst my closest friends, though I recognize that my leaving probably hurt him, too.

"Cowboy?"

"Yeah," he replies, his tone sharper than a razor blade.

"And this here is Tank." Sawyer clasps Ryker on the shoulder.

"We've met," he replies.

"That's right," Sawyer says. "Because you and Cowboy got to ride into the rescue last night."

Weston rolls his eyes. "We were together when Cap called," he says. "It would have taken extra time to grab the two of you. Besides, I called and clued you in."

"Yeah, after the fact," Sawyer replies. "Either way, I'm hurt. I considered us close as family."

The door opens again, and this time, a petite blonde strolls in, carrying three large shopping bags.

"Here, let me help," Sawyer says and rushes forward to take the bags from her.

I fight my own smile at his eagerness to help, something that isn't too difficult to do, when the woman turns toward me, and I see that she's none other than Anastasia Knox.

Zane's younger sister.

Her smile dies when she sees me, and the momentary joy I'd felt at seeing her again withers in my chest at the way she glares back at me. Of course she'd hate me, too. She and Zane are closer than most siblings. When I left him —I left her, too.

And according to him, he hasn't told her why.

"I brought you clothes and toiletries." She points to the bags Sawyer just set on the table.

"Thanks."

She doesn't respond, just turns toward Zane. "I'm going to put these down in your room. Come on, Tessa. I'll show you what I brought, and you can change out of Zane's baggy clothes." She grabs the bags and moves past me, toward the door that will take us down into the bedroom area.

I take a step to follow, only to have pain shoot up

through my thigh because—once again—I wasn't paying attention and put too much weight on it. I fall forward, and Zane's strong arms come around me, holding me up on my feet.

Heat explodes through me, and my heart pounds in response to the contact. As innocent as it is, I can't help myself.

"Let me help you," he says, voice little more than a low growl.

"I'm fine."

"You're not. And the last thing we need is you getting hurt worse." He wraps one arm around my waist and takes most of my weight as I hop toward the steps.

Anastasia is already inside, and she's set some clothes on the bed.

"I'll help her," she says. "Out, and I'll call when we need your muscles again."

Zane grins at her. No matter his mood, Anastasia was always able to bring a smile to his face. Seems like some things really don't ever change.

Zane releases me, and I take a seat on the edge of the bed. "Thanks, Anastasia," he says.

"You're welcome," she calls out as he closes the door. Then, she turns to me, though she avoids eye contact like I'm enemy number one. "Since I didn't know your sizes, I stuck with leggings and baggy t-shirts. If you get me your actual sizes, I can get you more fitted clothes. You look like someone who sticks to jeans."

My bottom lip quivers as emotion sears the inside of my throat. Since I can't trust myself to speak, I nod.

"Do you need help?" It's just like Anastasia to offer help even when she's furious with me. It's just who she is. It never mattered how she was feeling. If someone else needed something, she'd set aside her own issues to make sure they had what they needed.

Just like her brother.

Truthfully, I could use help. Trying to get changed is going to be a nightmare. But I don't want to ask for her help. Not now. I'd rather deal with the pain. "No. Thanks."

"Don't mention it." She starts to move past me, then pauses and turns back toward me. "It was an awful thing—what you did to him. If you truly changed your mind, you should have told him. He grieved you, Tessa. And I don't care what your excuses are; what you did to him was not okay."

"I know," I whisper as tears burn in the corners of my eyes.

The truth is, I've fought long and hard *not* to think about what Zane might have felt when I didn't show up. I'd hoped he would realize that he was better than me. Then find a woman and settle down without the weight of my baggage dragging him down.

I knew that there was no us without a fight, and he deserved so much better than to live in a war zone. Something I knew way too much about to let him shackle himself to me until death do us part. Which, if my dad had his way, would have happened even before we were married.

Anastasia turns and heads up the steps, leaving me alone in a room that smells like the only person who ever truly loved me.

I've been doing all I can not to look too closely at his space. Maybe it's because I'm avoiding going upstairs or trying to postpone the pain that I'm sure to feel as soon as I try to change my clothes, but I can't help myself now. It's neat, just like his room always was when we were kids. There's a framed photo of him, his sister, and both of his parents from back before his dad died.

I move forward to get a closer look at it and a smaller image pinned to the wall beside it. When I lean in enough to see the second photo up close, my heart flutters in my chest.

A young me is wrapped in his arms, staring up at him like he was my entire world. Which, he absolutely was.

Even standing here, jaded as I am, and outside of that moment, I can see the hearts in my eyes.

A tear slips down my cheek, and I reach up to run my fingertips over his smiling face. The pain in my chest isn't new, but it constricts the very beat of my heart.

I'd loved him.

He'd loved me.

And I'd broken it because I was so afraid that the poison in my veins would taint him, too.

Didn't I do that anyway?

He's not at all what I expected him to be. A doctor, living happily with his wife and two perfect kids.

Zane Knox does government work—whatever that means—and lives on his father's old boat all by himself.

How much of his current situation is because of what I did?

Guilt crushes down on me, and my father's voice as he'd stood over me, my blood on his fist, echoes through my mind. *"You'll never be good enough for a boy like that. He's too smart, and you're just a stupid, worthless girl. He'll get bored of you and then throw you out like the trash you are."*

The tears come faster now, so I angrily wipe them away, then step in to turn on the shower.

Stupid.

Useless.

I'd reached for the stars with Zane Knox. Went after a crown that glittered like gold. He was my ticket to a better life. My hope for a future where I wouldn't end up married to a man like my father or become the type of woman my mother was.

But he was more than that. He was my *everything*. My calm in the midst of a storm.

Then, just like my father said I would, I lost him. Because I couldn't understand why someone like him would *ever* love someone like me. And now he's insisting on helping me. Should I do as I said I would and let him?

Or is his best chance if I leave and never look back?

Zane may have been my calm all those years ago, but I'm still the hurricane that will rip his quiet life apart. And I want no part in destroying what he has. Not even if it means facing down my own death.

CHAPTER 11

ZANE

"She okay?" I ask when Anastasia steps into the main cabin and closes the door behind her. My team is waiting on the deck since I'd gotten the sense that Tessa was already overwhelmed enough.

"Sure. I brought her clothes and some toiletries just like you asked. I need to go now. I'm meeting Mom for—" She starts to push past me, so I reach out and gently grip her arm.

"Anastasia."

"What?" She whirls on me, tears in her eyes.

"Are *you* okay?"

"I'm not the one who nearly died last night, am I?" she snaps. All the guys go silent, their gazes trained anywhere but on us. Except Sawyer—he's watching Anastasia with his heart on his sleeve.

"I didn't nearly die," I tell her. "It was a scratch."

"Let's go get some sun," Weston says as he stands. Ryker and Garrison follow, with Sawyer hesitating just a moment before doing the same. He offers me a tight smile in support before closing the door behind them.

"Are you *kidding* me, Zane?" she yells as soon as the door closes. "One more centimeter and it would have taken off part of your face! You keep throwing yourself in these situations, and one of these days, you're not going to walk away." Anastasia wipes her cheeks. "Look, Jon showed me pictures of the trailer when he came in this morning. The fact that you survived—"

"I know." I make a mental note to tell Jon that, next time, he needs to keep things like that to himself. Never mind the fact that it's an active crime scene and he had no business being out there. "I'm okay, Anastasia."

She takes a deep breath. "This time. But what about next time? Can't you just let the police handle this?"

"Who says I'm not?"

She glares at me as she crosses her arms. "Oh, I don't know, the nine hundred pounds of muscle sitting behind me?"

I laugh and pull my sister in for a hug as I sense some of her anger dissipating. "We're not diving headfirst into anything, but I'm not going to send her out on her own."

"I can't lose you," Anastasia says. "Mom and I already lost Dad. Please don't make us bury you, too."

A lump forms in my throat, and I swallow hard. "I can't let her fend for herself."

She pulls away. "I know you can't. But don't lose yourself in the process. That's all I'm asking." Anastasia wipes her cheeks. "Sorry. I guess I needed a good meltdown. When I heard what happened—" She shakes her head. "Nope. You're fine. God protected you both, and I'm going to focus on that."

"Good."

"Okay. Call me if you need me. Mom and I are headed to dinner and a movie, but I'm reachable by phone."

"You've got it, sis. Thanks."

She offers me a quick hug, then turns and leaves the cabin. I hear the guys greet her as she does, so I turn back toward the closed door leading down to my bedroom. Since Anastasia wasn't in there long, I imagine Tessa insisted on getting dressed on her own.

With the pain she's in today, I don't know that that's possible, so I step forward and knock, my chest tightening as I wait for her to answer. I barely managed to keep my head last night when she'd needed help, and today we don't have the distraction of being at the trailer. But the idea of her hurting herself simply because she's being stubborn is too much.

She needs help. And I need her to see that I'm here. In whatever capacity she wants me. I knock again. "Tessa?"

A shrill yelp echoes through the door less than a heartbeat before something—or someone—falls over and hits the ground with a thud. I don't think, just burst through the door. "Are you okay?"

"Fine. I fell." Tessa waves a hand from the other side of my bed. I can't see her, but the sweats she'd had on are lying on the ground.

Heat slips up the back of my neck as desire punches me in the gut. "I'll go get Anastasia. She's probably still close enough that I—"

"No. I'm fine."

"Tessa."

"I don't want her help," she snaps. "She's done enough."

I turn away to give her some privacy. "Can I help?"

She takes a deep breath. "You've done enough, too."

"I'd really rather you be fully dressed when you meet with my team. So I'm happy to lend a hand."

"Keep your eyes closed."

"Deal."

I hear some rustling behind me. Then Tessa's hand grips mine, and she pulls me back a few steps. Heat spreads up my arm at the contact, but I keep my eyes shut tightly, trusting her to guide me.

"Okay. Here." She shoves a pair of pants into my hands, so I turn around and open my eyes just to make sure I don't put them on backward, then close my eyes before turning again. Just like last night, I drop to my knees and hold them open so she can slide her legs into each of the holes.

"Good?" I ask.

"Yeah. I can do the rest. Thanks."

"You sure?"

"Yes. I'll be out in a minute." Her tone is clipped, frustrated, so I don't press. Instead, I turn and open my eyes again, then head up the stairs and close the door behind me.

As soon as it's closed, I take a deep breath and rest both hands on my counter as I lean my head forward. My cheek aches, but it's nothing compared to the burning in my heart.

The desperation to still be everything she needs despite our history.

Behind me, the door opens, so I turn to face her. As she limps out and closes the door. Both eyes are red and swollen. "Are you okay? Do you need pain meds?"

"No. I'm fine." She forces a smile. "Let's do this."

"Look, Anastasia is—"

"Zane, you don't owe me anything, okay? Anastasia is protective of you, and what I did was wrong. She's right. You nearly died *because* of me."

"I'd gladly give my life if it means saving yours." The words are out of my mouth before I can stop them.

"That's not a fair trade, Zane," she says. "Because yours is far more valuable than mine."

Her words are more of a hit than any fist has ever delivered. Not because of the words themselves but because of the utter belief behind them. Tessa truly *believes* that her life is not worth what mine is.

How can she not see?

How can she be so blind to her own worth?

Gently, I place a hand on her arm when she starts to

limp past me, and she stiffens. "You've forgotten," I say softly. She tips her face up to look at me. "Just how much you're worth. And even if it takes every moment of the rest of our time together, I'm going to make you remember."

She takes a deep breath, her gaze never straying from mine. Tessa's confidence had been at rock bottom when we met. She literally had to fight to survive, and neither of her parents ever told her she was worthy of anything.

I'd made sure I told her just how wrong they were, every opportunity I got.

Then, she'd been a young teenager with a heart open to love.

Now, she's a woman who has built thick walls around that heart.

Walls I intend to demolish.

I release her, then wait until she's moved past me before I follow. Because I sense she doesn't want me to offer, I don't ask if she needs help as she limps toward the bench seat of the table that doubled as my bed last night.

As she sits, she keeps her gaze away from me.

I pull the door open, and my team glances down at me. "Ready," I tell them.

One by one, they get to their feet and come inside the small cabin. With all of them in here, it's crowded, but I thought Tessa would be more comfortable here than anywhere else—at least, right now.

"Must be nice to be out of his rags," Sawyer jokes.

Tessa smiles. "Something like that."

Truthfully, I wish she were back in my clothes.

"Okay, so let's get the big thing out of the way." Weston leans back against the counter. "Does this have anything to do with why you left originally?"

Tessa's smile falters, and I glare at Weston.

He simply shrugs, completely uncaring that he just dropped a stick of dynamite into an already tense situation.

"Since the reason I left is six feet under, I'm going to go with no," Tessa says.

Weston nods. "It was your dad then?"

"We're not here to discuss why I left," she shoots back. "And if you are, you might as well leave."

"We're not," I say quickly, shooting a glare at Weston. "Tell us about the company you worked for."

"Southeast Environmental Commission?" she asks. I nod. "I don't know much. I was only there a few months before everything went sideways."

"Just tell us what you do know. Right now, that's our best lead," Garrison says softly. If anyone can get Tessa to open up, it's him. Considering his day job is as a counselor for troubled teens, she's right up his alley, albeit slightly older than his typical clientele.

"I was working two different jobs. One was as a night shift waitress for a twenty-four-hour diner. One night, we had a couple come in. They seemed happy and were really kind. The wife asked me if I enjoyed what I was doing." She fidgets with her hands in her lap. "I told her that it was just a means to an end, until I figured out something better.

She said they were looking for someone to work the front desk at the environmental firm and said that she had a good feeling about me." Tessa chews on her bottom lip. I shift my attention away because, when she does that, her mouth is *all* I can focus on. "Anyway, I accepted on the spot."

"Without learning more about the position? The pay?" Weston questions.

"I was making barely enough to cover my rent, and my day job was seasonal. I was going to be looking for another one soon enough and figured it couldn't pay any less since I was making the bare minimum."

"Keep going," Garrison offers with a smile.

I cross my arms, trying to keep my head while she recounts a life of barely making it. How many nights did she lie awake at night, wondering if she was going to have a place to sleep tomorrow?

"When I went in to meet with their human resources woman to go over all the details, I half-expected her to slam the door in my face. Instead, she welcomed me in and ushered me into a conference room where platters of fruits and vegetables waited. They had a spread of juices, too. It was the most food I'd seen in a long time." Her gaze flicks to me, and it's a fight to keep my expression neutral.

"Then what happened?" Garrison asks.

"The monthly pay was more than I'd see in three months working two jobs. They even gave me the first month up front and told me to consider it a bonus. Everyone was really kind and doing what they could to make a difference. Money aside, I wanted to be a part of doing something good."

"Did the company seem legitimate?" Sawyer asks. "Were there any red flags?"

She shakes her head. "They seemed great. Right after I was hired on, the Bensons went on a trip overseas to see about getting clean water into some South American villages. While I was there, I answered phones, took notes in meetings, and that was about it. All in all, it was a great place to work."

Except, based on what Tucker found, something's off.

"What did the company do?" I question.

"They handled soil and water testing in residential areas as well as fighting to maintain nature preserves when big corporations tried to come in and buy the land."

"That's it?"

"They planted community gardens all over the city and were working to expand to other places, too. Why are you asking about them?"

"Because I have a guy looking into them, and he thinks something's off."

"What?" Her brows draw together. "What do you mean?"

"He said the company doesn't look like a traditional environmental agency."

"But that doesn't make any sense. They were good people doing good work." She shakes her head.

"Maybe," I say, though my gut is telling me something

else is going on. They grabbed a night waitress from the middle of her shift and offered her more money than she'd seen in a long time? It's possible they were just being kind and trying to offer her a fresh start, but I don't know that I'm buying it. "We'll continue looking into them. What were the first names of the people who hired you?"

"Karver and Alara. Benson," she adds.

The names don't ring a bell, but that doesn't necessarily mean anything. Could just mean they're not high-profile enough to have wound up on the radar. "Tell us about the day your apartment was ransacked."

"I already told you what happened."

"I mean your routine. Was anything different? Did anything feel off?"

She shakes her head. "I went to work like normal. Answered phones, then headed home with my dinner."

"That's it?"

"That's it," she repeats. "Nothing was off. Nothing felt different."

"Okay."

"Do you really think they have something to do with this? It just doesn't fit."

"Sometimes it doesn't until it does." Sawyer stands. "I'll start looking into the Bensons. See if I can find anything worth surveilling."

"Great, thanks."

"Yup." He offers a salute then slips out of the cabin.

"What do you need me to do, Cap?" Ryker questions.

"Just keep your ear to the ground. If the guy who shot up the trailer is still here, I want to know about it."

"On it."

"I'll do the same," Garrison says. "And I'll check in with my contacts to see if they know anything about anyone hired to do a job in this area."

I offer them both nods, and they leave. Soon, it's just Tessa, Weston, and me.

"You really should let this go, Zane," Tessa says. "This guy tried to kill me—and you alongside me. They're clearly dangerous. Killers."

Weston laughs, then leans forward. "Depending on who you ask, so are we."

CHAPTER 12

TESSA

Killers.

I look from Weston to Zane, searching for any hint of amusement in either of their gazes. Since I never bothered to check in on Zane, no matter how badly I wanted to, I have no idea what he's done with his life since the day I walked away.

"What's that supposed to mean?" I demand, my gaze shifting between Weston and Zane. Fear momentarily creeps into my mind, but I shove it aside. Weston always had a bit of trouble in his veins, but Zane was as upstanding as they come.

The guy literally spent most of his free afternoons hanging out at the grocery store to help little old ladies carry their groceries to their cars—for free. So Weston *must* be messing with me. There's no other explanation.

Killers? Not possible.

"You're safe here," Zane tells me, completely ignoring my question. His deep voice still wraps around my heart, a familiar and safe place to fall when my world is crumbling around me.

How many times did I run to him, terrified after one of my dad's benders? It didn't matter that everyone in town tried to warn him against me. I was the trouble that would break his heart. Yet, he *never* wavered. Not once. Zane Knox was the only constant in my life.

If only we'd have known back then that everyone had been right.

That I can do nothing but destroy.

Would I have had the strength to walk away, even if I'd have known how it was going to end up? The selfish side of me wouldn't trade the time we did have together for anything. Even the pain I know I caused.

I don't think I'm safe anywhere. And the closer you are to me, the greater the collateral damage will be.

"I really think this is a mistake. I can take all of this to the local police in Savannah and let them sort it out." The sudden urge to get away from this place—from him—is so strong it nearly chokes the life right out of me.

"You're not going anywhere," Zane says, then reaches into his pocket and withdraws his phone. "I have to take this." He steps out of the cabin and onto the deck, closing the door behind him. It shuts hard, and I flinch. I hate that I do, but that little abused girl inside of me is still very, *very* aware of everyone and everything around her.

And he'd been aggravated when he'd closed the door. Who called?

Weston remains where he is, his focus on me.

We always got along before, but I knew that, if things went sideways and it was because of me, he'd back Zane one hundred percent. They've been best friends their entire lives, and it seems that, just like so much in this town, that hasn't changed.

"You know him well enough to know that he's not going to let this go. He's too good to let you walk away, knowing you're in danger, even after you abandoned him. You never should have come back."

"I know." The two words are barely above a whisper. "I didn't come here for his help."

He snorts. "No, you've never been interested in anyone's help, have you? Not when your dad was beating you and we all begged you to tell someone who could do something about it, and not when you decided to walk away from Zane and everyone in this town without so much as a note." He takes a step closer, his large frame dwarfing the small space. "He thought you were dead. If you knew what he did after you left—" he trails off, shaking his head. "When you leave this time, Tessa, do him a favor, and don't come back."

He turns and leaves, closing the door hard behind him.

The tears begin to fall, so I slide out of the seat and limp toward the door leading down to his bedroom. Once inside, I flip the lock and let the pain hit me with the full force of a tidal wave.

"You keep throwing yourself in these situations, and one of these days, you're not going to walk away."

"Do him a favor, and don't come back."

Words from those closest to Zane haunt me in this small room.

It never occurred to me that I'd gotten myself into whatever this is. I've tried to keep my head down, done what I could to not make waves anywhere I went. Of course, things went sideways a few times, but I made *sure* it couldn't follow me.

Yet, it's starting to feel like I brought the biggest danger right here to the doorstep of the one man I never wanted to hurt. This isn't some drunk slob with angry fists; instead, it's someone who isn't afraid to use bullets to silence me. The *why* doesn't matter when Zane's in the line of fire, and I could save him simply by removing myself from the equation.

"Tessa?" Zane calls through the door.

"I'm tired," I say. "Just lying down."

"Okay. I'll let you rest." Footsteps carry him away from the door, so I bury my face into his pillow and scream.

As soon as the cabin has fallen silent, I carry my shoes in one hand and gently slide the door open. Zane is sound asleep on the fold-out bed he made by lowering the table. One muscled arm is draped over his eyes, and his bare chest is on full display, thanks to the blanket pulled down to his waist.

My mouth dries, and I drink him in through the dim light cast through the thin window shades due to the marina lamppost beside his docked boat. The tattoos on his arms climb up over his chest, but it's not even the dark swirls of ink that have my attention.

It's the giant scar running from his left pec and disappearing down beneath the blanket.

A thick, jagged scar that doesn't look like the owner should have survived whatever happened to him.

"Someone tried to rearrange my organs."

His deep voice through the otherwise silent cabin has me jumping a step back. "Sorry, I—" I lose the ability to speak as Zane sits up and the blanket falls completely away, revealing a toned abdomen. The scar stops just above the waist of his pajama pants.

I can't breathe.

Can't tear my gaze from him.

"Going somewhere?" His gaze flicks to the shoes in my hand.

"Yes. I—" I shake my head to clear it.

"You were going to run again."

I hold up a piece of paper in my hand. "I was going to leave a note this time."

His nostrils flare. "You think that makes it better?"

I start toward the door. Outside, lightning splits the sky, filling the cabin of the boat with a bright flash of light. "Yes. Because now you know why I left, and you can finally let go. Something you can't do if you're dead." Tears sting the corners of my eyes as I pull the door open.

Another storm has rolled in, and more lightning flashes. The boat rocks harder now.

"Tessa, you can't leave like this again," Zane insists, following me out onto the deck.

"If I don't, then something could happen to you. I'm good at disappearing. I've done it before, and I'll do it again. They won't find me."

"Except this time, it isn't just changing your name. They found you here. In the town you grew up in. It won't be as simple to vanish this time. They're hunting you."

"Simple?" I whirl on him right as the storm dumps rain down on top of us. It soaks me near-instantly, and the whipping wind chills me to the core. "Nothing I've done in the last eighteen years has been simple! But I refuse to drag you down with me. If I do, then—" I trail off. "What was the point of me leaving in the first place?"

Lightning splits the sky seconds before deafening thunder shakes the world around us.

Zane takes a step closer and points to his bare chest. "Does what I want matter? Has it ever mattered?"

"Of course it has. But you're too good to know what's best for you." My tears mix with the rain. This is why I disappeared without a word last time: Because the longer I stand here with him, the more desperate I am just to fall into his strong arms.

"Stop saying that," he growls, taking another step closer. Rain drips from his short beard down onto his chest. It slides over the ink and scars on his chest.

I retreat a few steps, needing the distance between us as the storm continues to hammer the boat we're on. I should be afraid, but it's nothing compared to the turmoil tearing me up inside.

"Stop saying what? The truth? Is it too hard to hear? You were always too good for me, Zane! I was always trouble!" I retreat another couple of steps.

"Stop saying that!" he bellows.

I close my eyes and take a deep breath. "Everyone else sees what you're too stubborn to."

"And what's that?"

"That you would be better off if you'd never met me."

He moves forward, and I step away. The backs of my legs hit something, though, and I fall backward—into the raging sea. There's a split second of shock before I'm painfully aware of the danger I'm in.

The scream barely has enough time to leave me before the cold water wraps around me, its icy fingers ready to pull me down into the stormy depths. I kick, trying to fight my way to the surface, but the searing pain in my leg makes it nearly impossible to do much else.

My lungs burn. Spots invade my vision.

And then, strong arms come around me, and I'm

propelled out of the water. I suck in a ragged breath as Zane swims us both back to the tanning ledge of his boat. My hand grips the ladder, and he shoves me up, holding me steady as I climb.

As soon as I'm out of the water, I collapse, my body shaking violently. Zane pushes out of the water, his expression unreadable as he reaches down and gathers me into his arms, then shifts me so he can get up the ladder and onto the main deck.

I keep my eyes closed as the rain continues to pelt us.

Zane doesn't stop once we're out of the storm; he continues down into his room, sliding the door open and stepping into the small bathroom. It's barely large enough for both of us when he sets me down on top of the closed toilet seat.

"What are you doing. I'm f-f-fine," I stammer.

"You're going to get hypothermia if we don't warm you up slowly. For once, Tessa, stop fighting, and just accept the help!" There's a desperation in his voice that wasn't there before, and it silences me as the water from his shower comes on.

I can barely keep my eyes open; my body is trembling so hard in his arms. The cold has seeped down through my bones and might as well be wrapping around my heart—ready to stop it for good.

Zane reaches in and tests the temperature, then gathers me back into his strong arms and steps beneath the spray.

The heat is searing even though I know the temperature is barely above lukewarm.

"Keep breathing, Tessa," he says.

I rest my head against his shoulder and take a breath, but it's shallow. My chest is just so heavy. Exhaustion tugs on me.

"Just a few more seconds, okay? Then we'll get you dry."

The seconds tick by, but I can't even begin to care. Because being held in Zane's strong arms is more than I ever thought I'd get to experience again. It's all I've dreamt of. All I've wanted.

But not at all what I can have.

He turns the water off, then carries me out and sets me back on top of the toilet before wrapping a towel around me. "I'm going to get you warm clothes." He leaves for a moment, then returns with a pair of sweats and a sweater that Anastasia brought me.

After setting them on the counter, he steps out and closes the door behind him, though I know he stays right where he can hear me.

My fingers are shaking so violently that I can barely grip the hem of the t-shirt and pull it over my body. I toss it to the floor, and it makes a loud *slap*. The sweatshirt is soft against my skin but offers no warmth when I put it on.

With a hand on the counter to steady me, I try to slip the shorts down.

My legs give out, and I fall over toward the side, barely catching myself on the wall.

"Are you okay?"

"Y-y-yes," I stammer. Thankfully, the cold has numbed the pain in my leg, so with careful precision, I'm able to slip out of the shorts and pull the sweats on. My hair is soaking wet, though, and no amount of towel drying is pushing away the chill in my bones. "D-d-done," I call out, afraid to move just in case I fall again.

The door slides open, and Zane moves into the small space, having already changed into a t-shirt and dry pajama pants.

With the boat rocking violently, I let him help me walk toward the bed. He's already pulled the blankets down, and I slip inside. But even when I pull them up to my neck, I can't stop shivering.

I bite my tongue, thanks to my chattering teeth, and my head begins to pound.

The bed dips as Zane sits down beside me, though he stays above the covers.

"H-h-how are y-y-you not c-c-cold?"

"Tolerance," he says.

"I c-c-can't s-s-stop."

He lets out a low groan, then adjusts to climb beneath the covers alongside me. I turn on my side to face him, and Zane pulls me in. I bury my face in his strong chest, and his large hand rubs my arm in an attempt to create warmth through friction.

Once again, my poor decision put him in danger.

He could have drowned trying to rescue me.

Why won't he stop following me into danger? Why won't he just let me go?

Warmth begins to spread through my body, and the shivers fade. Every muscle in my body is tense, though, and even that is nothing compared to the exhaustion. It pulls me under, removing my ability to recognize just how dangerous this situation is for me.

Wrapped in Zane's warm embrace, I can almost let myself believe we could have been great.

I close my eyes.

"Thank you," I whisper as I begin to drift. "I'm sorry."

"I will never let you suffer, Tessa," Zane replies, his chest vibrating with each word. "I'll always be here when you need me."

That's what I'm afraid of.

CHAPTER 13

ZANE

Looking at the horizon now, you'd never know a storm blew through town last night. My heart is still racing with the image of Tessa, wide-eyed and terrified, stumbling overboard into the raging sea.

She could have died.

But she didn't.

Thank God, she didn't.

I'd drifted off with her in my arms and woken as the first ray of sunshine snuck in through the window. Tessa had still been pressed against me, her head on my chest, her arm wrapped around me.

I'm ashamed to admit—even to myself—that it took every bit of strength and willpower I had to climb out of bed instead of pulling her in closer. She'd been so warm against me, her cheeks pink, expression soft.

Keep it together, Knox.

Turning away from the ocean, I pick up the pace again, sprinting until my body aches. Weston is at the boat this morning, keeping an eye on her until I get back. It was an offer I took him up on because, if I don't stop looking at her like the one who got away, then I'm going to be left broken all over again when she leaves.

Taking the steps quickly, I ascend the beach hill and step onto Main Street. The bookstore is straight ahead, so I check for cars then jog across.

The bell dings when I open it.

"Morning, Zane!" Maria Santos greets, her dark hair in a high ponytail. She offers me a bright smile and a friendly wave. Two years younger than I am, she's been close friends with my sister since they were in kindergarten. Though I've always known she's had a thing for me, things were never weird between us.

Something I've always been grateful for.

"Morning, Maria."

"What can I do for you?"

I consider. Is this a mistake? But I shove those thoughts aside. "I need a Bible."

"Of course." She moves out from around the counter, and I follow her toward a large display near the middle of the store.

After surveying the different covers, I choose a leather-bound Bible with a cross imprinted on the front, handing it to Maria. She takes it back toward the front and rings me up.

"Do you want this gift wrapped?"

"Nah. A bag is fine." Tessa has never been great at receiving gifts, so if I wrap it, it'll just make her uncomfortable.

"You've got it." She sticks it into a bag. "Thirty-nine, ninety-five."

I hand her my card, and she runs it, then hands it back to me.

"That was some storm last night, right? Did you end up staying with Anastasia?"

"No. I stayed on the boat."

"Really?"

I nod. "I was monitoring the weather, and it wasn't supposed to get bad enough that it would have been unsafe. Just slightly uncomfortable." I force a smile. It *was* dangerous, though, because I nearly lost someone who matters more to me than she probably should, considering the circumstances.

"Well, I'm glad you're okay." She offers me the receipt and bag. "Anything else?"

"Nope, that's it."

She grins. "You headed to Anastasia's next?"

"I am, need something?"

"Just let her know I'm looking forward to tonight! It's girls' night, and I am in desperate need of it." She laughs. "It's been a rough month."

"I'm sorry to hear that." Her dad has been battling

early-onset dementia, and Maria spends nearly all of her spare time with him.

"Thanks. It'll all be okay. God is good, and I know He can make something beautiful out of this. Even if I can't see it."

"Amen to that." I smile, then push the door open. "Thanks again, Maria."

"Anytime, Zane. Let me know if you need anything else."

"Will do. See ya." I push out onto the street and head toward Anastasia's coffee shop so I can pick up two cups of coffee and some breakfast for Tessa. She was still asleep when Weston showed up this morning and took my place, granting me the opportunity to slip out for a run and get her a Bible.

What if she never reads it? What if it's a waste?

I shut those thoughts down the moment they cross into my mind. She *will* read it. And offering someone the Word of God is never a waste. She'd been getting close to God before she left, which means the seed is there.

I just need to help her find it again.

With a smile on my face, I breeze into the coffee shop. It's relatively empty this morning, which is not super unusual for mid-morning on Saturday around here since most people are out on the water, even given the cooler temperatures this time of year.

"Morning," I greet Pastor Reeves and his wife, Helen, as they sit at a small, round table near the entrance.

"Morning, Zane. How are things?" Pastor Reeves stands and offers me a hug.

"Not too bad. I'm alive and can't complain," I reply, then embrace his wife when she stands as well.

"We are so glad to hear it," Helen replies. "How is your mom?"

"Good. I'm nearly done renovating the other side of her duplex, so she should be ready to rent it out again soon."

"That's so great to hear. You'll give her our love?" Helen asks.

"Absolutely. We'll see you guys tomorrow for church."

"Looking forward to it." Helen smiles. She and Mom were thick as thieves growing up. The absolute best of friends. And when my dad died, Pastor Reeves and Helen were right there, helping us the best they could.

They're family. The fact that they don't bring up Tessa either means word hasn't spread through town yet—which is surprising—or they don't want to risk upsetting me. Either way, I appreciate it.

With a final smile, I turn around and scan the bakery for my sister. When I see her talking to a man I've never met, though, a shiver of unease runs up my spine. It doesn't matter that she's only two years younger than me and going on thirty-four years old; she's still my baby sister.

She glances up from her conversation with him and beams at me. "Hey there, Big Brother!"

"Hey." I cross over and stand beside the man. He smiles at me, his grey eyes friendly.

"Zane, this is Jack. Jack, Zane." As Anastasia does the introductions, I reach out my hand to shake his. Unease continues to spread through me, and while he doesn't look overly menacing, I can't shake the feeling that this guy can't be trusted. Though that could absolutely be due to the way he's watching my sister as though she's the single point of focus for his day.

"Nice to meet you," Jack greets, shaking my hand tightly.

"You, too. I haven't seen you around before. Are you new in town?"

"Just passing through," he replies. "My parents used to bring me here as a kid every summer. They passed suddenly a few months ago, so I'm here trying to connect with old memories." His expression turns sad, and a bit of my unease dissipates.

"I'm sorry to hear that."

"Thanks," he says. "Your sister here makes the best coffee around, and I was just telling her that." He turns back to Anastasia, whose cheeks flush with color.

Oh boy.

"Well, I appreciate your compliment." She turns to me. "Your usual?"

"Yeah. Thanks."

She smiles. "You've got it."

As she turns away, I fix my attention on Jack. "So, where you traveling from?"

"California," he replies. "Just outside of Sacramento."

"That's a long way."

He laughs. "Don't I know it. Didn't seem like that long of a drive when I was doing it with my parents. We'd make a whole road trip out of it, stopping at a lot of sightseeing places along the way."

"Sounds fun."

"It was." He smiles wistfully, then takes a drink of his coffee. "I'm in town for a few more days, so maybe I'll see you around."

"Yeah, maybe," I reply.

"Any recommendations as to what I should do while I'm here? Anastasia says I need to get out on the water. But I've never actually sailed a boat myself."

"You can rent smaller boats at Nina's Bait Shop. It's down near the marina. She'll give you a crash course on sailing, too."

"Nina's Bait Shop? Got it. Thanks." He raises his coffee toward me, then calls out, "It was great to meet you, Anastasia! I'll see you tomorrow."

"See you tomorrow, Jack!" she calls out as she preps the two lattes I ordered.

One cinnamon vanilla. The other vanilla lavender—Tessa's favorite.

As the bell above the door dings, I shift my attention back to Anastasia. "I thought you knew better than to talk to strangers."

She laughs and rolls her eyes. "If that's the case, then I went into the wrong line of work."

"Seriously, Anastasia—" I let my attention shift back toward the door. "He didn't seem off to you?"

"Nothing is off about him," she replies. "You're just mad because you don't like me talking to handsome men."

"Handsome men? No. It has nothing to do with that." *Right?* "Either way, just watch yourself, please. I've got enough trouble in my life right now. I don't want to have you get into any."

"Ahh, yes. *The* infamous trouble. How is *she* doing?" she asks me, low enough that no one can hear.

"She's fine." I leave out the fact that she tried to leave last night and then nearly drowned because of it.

"Great," she says dryly.

"Go ahead. Give it to me. I can take it." I wave her on, letting her know that whatever is on her mind, she can feel free to speak it.

"Fine." She leans in closer. "The more I think about it, the angrier I get. You are going to let her back in just so she can destroy you again. I see it all over your face."

I lean in closer. "No, I'm not. And there's a lot more to the story than either of us knew."

"Yes, you are! See, you're already defending her!"

Taking a deep breath, I contemplate what I'm about to do for all of two seconds before I do it. Anastasia was hurt when Tessa left, too, and she needs to know that Tessa didn't just walk out without reason. Even if I don't agree with it, she thought she was doing the right thing.

"She went over to her dad's that night," I tell my sister, keeping my voice low.

Her eyes narrow, but she doesn't speak.

"He told her that he wanted to make amends and be a part of the wedding. When she got there, he beat her, Anastasia. *Badly.* She was afraid that I would do what I promised to do the next time he put his hands on her—and kill him. She was scared that, if I saw her, bruised, bloodied, and broken, I would snap. So she left."

Anastasia's eyes are full of tears, her mouth slack. All anger has vanished from her expression. "Are you serious?"

"Yes. Now, I don't agree with her leaving like she did. She didn't even give me the chance to protect her. To defend her." Even as I talk about it, anger rushes through me. I would have done anything to keep her safe. To make sure she never suffered again.

"Would you have done what she was afraid of?" she asks.

"I would have done something," I reply. "I'm not sure what, but I know the headspace I was in back then, and it wouldn't have been pretty."

"Vengeance belongs to God."

"I know that now. But I was a nineteen-year-old boy about to marry the woman I loved, and her father beat her bloody." I leave out the part about him trying to set her on fire because Anastasia is horrified enough.

She's quiet for a few moments. "I guess I owe her an

apology. Maybe even a thank you for sacrificing her happiness to save you. I was pretty rude the other night."

"I'm not letting her back in, Anastasia. Even if I wanted to, I can't. But I do think we can find some closure before this is all said and done."

"I hope you're right," she replies, then offers me the two coffees she'd finished right before I told her about Tessa's reasons for leaving. "Just watch yourself, okay? I don't want to see you get hurt again. I love you and stuff."

I laugh. "I love you and stuff, too, Anastasia. And I'll be careful."

"Not just with your heart, Zane. After what happened the other night—" She shivers. "I just have this sick feeling in my gut."

I set the coffee down and cover her hand with mine where it rests on the counter. "I'll watch myself, okay? You know I'm good at what I do."

"I know." She smiles softly. "But you're not bulletproof, Zane Knox. And these last couple of years, you've been walking around like you are."

CHAPTER 14

TESSA

"What are you reading?" I ask Weston. He's sitting on the deck of Zane's boat, a good two yards from me, and has been silent since I woke up this morning and found him here instead of Zane.

The disappointment I'd felt when I realized he wasn't here is something I'm trying really hard not to think about. I step out of the cabin and limp up onto the deck. The waters are calm today, the sky clear.

But I can still feel the icy depths surrounding me when I fell.

He doesn't respond.

"You know, you didn't like me when we first met, either. Then we became friends."

He glares at me over the book. "I'm reading."

"Are you, though? Seems like you're talking to me." I woke up with a bit more fire than I've had in—well—as long as I can remember. Could be that I slept better than I ever have and woke up feeling rested despite the pain in my leg and the ache in my heart.

Weston growls and shifts his attention back to the book.

"Look, I didn't purposely set out to hurt him. I was trying to protect him."

"Yet, you did hurt him."

"Things were out of my control."

"Did you leave of your own volition?"

"Has Zane not told you why I left?"

Weston slams his book closed. "Believe it or not, Princess, we don't sit around gabbing about you all day." He opens the book and turns the page, even though I'd bet every cent I have that he didn't read a single printed word.

"No? That's surprising. You've always been so chatty."

The ghost of a smile tugs at the corners of his lips, but it dies quickly. "There were at least three other ways you could have handled what happened that night, yet you chose a coward's way out. Any respect I had for you died when you left my friend heartbroken and standing at the end of an aisle you were never planning to walk down."

So he did finally tell him.

His words bloom a familiar ache in my chest. "I didn't want him to throw his life away."

Weston glances up at me. "That was his decision to make. Not yours."

"What would you have done? Would you have let him throw his future away? His dreams of becoming a doctor?"

I'm not sure why it matters so much to me that Weston understands. Whether it's because I miss the days when he didn't hate me or because things are awkward right now, I need him to understand.

To know that I didn't mean to hurt anyone.

"No, because I would have handled it before he could."

The simple way those words are spoken does not match the underlying threat. Weston always stood beside Zane. Even though I know he's also felt like he would never match up to Zane, given their different backgrounds. It's something he and I always had in common.

But would he really have sacrificed his own future to keep his friend safe?

"I'm sorry, Weston. I really did think I was doing what was best."

"Well, you were pretty far off." He glances off into the distance, then closes his book. "Get in the cabin."

"Why?"

"Someone I don't recognize is headed this way."

I don't wait for him to elaborate, just get up and limp my way into the cabin.

"You look lost," Weston calls out.

"I'm looking for Nina's Bait Shop?" A man laughs. "I was told to check it out, and I'm afraid I didn't listen to the directions very well."

"Back toward the entrance," Weston replies, pointing to the left. "Hers is the first boat you pass. There's a faded sign in front of it. Pretty impossible to miss."

"Great, thanks so much. I think I'm just so in awe of how gorgeous everything out here is. I didn't remember."

"Yeah. Well. Pay better attention next time."

The man laughs. "You're not wrong there. Have a great day."

Even as the man's bootsteps fade in the distance, Weston keeps his attention straight ahead.

"Is everything okay?" I ask after a few minutes have passed.

"He went inside Nina's," Weston replies, then returns his attention to his book. Minutes tick by as I remain inside the cabin, staring out the window toward the ocean.

I'd always loved being out here on the boat. Zane and I spent nearly all of our free time out here. Even if we remained in the marina, I'd pretend we were sailing far away from this place and all the darkness that waited for me whenever I went home.

"Hey there, Cap, good outing?"

My heart jumps when Zane comes into view. He shakes Weston's hand. "Yeah. Thanks."

"Anytime."

Zane turns to me, and our gazes hold. I can still feel his arms around me. The warmth of his body battling the cold in mine.

"I'll check in later. Have some ranch errands to take care of."

"Great. See you then."

Weston offers me a nod, which is technically progress

when I compare it to the cold shoulder he offered me the last time he left, so I raise my hand in a slight wave, and he steps off the boat.

Zane comes inside and sets a bag down. "I need to run to my mom's and help her with some stuff. I'd like you to come with me."

"I don't think that's such a good idea."

"I think it's a great idea. You can't be happy sitting on this boat constantly."

"Weston made me get back inside because some guy was coming toward the boat, looking for Nina's. Do you really think I should—"

"Someone asked for Nina's Bait Shop?"

I nod.

"What did he look like?"

"I don't know; I was inside. Weston said he went inside, though."

Zane relaxes slightly.

"Why? What's wrong?"

"Probably nothing. He was inside Anastasia's place and was asking about where to rent a boat. I pointed him to Nina's. If it was the same guy, at least."

"That's good then, right? He was looking for Nina's and just walked past it."

"Yeah. Maybe." He keeps his attention focused there for a moment, then shifts it back to me and claps his hands. "Come on, let's get you out of here. She's making dinner, and I have some work I need to do over there."

"Zane—"

"Tessa. I will be with you the whole time." His tone is firm but understanding. "I promise, I won't let anything happen to you."

It's not me I'm worried about.

Then there's the fact that I'm already getting too used to having him around. I can't afford to become so reliant on the warmth he offers that I forget how to handle the cold. "Okay. If you think it'll be fine."

"I do." He reaches up on top of his refrigerator and pulls down a blue baseball cap. After tucking it low on my head, he grins in such a way that makes my heart flip in my chest. "Perfect. I barely recognize you."

I roll my eyes, but don't take it off. It's a running joke between us after we bonded over the whole superhero thing where people hide their eyes behind a pair of glasses. Who would have thought I'd be trying to shield my identity one day? Turning toward the door, I look for my shoes. And then remember what happened last night. "Um, I don't have any shoes."

"Sure you do," He raises one of the bags he'd carried in and pulls out a shoebox. He opens the lid and reaches inside to pull out a pair of boat shoes with pink plaid on the side.

"You bought me shoes?"

"I did."

"Why?"

"Because yours fell in the ocean last night." There's no

frustration in his tone, no anger. Just a simply stated fact that hits me like a bolt of lightning to my heart. I don't know why I'm surprised. Zane has always been thoughtful, but it catches me off guard.

"Why are you doing this? Why are you being so kind to me?" I rip the baseball cap off my head and set it aside. "You could have drowned last night."

"Out of the two of us, I was not the one at risk," he replies smoothly. Zane takes a step closer, his expression full of emotion I don't trust myself to see. Because if I fall again, I don't think I'll ever stop. "Navy SEAL, remember? And I'm doing this because I *want* to."

"Why? I left you, Zane. And since I've been back, you've been shot and had to retrieve me from the ocean in the middle of a storm. You've given up your bed, your space, your time—I just don't get why." My throat constricts.

"I already told you, Tessa." He takes another step closer, those gorgeous green eyes piercing straight through to my soul. "Because I want to keep you safe. Because I want you to see what I always have."

"This is a mistake. All of it is a mistake." My throat burns with raw emotion and the weight of this moment. Of his declaration.

Zane's hand cups my cheek, his calloused palm scraping delicately against my skin. I freeze beneath the contact, terrified that, if I move, if I breathe, he'll pull away. "Tessa Lane, I made you a promise. That I am going to make you see just what you're worth. I'm helping you because I *want* to," he repeats. "Because even if I can't keep you when this is all over, having you here is soothing an ache that nothing has touched since the day you disappeared."

His thumb caresses my cheek, and I close my eyes as a tear slips free. His touch feels so right. It's the absolute last thing I deserve, but I never want him to stop. Even though I know without a doubt that this is going to end badly.

Even if whoever is after me doesn't succeed, leaving this man is going to kill me.

"More coffee, honey?" Linda asks as she comes back toward the table and retrieves our empty mugs.

"No, thank you. I'm okay." Sitting here at the small four-seater table in her tiny kitchen is the most at home I've felt in a long time. It's a different house, but there are so many similarities in the décor that it's like stepping back into a happy memory.

The lemon curtains she had in the house Zane grew up in are over the main kitchen window, the large cross Zane made for her in woodshop is hanging on the wall beside the table, and a vase Anastasia made for her in art class is over-flowing with wildflowers on the counter.

There are pictures everywhere. The walls are covered in happy moments frozen in time. It was one of the first things

I noticed when I went over to his house for dinner that first time. In my house, the only things that made it up on the walls were holes from fists and inappropriate posters my dad hung for his own enjoyment.

Walking into the Knox home had been my first look at what a family truly could be. Even as they were still reeling over the death of Zane and Anastasia's father.

Linda hums as she chops potatoes. I remember how kind she was that night, too. How welcoming. Linda Knox is the strongest woman I've ever met, and I aspired to be half the wife and mother she is.

And then I failed before I even had a chance to be either. *Get out of this pity party, Tessa. It is what it is.* I clear my throat.

"Can I help?" It's been a *long* time since I cooked, but I used to love cooking with her. She taught me everything I do know.

"I would love that." Linda beams at me over her shoulder. "Do you remember how I slice the Brussels sprouts?"

"I do." With a smile, I get up and limp over toward the counter. My leg is doing better this afternoon, though the soreness from last night's unplanned swim definitely makes movement harder than I would like.

"Honey, sit. I can bring them to you."

"No, please. I've been sitting a lot the last couple of days, and it's starting to drive me crazy."

Linda chuckles. "Fair enough."

The Brussels sprouts are in a colander beside a cutting

board, so I take them out one by one and remove the loose leaves around the outside. Then, after cutting an X in the stem, I slice it in half and lay them on the prepared baking sheet beside me.

It feels so *good.*

"How long have you lived here?"

"Seven years," she replies. "The tenant I had next door moved out and left the place a mess, so Zane's been helping me fix it up."

"I'm sorry to hear that."

She shrugs. "It happens. They were friendly enough, but the husband was a mechanic, and he worked on engines in the living room."

"Are you serious?"

She laughs. "I am. And he didn't put anything down first. The carpet was destroyed."

"Did they at least pay for that?"

"I kept the deposit, but it wasn't enough to cover the damage. It's okay, though; my sweet boy has been helping." She beams, so proud of her son. And why wouldn't she be? Zane is the best man I've ever known.

"That's great that he's helping you."

"He always does."

Silence wraps around us as she continues chopping potatoes and putting them in a pot of water heating on the stove.

"I'm sorry that I left the hospital the way I did. I—uh— I wasn't sure how to face you after what I did to Zane."

Linda sets her knife down and turns to face me, so I do the same. She reaches out and grips both of my arms. "You don't need to apologize to me."

"Did he tell you? Why I left?"

She nods. "He did. But I didn't want to bring it up unless you wanted to talk about it."

"I didn't want to risk what he'd do when he found out."

Linda smiles, tears filling her eyes. "As his mother, I can appreciate the sacrifice you made. But as a woman who loves you like a daughter, I wish you would have come to us so we could've helped you. I like to believe Zane had a steady enough head on his shoulders he wouldn't have run off without a thought to the consequences."

Loves. Not loved. Loves. The dam I've used to hold back my emotions since I walked into this place shatters, and tears fill my eyes.

"Oh, come here, sweetie." Linda pulls me in and wraps her arms around me. I hug her back, the embrace more than I've had in years. "You're safe now. No one will hurt you again, okay?"

I wish that were true.

Because I sense that my greatest heartbreak is still on the horizon.

CHAPTER 15

ZANE

"I got you something." I set the Bible down in front of Tessa, then slide into the booth across from where she's sitting.

She stares at it as though it's going to jump toward her. "What's this for?"

"You."

"I heard you. But why?"

"Because you don't seem to have one anymore."

Tessa's hands remain firmly clasped in her lap. "What made you think I want one?" Her voice is barely above a whisper. Shoulders slumped, she doesn't look like a thirty-six-year-old woman.

Instead, all I can see right now is that terrified teenage girl I'd first met.

Has she truly regressed that far? How can I make her see what I do when I look at her?

"If you don't want to read it, then don't. But no matter what happened to you, Tessa, the Lord never left you."

She closes her eyes and shakes her head. "You don't understand. The things I did."

"I've been there, too. And I found my way back."

Tessa's gorgeous dark eyes open, and she stares back at me. "There's no way you would have done anything close to what I did."

"Sin is sin, Tessa. But I'm starting to think you are holding onto the view you had of me when we were teenagers."

"What view is that?"

"You once called me the Golden Boy of Stormwatch Landing."

She smirks, but it fades. "Sin may be sin, but I've—" She trails off.

"You don't owe me an explanation, Tessa."

"You need to know who you're protecting, though. Who you're risking your life for."

"I already know."

She shakes her head.

"You're Tessa Lane, an imperfect daughter of the King. You love Brussels sprouts, pineapple on pizza, and cheesy rom coms, but dislike scary movies, when people put marshmallows on top of sweet potatoes, and small spaces."

A tear slips down her cheek. "It's not that simple anymore."

"It *is* that simple, Tessa. Jesus died for every sin you

committed and every sin you will commit. All you have to do is repent and believe in Him."

"I don't know what I believe in anymore."

"Then start here." I gently push the Bible toward her. "And find your way home."

She closes her eyes, and more tears fall. Even though I'm not sure she wants me to, I get up and slide into the booth beside her. She's all the way near the wall, so we're not quite touching, but when she doesn't pull away or shove me off the side, I move a little closer.

I'd prayed this morning. Harder than I've ever prayed, that He would use me to bring her back to Him. Even if that's all my purpose is in this life, I can die a happy man knowing that Tessa realized just how much she's worth.

That she found her way back to Him.

Because I know she won't do it herself, I open the Bible and turn to Psalm 139.

"O Lord, You have examined my heart and know everything about me. You know when I sit down or stand up. You know my thoughts even when I'm far away. You see me when I travel and when I rest at home. You know everything I do."

Tessa swallows hard, her eyes still closed, but tears continue to stream freely down her cheeks.

I keep reading, "You know what I am going to say even before I say it, Lord. You go before me and follow me. You place Your hand of blessing on my head. Such knowledge is too wonderful for me, too great for me to understand. I can never escape from Your Spirit. I can never get away from Your presence."

She leans toward me, so I wrap an arm around her shoulders and hold on, basking in this moment where her walls are down. Where she's seeking comfort in my arms.

"If I go up to heaven, You are there; if I go down to the grave, You are there. If I ride the wings of morning, if I dwell by the farthest oceans, even there Your hand will guide me, and Your strength will support me. I could ask the darkness to hide me and the light around me to become night—but even in the darkness, I cannot hide from You."

My throat tightens, and I swallow hard, hoping to push the lump aside so I can continue. "To You the night shines as bright as day. Darkness and light are the same to You. You made all the delicate, inner parts of my body and knit me together in my mother's womb. Thank You for making me so wonderfully complex. Your workmanship is marvelous—how well I know it. You watched me as I was being formed in utter seclusion, as I was woven together in the dark of the womb. You saw me before I was born. Every day of my life was recorded in Your book."

I clear my throat again, and Tessa remains where she is, her shoulders shaking softly as she cries. It's not a complete break, but the fissures are there. Only God can fully remove those walls she's built, and I pray He does.

"He has always been with you, Tessa," I say again.

"He gave me a second chance, and I threw it away."

"We all do. There's not a single person who walks this

world and doesn't sin. Just because You accept Jesus doesn't mean you're perfect. Only He is."

"I've hurt so many people. I've done so many things I can't take back."

"But you *can* move forward. You don't have to live in the past."

"Well, when it's literally trying to kill me, I'm not so sure about that." She straightens and wipes her eyes, so I reluctantly remove my arm from around her shoulders and turn slightly to face her.

"You let me worry about that."

She looks up at me, and in her eyes, I see a bit of the light that once shone so brightly. "Will you keep reading?"

"Absolutely."

Soft creaking pulls me out of sleep, but I don't open my eyes. Keeping my breathing steady, I listen for the source of the sound. *Footsteps.* The door leading into my cabin slides open, meaning someone picked the lock.

Moving slowly, I slide my hand beneath the pillow and retrieve my gun. Then I wait. Footsteps move farther inside the cabin of my boat.

Nearly there.

A shadow passes over the top of me, so I lunge up, bringing my gun with me. An arm comes down on top of mine, knocking it free. Pain radiates up through my arm as I slam my fist into the masked assailant.

He stumbles backward, falling against and splintering my door.

Loud enough that I know it will have woken Tessa.

I can't see his face due to the mask, but he withdraws a knife and snarls at me. "You have no idea what you're up against, SEAL."

"I know that you're not walking off this boat." I square off, ready to end his life if it comes down to it. "And that's enough right now."

The man charges forward, slashing out with his knife. I move to the side, but because of the small space, it slices into my arm. Pain radiates from the source of the wound, but I ignore it as I turn to the side and slam my bare foot into his chest. He falls back, so I rush forward, gripping the arm that's holding the knife and slamming him to the deck of my boat. I keep a firm hold on his arm as he thrashes beneath me.

A bullet whizzes past my head and hits the bench seat just to my right.

Two attackers. Keeping myself as hidden as I can, I grip the throat of the man beneath me and squeeze.

He thrashes, arching up to put me in the line of sight for his partner, but I remain low.

"Zane!" Tessa screams.

"Stay out of sight!" I yell. "Get inside! Lock the door!"

Something slams into the back of my head, knocking

me to the side. *Three attackers.* I'm dazed, spots in my vision, but I don't stay down long.

Gripping the knife that the man on the deck dropped, I rush back toward the cabin.

Tessa screams, and my blood runs cold.

She's back against the wall, a masked assailant pinning her there. She fights for breath as his hands tighten around her throat.

Red invades my thoughts, and a fury unlike anything I've ever felt consumes me.

I rush forward and drive the blade down into the side of his neck as I wrap an arm around him and yank him backward. He falls back, so I wrap both legs around him, pinning him to my body as he jerks to break free.

Warmth trickles down my hand, sliding over me.

My stomach twists as bile burns, but I don't relent.

He jerks, fighting against me, but I remain where I am until he falls still. Tossing him to the side, I search for Tessa. She's curled in the corner, her hands on her throat. Her eyes are wide and full of tears, but she's alive.

Breathing.

Immediate threat neutralized, I rush back onto the deck of my boat. The man who'd initially attacked me is gone, and since no one takes another shot at me, I can assume that—at least for the moment—we're in the clear.

Heading back inside, I grab my cell phone from the counter and call 9-1-1.

"What's your emergency?" Lynette, the local

dispatcher, asks. Her voice is one I recognize easily since she's close friends with my mom.

"It's Zane Knox. I was just attacked on my boat. A shooter and two others. One is down; the others are gone."

"Your boat is in the marina? Normal spot?"

"Yes." Breathless, I brace one hand on the counter and stare out the door. "I don't know if they're going to be gone for long."

"I'm sending help right now."

"Thank you." I end the call but keep the phone in my hand as I turn and sink to the ground beside the man who'd attacked Tessa. Using two fingers, I feel for a pulse, but I'm not surprised when I find none.

"Is he dead?"

"Yes." Setting the knife aside, I retrieve the gun I'd dropped and crawl over in front of her. Since I don't want to risk our shadows from turning on the lights, I turn on the flashlight on my phone and study the red marks on her throat. "Are you okay?"

She nods. Her gaze leaves my face and fixates on my arm before it widens. "You're bleeding!"

I study the gash in my arm. It's decent-sized, but not fatal. "I'll be fine."

"We need to put pressure on it." She starts to push up from the floor, but I yank her back down.

"You have to stay out of sight."

Her gaze lifts from me to the towel hanging on the front of my small oven. She reaches up and pulls it down, then presses it to my injury. Pain shoots up from the pressure, but I don't make a sound.

Sirens wail outside, and flashing red and blue signifies we're no longer alone, so I flip on the lights.

"Are you okay?" she asks.

I nod even as my gaze drops to the dead man on the floor of my boat. It's not the first life I've been forced to take, but that doesn't make it any easier.

Lord, please forgive me.

CHAPTER 16

TESSA

I can't stop shaking.

Even with a warm blanket wrapped around my shoulders, my body continues to tremble. I can still feel those hands wrapped around my throat. I can still feel the weight of his body as he pressed me into the wall, holding me there as he choked the life from me.

Red and blue lights cut through the darkness, and my gaze lands on the black body bag being carried off Zane's boat by two men wearing coroner's office jackets.

Dead.

"Depending on who you ask, so are we." Weston's words, when I'd said these men are killers, echo through my mind now, and my gaze lands on where Zane is standing with Officer Leopold. Weston, Ryker, Garrison, and Sawyer are here, too, though they're talking to another officer over to the side.

Garrison glances up at me, then excuses himself and crosses over to take a seat on the marina bench beside me. "How you holding up?" he asks.

"Not great," I admit. We'd gone to sleep after Zane read more of the Bible to me. I'd had a peace that I haven't had in quite some time, only to have it robbed from me in the middle of the night.

"Zane!" A shrill feminine voice cuts through the night, and Anastasia sprints down the marina dock toward him.

"I'm okay," I hear him tell her as she wraps her arms around him and squeezes.

My throat constricts.

"Hey, this isn't your fault," Garrison says, as though he can read my thoughts.

I can't even find the words to argue.

Anastasia releases Zane and turns toward me. As she crosses over, I prepare myself for her anger. She's never quick to it, but when that temper is released, the entire world shakes.

Garrison offers me a quick smile, then gets up so Anastasia can sit.

"Are you okay?" she asks.

I nod.

"I saw the lights when I came downstairs to open the bakery." She runs her hands over her face. "I'm so glad you guys are okay."

"I'm sorry. It's my fault."

"It is not your fault," Anastasia counters.

"I know that you're worried I'm going to cause him to get hurt. And you're right. He keeps getting pulled into it because of me."

Anastasia studies me for a moment. "You overheard our conversation. Of course you did. I wasn't exactly quiet. I'm sorry." She sighs. "I *am* worried about him—he's my brother. But you aren't the one getting him into these situations. He's been getting himself into life-or-death instances long before you came back."

"He killed someone," I whisper.

"From what I hear, it was that or your life. Tessa, he'll always choose you."

My eyes fill. "I left so he wouldn't kill my dad and throw his life away, yet here he is, doing it anyway. Eighteen years later."

Anastasia wraps an arm around my shoulders. "This pity party you keep throwing for yourself has to stop. It's not doing you any favors, and it'll only keep you rooted in the past. Zane killed a man who was going to kill you *both*. It was self-defense."

Pity party. Didn't I just tell myself that same thing last night? That it was time to stop throwing one for myself?

Before I can respond, a black SUV pulls into the parking lot. Two men in suits climb out before one opens the back door, and a leggy brunette in a pencil skirt climbs out of the back.

Her gaze travels over the scene before her until it lands on Zane.

"Uh-oh," Anastasia grumbles.

"What? Who is that?"

"Zane's boss. I've only met her once, and it was by accident, but she's a walking nightmare."

Approaching on heels so high it should be impossible to glide the way she is, she moves toward Zane. Officer Leopold offers him a wave, then walks away, and Zane crosses his arms. They have a heated exchange before he turns and walks back toward me, leaving her behind him.

"We're going to go stay at Anastasia's," he tells me. "She has a guest room available."

"I'm not done speaking to you, Knox," the woman demands, her tone sharp, as she stops right behind him.

He takes a deep breath and whirls on her. "We are done because I say we are."

"Do you really think I wouldn't find out? Two incidents requiring police presence. Both of them with you as the headliner. I expect an explanation. You're supposed to be flying under the radar, not setting it off."

"As I said, they were misunderstandings."

"Misunderstandings." Her gaze shifts from him to me, and she pins me with an ice-cold glare. "This have something to do with your new houseguest?"

"Hey, watch it." Anastasia stands and crosses her arms. "You don't get to talk to him that way."

"I'll do whatever I need to do," she replies.

Zane takes a step in front of his sister. "You do not address her. Period. My family has *always* been off-limits."

Weston, Ryker, Garrison, and Sawyer all flank us, with Sawyer pulling Anastasia behind him.

The woman looks from them back to Zane. "I expect an explanation, Knox. I can't have you distracted." She glares at me. "Something you clearly are."

"Like I told you. Unless you have orders for us, we have nothing to talk about." Zane turns toward me. "Come on, Tessa." He reaches out, so I take his hand. The blanket slips from my shoulders, but Weston grabs it before it can hit the ground.

He offers me a soft, understanding smile, and I can't help but wonder if tonight somehow changed his outlook on me. I'm not sure why it would have, given his friend nearly died—again, but I'm grateful for it.

Zane scoops me into his arms and carries me the rest of the way to his truck, while Anastasia and the rest of the team follow.

I want to argue. Want to insist that I can walk.

But when that woman's gaze pins me again, I'm grateful for the speedy retreat.

We reach Zane's truck, and he helps me into the passenger seat. Anastasia climbs in, too, so I scoot over to the middle of the bench seat as Zane climbs behind the wheel.

My thigh brushes against Zane's, and despite everything that's happened tonight, the contact sends a wave of warmth through me.

Less than two minutes after we leave the marina, we're

pulling around the back of an old house on Main Street. Zane climbs out first, then reaches back in for me. Instead of going out the passenger side, I scoot beneath the steering wheel and let him help me out on the driver's side.

The rumbling of a motorcycle has me turning toward the left as Weston pulls in, a truck right behind him. Thankfully, it doesn't look like the black SUV is anywhere to be seen.

Weston turns off the bike and climbs off, setting his helmet to the side as the rest of the guys get out of the truck Ryker was driving.

"I need to get things going this morning, but I'll bring up coffee as soon as I can." Anastasia groans. "Karly picked the perfect day to start her vacation."

"I can help," Sawyer offers, clapping his hands together. "Put me in, coach."

Anastasia grins at him. "No offense, but I don't even think the apron will fit you."

He smiles. "You saying you like my muscles?"

"Before we all get nauseated, how about we get inside?" Ryker comments with a roll of his eyes.

"Yeah, we need to get off the street." Zane glances around, his head on a swivel, body between me and the building. It makes me sick to think that someone wouldn't hesitate to take him out—to take them all out—just to get their shot at me.

Who did I anger? Why is someone trying so hard to kill me?

Zane's hand goes to my lower back, and he guides me toward the building while Anastasia moves ahead and unlocks the back door. We all file in behind her, but instead of following her and Sawyer into the front, Zane leads me toward a staircase.

It's not until we get to the top that I realize we're alone and the others remained downstairs.

He closes the door behind us and leads me toward the couch where I take a seat. Without a word, he moves into a small kitchen and fills a glass with water before bringing it back over to me.

I can't even focus on the room around me. Not while my mind is running a million miles a minute.

Zane takes a seat beside me. "Talk to me."

"You—"

"Tessa."

"You killed him."

"Because, if I hadn't, he was going to kill you."

Aside from the time he punched my dad, I'd never seen Zane fight before. Not until earlier when I watched him take on two masked assailants and walk away with only a cut on his arm.

I've always felt safe with Zane. But after tonight? There's no doubt in my mind that he'll still be standing when this is over. The question is…will I?

"I'm sorry." My eyes fill with tears, and the adrenaline that's been with me since I woke to the sounds of fighting flatlines. My teeth begin to chatter as my body trembles uncontrollably.

Zane reaches over and pulls me into his lap. I rest my head against his chest, the steady beat of his heart easing the panic in mine. "You have nothing to be sorry for."

"I don't understand why this is happening. I don't know what I did to deserve this."

"You didn't do anything. And we'll figure it out."

"Before or after we're killed?"

Zane cups my cheek and tilts my face up to look into his eyes. "What about this morning made you think it's going to be easy to kill me?"

"Nothing," I reply without hesitation. "But that doesn't make you bulletproof. Or immune to bleeding out."

His smile falters. "I was terrified tonight. I don't think I've ever been that scared."

I snort. "I find that hard to believe."

"Don't." He strokes my cheek with his thumb. "You could have died."

My breath catches.

"When I saw him grab you—there was a moment there where I wondered if that was it. If you were going to be taken from me again."

Again.

"I won't leave without saying goodbye this time around." It's meant to be a light-hearted comment, but the weight behind it wipes the emotion from Zane's face.

Right as someone knocks on the door. Zane sets me

aside and crosses over to open it. Weston, Ryker, and Garrison are on the other side, all of them with paper cups of coffee in their hands. Ryker offers Zane a cup, then Weston hands me one.

"Thanks."

"No problem." He turns to Zane. "So, Cap, what's the plan?"

"We hope Leopold can ID the guy they took from the boat. And that he will lead us to the rest of them. Then, we take them out."

"Take them out?" I nearly choke on it. Surely he doesn't mean—

Zane turns toward me. "You wanted to know what I do? This is it, Tessa."

"You kill people?"

"Not if I can help it," he replies. "But I put a stop to violence."

"These guys," Ryker starts, "whoever they are, aren't going to stop until you're dead. We're going to make sure that doesn't happen."

I swallow hard. I'm living in another warzone. Where every day is a fight for my life. And now I have five new people in the line of fire.

My gaze lands on Zane.

There was never a doubt in my mind that he loved me before. That he wouldn't risk everything for me if he had to. Which is exactly why I had to leave before. And now, we're here doing the same thing.

Different fight.

Different enemy.

Same possible outcome.

It was self-defense, but what if they come for him for the death of that man? What if they decide it can't go unpunished?

How can I live with myself if my freedom costs him his?

CHAPTER 17

ZANE

After hanging the new door on the cabin of my boat, I step back and study the work. It's been freshly stained and will hold up for a long time…so long as I don't have to throw anyone through it again.

The last week has passed smoothly, while Leopold works to ID the guy who didn't make it off my boat. So far, his dental records, fingerprints, and DNA have returned nothing fruitful. Not that I'm surprised.

Hired killers rarely have paper trails.

Not even Tucker Hunt has been able to find anything based on his photos, meaning he was wiped from every database everywhere. This guy is even more of a ghost than I am.

Things with Tessa have also been weird, though that's more to do with me than her. When she told me she wouldn't leave without a note, I knew she was trying to put my mind at ease, but all it did was remind me that she's still planning to leave when all of this is over.

No matter what the outcome, I'll lose her again. And that's been a tough one to swallow. But I've since realized that, even though that's true, I want her to leave knowing just how important she is. That way, she can finally stop living in the past. I want her to have a good life, even if it's not with me.

My cell rings, so I reach down and pull it out of my pocket. When I see Anastasia's name on the screen, I can't keep the grin off my face. "Hey."

"She's on her way with Sawyer."

"Great. I just finished."

"I don't think she even realizes what today is."

"It wouldn't surprise me. With everything we've had going on, I barely notice the days as they pass."

"But you remembered today."

"How could I not?"

She laughs softly. "Well, give her my love, too."

"I will. Thanks for your help." I eye the white box on the counter inside the cabin.

"Anytime, Big Brother. Have fun." She ends the call, so I shove my phone back into my pocket and work quickly to clean up the tools. I'm just finishing when Sawyer and Tessa step on board. The last week has given her leg time to heal, and her limp is gone for the most part. Though I do notice that early in the morning and late at night, she seems to be in pain.

"This is where I leave you, My Lady." Sawyer bows dramatically, and Tessa smiles.

"Thank you, Sir."

He grins, clearly happy that she's playing into it. "Cap." He salutes me, then turns on his heel and heads back down the dock.

For the first time in a week, Tessa and I are alone. She turns to face me, her smile falling slightly. It makes my chest ache to know that she's still awkward around me, but I hope today will change that.

Maybe. It may also make it worse.

Either way, it's worth the risk.

"The new door looks nice," she comments.

"Thanks. Well, are you ready?"

Confusion mars her expression. "Ready for what?"

"Wait up there; I'll be right back." I gesture toward the pilothouse, then quickly untie the dock line securing the boat to the marina.

"So where are we going?"

"You'll see," I reply with a grin, then start the motor. It rumbles to life, and I guide the boat out onto the water with the precision of someone who has been doing just that nearly his entire life. Even as young as I was when my dad passed, he'd taught me to sail. In a lot of ways, I'm more comfortable at the helm of a boat than at the wheel of my truck.

Tessa stands at my side, her gaze fixated straight ahead. Although I know it's treading dangerous waters, I can't help but imagine what it would have been like if we'd gotten married. Would she have been happy for the year we sailed around the world?

Would we have kids now?

Would I have gone to medical school and become a doctor?

Focus on the present, Knox.

"I thought you could use some distance," I tell her, my voice louder than normal so she can hear it over the rumbling motor.

"You thought right," she replies with a wide smile that has my stomach twisting into knots.

Twenty minutes pass in silence with just the sound of the rumbling boat motor to keep us company. But soon, we've reached our destination, and I guide the boat toward the small island, staying as close as I can while also avoiding the rocks.

Tessa turns to me, a wide smile on her face. "Really?"

"You recognize it?"

"Of course I recognize it! Some of my best memories are out here." She follows me down toward the bow of the boat, where I drop the anchor.

Warmth spreads through my chest as I take in the sight of her bright smile.

"Well, I figured it was the best way to spend your birthday."

Her brows draw together, and her smile falters. "What?"

"Do you not know what the date is?"

She continues staring at me, clearly trying to decide whether or not it really is her birthday. "I didn't even real-ize. I haven't celebrated since—well—since we did the last time."

That warmth I'd experienced moments ago dissipates. "You haven't celebrated your birthday since you were nineteen?"

She shakes her head. "I never saw a reason to. We didn't celebrate it when I was a kid, and I guess I was just focused on surviving."

"Tessa." My heart breaks for her. For the loneliness she must have experienced since she left.

"It's fine." She forces a smile. "So it's my birthday, huh?"

"Yeah. Anastasia brought over something for you to swim in, and I figured we could—" I trail off, shaking my head. "I'm sorry. If this isn't how you want to spend today, we can head back."

"Are you kidding? I think this is perfect. Is what she brought me back in your room?" When I nod, she turns away and heads down into the cabin of the boat.

I'm paralyzed as she leaves. Completely and utterly unable to move from the spot I'm standing in. When we'd first met, she told me that, aside from parties the teacher threw at school, she'd never celebrated her birthday. I'd made it a point to do something every single year for her.

Even after she went missing, I'd come out here with a cupcake and wish her a happy birthday. It was my way of being close to the woman I thought I'd lost forever. And now I find out that, this whole time, she'd been out there, surviving, not even taking the time to celebrate the day she was born?

Emotion burns my throat, and I force myself to turn away so I'm not standing in the same spot when she comes out. I strip out of my shirt and kick off my shoes. I've just finished lowering the ladder on the sundeck when she clears her throat behind me.

I turn, and my mouth dries.

I'd specifically told Anastasia to make sure she grabbed something modest for her. Mainly because I have a feeling the sight of Tessa in a bathing suit will be enough to drive me wild.

But when I get my first look at her in a pair of swim shorts and a rash guard t-shirt, the punch to my gut is enough to knock me overboard.

She's *stunning.*

Dark hair braided down her back, feet bare, it's all I can do not to close the distance between us and pull her against me. Would she shove me aside? Or is there a part of her that misses what was between us, too?

"Look okay?" she asks, arching a brow.

I clear my throat. *If by 'okay' you mean perfect.* "Yeah. Great. Fit okay?"

"Like a glove."

I'll agree with that. Holding out a hand, I wait for her to cross over and slide hers into mine. The feel of it is so right, so perfect, that it momentarily transports me back in time to when the whole world hadn't been between us.

When it was just her and me.

I lead her toward the back of the boat, then release her long enough to climb onto the tiny sun deck off the back.

"You ready for this?" I ask her once she's joined me.

Her dark eyes are wide with excitement, her cheeks flush with color. "It's been a long time since I went swimming. Last week's stormy dip aside," she adds with a laugh.

I lean in closer, desperate to erase at least some of the distance between us. "I won't let you drown."

Her gaze locks on mine. "I know you won't."

The tension between us increases tenfold, and I have to clench both hands into fists at my sides to keep from giving in and crushing her against me.

Get it together, Knox. I grin at her, then dive into the cold water. It envelopes me, ripping away all unwelcome thoughts about a gorgeous brunette and how desperately I want to make things work, even though they never will.

It shoves aside the constant stress I carry, and offers me the rare opportunity to focus only on the feel of my body moving through the water as I swim. I come up to the surface and take a deep breath before grinning up at her.

Tessa's expression steals my breath. *Unguarded.* For the first time since she came crashing back into my life, she looks free.

"You coming in?" I ask.

With one final, heart-stopping grin, Tessa leaps into the water.

When she doesn't immediately surface, though, worry pushes through the joy. I start to dive down to look for her when a hand grips my ankle. The contact sends a spike of heat through me, and I still haven't pulled myself together when she surfaces with a laugh, her eyes bright with joy.

"Did I scare you, Navy man?"

I'm unable to tear my gaze away from her. "Something like that. Wanna race to the island?"

"I think you have an unfair advantage over me," she replies.

"You used to win."

"Because you'd let me."

Truth be told, I'd been too afraid that something would happen to her if I got out of the water first, so I'd always let her remain in front of me. That way, I never took my eyes off her. "I'll even give you a head-start if you're scared."

"Not a chance," she says. "You ready?"

"One. Two—"

"Three!" she yells, then starts swimming as fast as she can through the water. I laugh and follow, stride after stride, moving through the water with the proficiency that comes from spending a lifetime swimming. First as a kid living on the coast, then as a Navy SEAL.

And no matter how many swim minutes I log, I'll never get tired of it. Being out on the water has a way of putting things into perspective. Especially when I think of Peter and the apostles as they were out on that storm-tossed lake.

It's a reminder that, no matter how stormy things get, Jesus is always there.

I fix my attention back to Tessa. She's leading us, with me keeping pace a few feet back.

In her darkest moments, she turned away from Him. Is that why she's here? Did He give her a nudge back to Stormwatch so she could find her way home again?

CHAPTER 18

TESSA

Being out here with Zane is soothing an ache I hadn't realized was there. My entire existence over the last eighteen years has been simply surviving. Day after day, it's all I could focus on because daring to think about anything but rock bottom was too dangerous.

I move along the rocky beach, scanning tide pools for signs of life. Out here, surrounded by clear water, it's easy to forget all of the things waiting for us back in the real world.

"Look what I found."

I turn as Zane crosses over, his sun-kissed olive skin so distracting it should be illegal. Seriously, it's all I can do not to reach out and run the tips of my fingers over the ink swirling on his chest. In his hand, he holds a sand dollar, and he takes a seat on a chunk of rock.

Sitting beside him, I look at the sand dollar in his hand. "We used to find these all the time."

He smiles. "Did you know that when the Keyhole Urchin who called this home dies, and the sand dollar dries, it leaves behind tiny doves?"

"What?" I arch a brow.

Zane grins, then snaps the sand dollar in half. He gently shakes it, and five tiny white dove-shaped things fall into the palm of his hand.

"Those were inside?" I reach out and pluck one from his palm, letting it rest in mine.

"Yeah. Sand dollar doves. I didn't know about them either. Not until Anastasia showed me before I'd left for training. We were out on the beach with Mom, and she found one. These doves are said to symbolize peace and joy that spread throughout the world when Christ rose from the dead."

Captivated by what he's saying, I hang on every word.

He sets the rest of the doves into my hand, then gently arranges the broken pieces of the sand dollar in his hand. "These four outer holes here are said to symbolize the four wounds in Christ's hands and feet when he was nailed to the cross, while this fifth one here is from the Roman's spear."

"I never would have thought of it like that."

He chuckles. "Me neither. Like I said, Anastasia is the one who told me. I took one of the white doves with me and still have it. It's gone with me on every mission, and somehow—it's still not broken."

"Have you been on a lot of them?" I ask, tipping my face to look up at him. "Missions?"

"More than I can count." He swallows hard, his gaze fixated on the water. "I've done things I wish I could take back, and I know that a lot of people would be put off by the violence I've carried out—and rightfully so. But I do feel like I've made a difference."

"You made a difference in my life."

He shifts his attention to me now. "I hope so."

"Whatever happiness I've had in my life, it's because of you. Then and now."

Zane smiles softly, then gently sets the sand dollar aside. Meanwhile, I cling to the tiny white doves in my hand.

"I've killed people," he says. "More than last night. But I only ever took a life when there was no other choice."

"I believe that."

There's a weight on him now, something that wasn't there only a few moments ago, so I remain quiet as he gathers his thoughts. Zane has always been careful to think through things before he speaks.

It's something I've always admired about him because it's something I struggle with. Anger is as familiar to me as breathing.

"Six years ago, I made a mistake that led to the deaths

of three civilians. It's why I'm not in the Navy anymore."
He takes a deep breath. "My team and I—we were
supposed to get in, gather intel, and get out. I made a call to
rescue half a dozen women who were being held against
their will. On the way out, two of them and our translator
were killed."

The weight of that one call weighs on him like cement.
I can see it all over his face. "It sounds to me like you
saved four lives."

"My orders weren't to pull them out."

"Then they were not good orders."

He smiles softly at me. "That's not my call."

"What about now? You said you do government work.
That you put a stop to violence."

"I work for a branch of the government that doesn't
technically exist. They were going to court-martial my
entire team, and to avoid prison sentences for all of us, I
agreed to a no-end-in-sight contractual obligation to do as
I'm told without asking questions."

"Zane."

"It's a glorified prison sentence, but at least I get to be
here." He gestures toward the open ocean.

"And the others? Weston, Ryker, Garrison, and
Sawyer?"

"They won't let me serve it alone, though they're not
tied to it like I am. It was the one request I made before
accepting."

"They were the team on the ground with you?" He nods, and my respect for the four men grows substantially.

"I'm telling you this because I need you to understand that I'm not who I was before. And I'm not looking for anything romantic between us because it's an impossibility I can't have." He turns toward me, pain in his green gaze. "But I need you to see that you matter, Tessa. Because I don't want to lose you again. Even if we can only be friends, I want you in my life."

My breath catches, and my gaze momentarily drops to his lips. Soft, gentle lips that kissed away my pain for so many years that the feel of them is branded in my soul. "You can't have anything romantic, or you don't want it?"

"I don't have anything firm to offer someone," he says. "My life is fluctuating constantly. There is no future where I see myself free of these chains. Not until I'm in a wooden box and buried six feet down."

The crude truth of his statement makes my chest ache at the mere thought of losing him. "What if you found someone who wanted what you could offer? Who understood?" I'm approaching dangerous waters, but I can't help myself. Today has rooted just how important Zane Knox is to me. And the one thing standing in our way is gone—right? My dad's not coming back, and he's no longer an obstacle.

What if Zane could forgive me?

What if I could forgive myself?

"I honestly don't know," he says softly. Our gazes hold a moment, and the moment grows heavy with things unsaid. Until Zane claps his hands on both thighs, then stands. "We have to get back to the boat because I have cake."

"What kind of cake?"

"Double chocolate with peanut butter frosting. What else?"

I grin, delight rising inside my chest, creating a warmth that hasn't been there in quite some time. "Can I take these?" I ask, holding out the doves.

"Here." He holds out his hand, so I dump them inside. He slips them into the pocket of his shorts and zips it up. "I'll keep them safe for you."

"Thanks." Our gazes hold, and Zane leans down to take my hand. Connection shoots through me, desire coursing through my veins like lightning in a bottle.

The first time he kissed me was on this island.

Nearly in this same spot.

My breath catches when Zane takes a step closer, then brushes a few strands of my hair behind my ear with his free hand. "Ready?"

Clearing my throat, I force a smile that I hope doesn't scream *kiss me. I don't care if you don't feel like you have anything to offer me. Your love is all I need.* "Yeah. Let's go have some cake."

Feeling lighter than I have—in I don't even know how long —I stand beside Zane as he guides his boat back into its spot in the marina. The tension between us has lessened, though the same love I carried for him all those years ago has returned full force. Something I plan to keep to myself in hopes it'll simply fade away to friendship.

There's just too much hurt there. Too much history… right? The idea that he could forgive me—and try again—is a fantasy that I can't afford to get lost in.

I remain in the pilothouse even after Zane leaves, my attention captivated by a gorgeous sunset. Rays of orange and gold paint a masterpiece in the sky.

And as I sit here staring at it, I reach into my pocket and withdraw the five tiny doves he'd given me.

Who would have thought so much beauty could come out of something broken? Tears burn in my throat, and I take a deep breath. I hadn't missed what he was trying to tell me; I'm just not sure I can believe it anymore.

Not after everything I've done and all that's happened to me in the course of my thirty-six years on this earth.

"Tessa?" Zane calls out.

Quickly, I shove the doves into my pocket and wipe the tears from my eyes. With a smile on my face, I step down out of the pilothouse. Zane is standing on the boat deck, hands in his pockets, looking nearly as nervous as he was the day he first asked me to dinner.

"What is it?"

"My mom texted. She was wondering if we'd come over there for a late dinner."

Nerves twist my gut into a million knots. "A birthday dinner?"

"Probably," he replies, running a hand through his hair. "Look, if you want to say no, you can. Don't feel obligated."

I should say no. Should fight to keep these boundaries in place, especially with how desperately I want to see them slip, but the hope on his face is everything. "That sounds great."

"Really?"

"Really," I repeat. "Today has already been perfect, which means it can only get better." I move past him and step off the boat, every step weighing me down with fear.

I've been careful to remain hidden. Not just from whoever is trying to kill me but from the people I left behind when I fled this town. The questions they will have for me are too many to answer.

Zane locks up the cabin of his boat, then follows me onto the dock. "How's the leg?"

"Great," I reply honestly. "I'm actually surprised it's not aching after swimming."

He grins at me, and my heart hammers in response. *So gorgeous.* "Feel up for another adventure?" Zane pauses near a motorcycle parked on the dock close to his boat.

I arch a brow. "That's yours?"

"It is."

"*The* Safety Monitor, Zane Knox, has a motorcycle?"

His grin spreads. "Like I told you, I'm not the same man I was."

"Clearly. Tattoos, a motorcycle. You have any piercings I should know about?"

Zane's laugh tears me up on the inside. "No. I can safely say I have none of those." He unlocks a slightly rusted metal cabinet and reaches inside, then offers me a black helmet. "Unless the motorcycle is too much for you."

The challenge is there. Truth is, the motorcycle isn't what scares me. It's having my arms wrapped around Zane that has my pulse pounding. "Not at all, Knox. Let's do it." I take the helmet and slip it over my head.

He retrieves another one, then locks up the cabinet and climbs onto the bike.

I study it for a moment, trying to decide just how much danger I'm in right now. And before I can talk myself out of it, I place my hands on his strong shoulders and straddle the bike behind him.

The bike roars to life beneath me, the thrill of it outmatched only by the feeling of being pressed against Zane as I wrap both arms around him.

He takes off, guiding the motorcycle away from the marina.

With every passing second, the feeling of freedom grows within me. Heart-pounding, soul-stirring joy as I sit here with my arms wrapped around the boy who stole my heart all those years ago.

Though I'm finding quickly that adult Zane is even more of a threat to my heart than the boy version of him was.

I lean with him as he guides the bike along the coastal road toward his mom's house. The sun has already dipped beyond the horizon, but the rays of color are still there, one final show before night takes over.

When I was a kid, I dreaded the second that night fell. Because it meant there were no more reasons for me not to return home.

The library closed, so no more studying.

The grocery store shut its lights off, so no more late-night food runs.

Zane's curfew hit, so no chance he could rescue me.

It became a fight to survive every time the sun went down. But tonight, I relish the feeling that I have nowhere to be except right here…with Zane Knox.

He guides the bike down a residential street, then parks in front of his mother's house. Ryker's truck is here, as is Anastasia's car. Nerves overtake the freedom I'd felt with my arms wrapped around Zane, but there's something else there, too.

Something awfully close to happy.

I climb off and remove my helmet, though I can still feel the rumbling of the bike as I do. Zane does the same, then sets his helmet down before taking mine. "Looks like she has company, too. You okay?"

"I am," I reply, surprised that it's true.

Zane's hand falls to my lower back as he guides me up the steps. Heat swirls in my belly at the contact, and I fight the urge to lean back into it. Into him.

The door opens before we reach it, and Anastasia's smiling face swims into view. "It's about time!" she jokes.

"I didn't even know we were coming until five minutes ago," Zane defends.

"Excuses, excuses," Anastasia jokes.

We move into the house, and she closes the door behind us. Ryker is in the kitchen with Linda, as is Sawyer. The latter is sprinkling something on top of what looks a lot like a cobbler, while the former is stirring something that smells absolutely delicious.

My stomach growls despite the cake Zane and I had only an hour or so ago.

Linda turns toward me and smiles widely. "Happy birthday!" she exclaims.

"Thank you," I say, tears burning in my throat. "You really didn't have to do this."

"Nonsense." She waves it off and turns back to whatever she's prepping on the counter. "You go ahead and relax. Dinner will be ready in a few."

I don't deserve this. Those four words echo in my mind, so loud they might as well be accompanied by a drumline.

I left her son at the altar.

I lied.

I've stolen.

I don't deserve any of this.

With Zane's hand on my lower back, I can't run, so I remain where I am. Weston shakes Zane's other hand and offers me a smile, while Garrison crosses over to stand in front of me.

"Happy birthday, Tessa," he says with a kind smile.

"Thanks. I, uh, I need to use the restroom." I force a smile that I hope looks genuine, then steer away from everyone and head down the hallway toward the first door on the right. Once inside, I go straight to the window and throw the curtains open, then open it and breathe in the cold air.

It hits my face, alleviating some of the panic, though the anxiety is still clawing its way through my chest.

I deserve *none of this.*

Not what Zane did for me today.

Not his kind words.

And certainly not a birthday dinner thrown by his mother.

Outside the window, I can hear the ocean.

They would all be better off if I just took off right now. My leg is healed; I could hit the ground and run away. I'd be gone before they even knew to look for me.

"I won't leave without saying goodbye." I meant those words, and no matter how uncomfortable I am about tonight, I won't do that to Zane.

Not again.

So I remain where I am, sucking in breath after breath in an attempt to ease the panic in my chest. They all know —right? They all have to know why I left.

That I did it on purpose.

That I'm a woman too broken for this, and it's only a matter of time before the jagged pieces of me destroy Zane all over again.

CHAPTER 19

ZANE

While everyone is in the kitchen, visiting or finishing making dinner, my gaze remains fixated on the closed bathroom door. She'd been upset when she left; I could tell that much. And who can blame her?

This is a whole lot more than the small dinner with my mother I'd been led to believe we were having.

"Maybe you should go check on her," Garrison offers. "She looks a bit overwhelmed."

Weston grunts in agreement.

"Yeah. You're right. Be back." I move over toward the bathroom door. "Tessa?" I ask, keeping my voice quiet so I don't bring attention to us.

A few seconds later, she opens the door.

Her eyes are red-rimmed, and the bathroom window is wide open.

Momentary anger shoves through the concern, and I push into the bathroom, closing and locking the door behind me.

All while Tessa's expression remains the same— neutral.

"Were you going to climb out the window?"

"I thought about it," she replies honestly. "But, no." She swallows hard and closes her eyes. "I don't deserve any of this, Zane."

I cross my arms. "Why is that?"

"The list is too great to share right now. We'd never leave this room."

She's a few feet away from me, so I take a step closer. "I have no complaints about staying right here." Truth is, having her pressed against me on the back of my bike shoved aside any and all rationality about why a relationship between us won't work.

The *only* thing that matters is Tessa.

Everything else will work itself out.

"What if you found someone who wanted what you could offer? Who understood?" Her simple words have been running through my mind since she spoke them. Was she asking for herself? Because she understands?

Her eyes widen, pupils dilating, but she remains where she is. "Zane, your family knows what I did to you."

"They know that you left because you felt like you had no choice. They know that you were trying to save me. I may not agree with it, but I see it, too." I rest both hands on the bathroom sink on either side of her. She looks up at me. "You deserve all of this and so much more, Tessa." I whisper the words now, my gaze dropping to lips I long to taste.

But I won't take that next step.

It has to be her.

"I shouldn't have left." A tear slips down her cheek. "I wish that I had never gone over there. Then maybe—" She closes her eyes. "Maybe I wouldn't have lost you."

Reaching up, I cup her cheek, letting my thumb caress soft skin I've spent nearly two decades dreaming about. "Tessa."

She opens her eyes.

"I'm right here."

Her gaze drops to my lips, and it takes *everything* to keep myself rooted here with distance between us. *Please,* I want to beg. *Please drop those walls and let me in.*

Those gorgeous brown eyes widen, and she looks up at me. The moment between us becomes so heavy that I can hardly breathe. It's as though everything that's been building since I found her on my boat comes crashing into us like waves against a shoreline.

So close.

She's *so close.*

A heavy knock obliterates the moment, and Tessa looks away from me.

"Hey! Dinner is ready!" Anastasia calls out.

A laugh bubbles out of Tessa, and she covers her face

with both hands as she rests her forehead against my chest. I lean down and press a kiss to the top of her head. "Anastasia has a talent for ruining moments, doesn't she?"

Tessa's laughter dies as I pull away. "Maybe it's for the better." She wipes her eyes and takes a deep breath.

"No," I reply without hesitation. "We're not done here, Tessa. Not by a long shot."

They told me I'd be afraid standing here at the end of the aisle, but it's not fear that has my heart pounding or my palms sweating. It's anticipation because, any *moment now, Tessa will be walking through those doors and heading straight to me.*

The deed in my pocket is my gift to her. Land we can build a home on. A future. It'll be a while before I can afford to actually do anything with it, but it's a beginning.

Maybe once we get back from our honeymoon, we can get started.

My mom smiles at me from where she's sitting in the front row. Anastasia is in the back, likely getting ready with Tessa since she's the Maid of Honor. Beside me, Weston stands strong. My brother in everything but blood.

The double doors open, and my heart leaps into my chest. But instead of Tessa dressed in white, it's Anastasia who's coming toward me.

Her expression is enough to kill the joy in my heart as I rush down the aisle toward her. "What is it?"

"I'm sorry, Zane. I'm so sorry."

"For what? What's wrong?"

Her eyes fill with tears. "She's gone. Tessa is missing."

The coffee in front of me is not at all strong enough to combat the night of tossing and turning. I never thought I'd admit it, but I'm honestly missing my sister's couch. Because having Tessa only a few yards away, behind a single door, was nearly too much to handle.

Unfortunately, without knowing who's after us and realizing how far they've been willing to go up to this point, staying with Anastasia longer than we had to isn't an option. She may not care about the danger, but I do.

So much so that Weston is currently crashing in her guest room, just in case, while Sawyer spends his free time sitting in her café and keeping watch, and spends his nights sleeping in my mom's guest room.

I'd tossed and turned all night, playing that moment in my head over and over again until finally I had gotten out of bed just to peek in on Tessa and make sure she was still there.

My Bible is open to Ephesians 2, though I stopped reading about five minutes ago when my brain stopped processing anything I was putting into it. I bow my head. *Lord, help me, please. I'm drowning here.*

The bedroom door opens, and Tessa steps out wearing leggings and a long t-shirt that falls mid-thigh.

My mouth dries at the sight of her.

So absolutely breathtaking.

"Morning," she greets with a hesitant smile.

"Morning. Coffee?" I question as I get to my feet to prep her a cup.

"Thanks."

"Yeah." I plaster myself against the counter so she can move past me, but it's not far enough. Her shoulder brushes against my chest, and I have to fight the urge to pull her closer just so I can have more of it. More of her.

Strength. Lord, I need strength.

After getting her a cup of coffee and refreshing mine, I slide back into the booth. She takes her mug and sips from it while her gaze remains out the window at the bright sunshine reflecting off the ocean's glassy surface.

"How did you sleep?" I ask her.

"Not great," she admits. "Just had a hard time falling asleep."

"You and me both," I reply.

She offers me a partial smile, then shifts her attention to my Bible. "Ephesians, huh? I kind of remember that one. Armor of God, right?"

Hope surges through me. *An opening.*

"That's the one," I tell her. "Right now, I'm on

Ephesians 2. 'For we are all God's masterpiece. He has created us anew in Christ Jesus, so we can do the good things He planned for us long ago,'" I say, reciting Ephesians 2:10, a verse I've had memorized for as long as I can remember.

"How many times have you read through the Bible?"

"A few," I reply. "But that's the great thing about God's Living Word. Every time I read through it, I find something else that hits harder than it did before."

"What is it this time? Or is that verse it?"

"Actually, it's Paul's ministry I've been really focusing on lately."

"Paul?"

"He was Saul before and actively hunted and persecuted Christians until he was chosen to spread the Good News about Jesus. He did a lot of horrible things, but the Lord used him as an instrument to spread His Gospel. I guess it's really resonating with me lately that light can come from the darkest of places." My gaze locks on hers.

"You're a good person, Zane."

"I've done a lot I'm ashamed of, Tessa. And there are so many days when moving forward feels impossible. I guess I just wonder if Paul ever felt like that, too."

She doesn't respond, just takes another drink of her coffee and turns her attention back out the window. Silence descends upon us once more, and since I'm not really sure there's a great opening for what I want to ask her, I close my Bible and jump right in. "Will you go to service with me today? I haven't been in a while now, and I'd really like to go."

She turns toward me. "Church?"

I nod, trying not to hold my breath as I wait for her answer.

"I don't—I don't have anything to wear."

"No one there cares what you wear," I tell her. "But we can call Anastasia and see if she has a dress or something you can borrow if you want? If you're uncomfortable, then that's okay, too. We have about an hour before service starts."

Her gaze shifts from the Bible to me, out the window, then back to me. "No, it's fine. If you want to go, I'll go."

They're the exact words she spoke to me the first time I asked her to go to church with me. I know she'd only gone because she was afraid to go home, and maybe it's a similar reason here, but I can't keep the joy from saturating my heart. Maybe if I can remind her just how powerful her faith is, she can find it again.

She can find Him again.

"It's been a while for me, too," she says as she nervously toys with her mug.

"How long?"

Her gaze levels on mine, and the heaviness in it isn't something I miss. "Since the last time we went together."

It's a day branded in my memory, like so many others from that time of my life. The time I spent with her. Every moment is etched into the very fabric of my being. "The Wednesday night service before our wedding."

She nods. "I don't even remember what the sermon was, but I remember sitting there, wondering how I could speed up time so we could just be married already." Her soft laugh lacks all humor. "I guess it's a shame I couldn't figure it out."

Reaching across, I cover her hand with mine. "Things aren't set in stone, Tessa."

"In some cases, they are." She pulls her hand away, retreating even after the closeness last night, and stands. "I'll get ready to go. I'm sure I can find something to wear."

TESSA

The loud echoing of happy voices from everyone who has gathered in the fellowship hall for a Sunday potluck should bring me a bit of joy, too. But the weight of the sermon I just listened to, and the depth of my own sins, have me feeling a bit lost even in this place where I once felt more at home than anywhere else.

Everyone has been incredibly welcoming, telling me that they are so happy to see me and they're so glad that I'm home. How do I tell them that I feel more lost than before? More confused than ever?

"How are you feeling?" Anastasia asks as she links her arm through mine.

I glance over at Zane, who is in what looks like a happy conversation with Garrison and a teenage boy I've never seen before. Every now and then, he scans the room for me, smiling when our gazes lock. Almost like he's expecting me to disappear.

I've definitely thought about slipping out, but I just can't bring myself to do that. Not again. Running seems to be my default setting, and I'm trying so hard to change it.

"I'm okay. Why? Do I look that lost?" I ask, hoping that my tone is light-hearted instead of weighted down by the very real turmoil I'm in.

She smiles softly. "A little."

"Anastasia!" a woman calls out.

"Oh, sorry. Be right back." Anastasia squeezes my arm gently before veering off toward the right.

Unsure what else to do and desperate for some air, I move out of the fellowship hall and into the otherwise empty sanctuary.

Stormwatch Landing's church hasn't changed much over the years. Aside from the fresh altar flowers that get changed out with each new service, the place looks almost exactly the same.

I still remember the first time I came here.

It was with Zane and his family. I'd been so nervous—terrified, really—because everyone in town knew who I was and who my parents were. I was certain they'd judge me for being here. Maybe even mock me for daring to enter God's house, considering my bloodline.

But all I'd found was a welcoming array of people who were glad to see me.

The pews are lined up on both sides, leading up to an

altar that has a large wooden cross made from driftwood. There are broken chains beneath it, signifying the way Jesus broke our chains when He came to die for us.

I remember standing here in awe for the first time, trying to wrap my head around that type of love. Truthfully, I still don't understand it.

The balcony doors are wide open on both sides of the altar, giving a near panoramic view of the ocean out the back.

I take a step closer to the altar, and a side door that leads to the church office opens.

An aged man steps out into the sanctuary, his gaze trained on the Bible in his hands. Sensing he's not alone, though, he stops and looks up at me, his smile friendly. "Tessa Lane."

I should say hi and then turn back toward the fellowship hall, but the ache in my heart is only growing as I stand here.

"Hi, Pastor Reeves."

"You're—are you okay?" His light gaze darkens with concern.

"I'm okay. Just—" I take a deep breath and let it out with a soft sigh. "I'm not entirely sure why I'm in here, to be honest. I guess I just needed a few minutes of quiet."

"Something I understand quite well," he replies. "And I'm so glad you did find yourself in here." He starts to reach out, but I flinch, then instantly kick myself for it when he withdraws his hand. That friendly smile I've always remembered stays in place, though.

He'd been another one who tried so hard to get me to turn my dad in. Though he was far gentler than most.

"Come, sit, Tessa." He gestures toward a front pew.

I should head back. Zane could be looking for me.

So why am I following him down the aisle and taking a seat beside him on the pew?

"I don't know why I came here today," I repeat. "I don't even know what to believe anymore." I still haven't even touched the Bible Zane gave me. It just sits there on the table where I left it that first day…waiting for me.

"Why is that?"

"Life," I reply. "How could I believe a loving God is walking alongside me when I can't ever seem to stay on my feet?" My throat constricts, and I stand. "I'm sorry, I shouldn't have come here."

"You're lost." It's not a question.

I meet his gaze. "You're the second person to tell me that today." I take a deep breath. "But how can I be lost when I don't feel like I was ever found?"

"You know, I remember the day you first walked through those doors." He smiles at the memory, and I find myself sinking back into the pew. "You were afraid; I could see it on your face, but there was this light within you." He shakes his head. "It shone brighter than most I'd seen because, unlike some others, it had experienced true darkness."

My eyes fill.

"You were born into an incredibly dark situation, Tessa," he says softly. "But that has never defined who you are."

"I don't think I ever had a chance."

"That's not true," he replies. "Your parents may have chosen one path, but you chose another."

I shake my head. "I left. I ran like a coward, Pastor Reeves. I wasn't kidnapped. I wasn't killed. I ran because I was so afraid that my darkness would taint Zane. The truth is, I let my dad set me on a path, and I took it without looking back."

Pastor Reeves reaches over and takes my hand in his. He pats it gently as he did so many years ago. "I know you ran away. Or, at least, I assumed."

"What?" I turn toward him. "How?"

"I saw you at your father's funeral."

I stare at him, shocked that he saw me and didn't say anything. There were only four people in attendance that day.

Pastor Reeves.

Officer Leopold.

Zane Knox.

And me.

I'd hidden behind a tree, not wanting anyone to see me. Partly because I wanted to make sure my dad was dead and the other part mourning the man he could have been. A man who should have loved me as most fathers love their children.

"So you knew I wasn't dead."

"I did."

"And you didn't tell anyone?"

"It wasn't my story to tell. By the time your father died, you'd been gone sixteen years. The investigation had stopped, and I assumed, if you'd wanted contact, you would have stuck around once the casket was in the ground."

"I hurt people."

He takes a deep breath. "Zane struggled for years with your disappearance. By the time I realized you were alive, he seemed to be doing better, and bringing it back up felt cruel."

"What I did to him was cruel."

"We all make mistakes, Tessa. But you don't have to continue living in them."

"They might as well be cement around my ankles."

"There's only one way to break free."

I glance over at him. "How's that?"

"Him." He nods toward the cross. "Ask for forgiveness, and choose to live in the light. There will be moments where the darkness settles around you, moments of weakness where you slip and fall, but He is always there to pick you back up. You say that you feel like you can't stay on your feet? Then remain on your knees, Tessa, and pray."

The tears I've been fighting against begin to fall, and Pastor Reeves wraps an arm around my shoulders as I completely fall apart. Every single wall I've carefully built comes crashing down in this moment, and if it weren't for his arm around my shoulders, I imagine I would fall right out of the pew and onto the floor.

My entire life has been one battle after another.

From the *moment* I was old enough to understand my childhood wasn't like the other kids', to the first time my dad's hand knocked me to the floor, to this moment right now, it all comes rushing over me in one constant wave of emotion.

The pain of the abuse.

The guilt of believing it was my fault.

The agony of never feeling loved.

The anger of not knowing why they couldn't just *love* me.

I let it all out as I sit here on this pew in front of the cross.

"Lord, I come to You today, asking You to walk with Tessa. You know her heart, God. You know her pain. Please wrap her in Your loving embrace and help her see that she belongs to You. That You have always been here with her and that You will always be here with her. Lord, help her to find her way back to You and seek comfort in Your loving embrace. I pray this in Jesus' name. Amen."

"Amen," I whisper.

The weight that's been on my shoulders for the last eighteen years lessens, and I draw in a deep breath as I wipe my eyes and settle my gaze back on the cross. *Please forgive me, God. Please help me. I want to do better. I want to know You.*

The Bible Zane gave me sits in front of me, unopened. Reaching out, I run the tips of my fingers over the golden letters printed on the front. *Holy Bible.* I still remember the first time I ever held one.

Zane had given me that one, too.

"You okay?" Zane drops into the booth seat across from me and slides a mug of chamomile tea toward me.

"Pastor Reeves said that I don't have to continue living in my mistakes."

"You don't."

I look up at him. "I don't know how to move forward, Zane. I know it sounds pathetic, but that's the truth. Every time I close my eyes, they're there. The things I did to you, the things I did afterward...they haunt me."

"I know how that feels," he replies with an understanding smile.

"How did you do it?"

"I'm still trying to do it," he admits. "But I know that Jesus came here to die for all of my sins, and that brings me comfort in those moments when the enemy seems hellbent on using my pain against me."

My chest aches, so I rub the heel of my palm against it. "I'm just not sure how to forgive myself."

"If it helps, I've forgiven you."

He speaks the words so plainly, as if they don't carry the weight of the world. Eyes wide, I stare at him. "You have?"

He nods and takes a bite of an apple he'd sliced up and put on the table in between us. "Pretty much the moment you came back."

"Why?"

"Because it's what we're called to do." He swallows hard. "And because I care about you, Tessa."

The tension that was between us last night in his mother's bathroom returns full-force, and all I can think about is the way his muscled arms caged me against that countertop. He'd been so close. Close enough that I could see flecks of copper in his green eyes.

The way that gaze dropped to my lips more than once.

The way I nearly gripped the front of his shirt and yanked his mouth down onto mine, even if there's no real future for us.

Why can't there be, though?

Because the way he's looking at me now? I can't help but wonder if maybe, just maybe, there isn't still something there.

Another knock on the door slices through the tension,

and Zane chuckles, running a hand over his face. "One of these days, we're going to finish that conversation." He pushes up, and I turn in my seat, watching as his hand goes to the weapon holstered in the waistband of his jeans.

"Who is it?" he calls through the locked door.

"Someone tired of being ignored," a stern feminine voice calls back.

With a frustrated sigh, he slides the door open, revealing the brunette who'd shown up after we were shot at a week ago.

Her dark hair is slicked back in a ponytail tonight, and instead of a pencil skirt, she's wearing black slacks and a matching jacket as she strolls into the cabin on heels so high they should be registerable weapons.

"You've gotten yourself and him into quite some trouble," she snaps at me.

Anger flushes my skin, and I slide out of the booth and cross both arms to glare back at her. I will *not* be intimidated anymore.

"You're going to use respect when you talk to her," Zane says, crossing his arms. "Or you can leave, Brenda."

She rolls her eyes. "Did you even bother looking into your high-school sweet mess here before just letting her back into your life?"

High school sweet mess? Is this lady serious?

"As I said," he growls. "Respect. Or get out."

Brenda glares at me, then turns her attention back to Zane. I don't miss the way she eyes him like he's the last piece of candy in a candy store. Jealousy threatens to eat me up, but I beat it back down.

Not the time.

"The guy you killed? Former CIA." She shoves a manila folder at him, and Zane opens it.

"Who sent him?"

"I have no idea. There is literally *no* paper trail. Not one. He has no recent travels—aside from coming here—no known accomplices, no family, friends—nothing."

"Former CIA? Why? How?" I'm reeling. Why would the CIA be after me? Is it the name changes? But wouldn't they be trying to arrest me? I can't imagine that comes with a death sentence.

"I'm not sure." Brenda crosses her arms. "But that's not all." She opens the door. "Come in now!" she calls out. "Had to warm you up first," she adds just before a man I've never seen steps into the boat.

Based on Zane's furious expression, though? He's absolutely seen him before.

"What are you doing here?" Zane demands, his hands clenching into fists as he takes a step toward the newcomer.

"Meet Agent Jack Weathers," Brenda says. "FBI."

"Why were you in my sister's place? Once again, you've walked right past Nina's Bait Shop."

"I'm not a threat to your sister. I was just trying to get information."

"My sister is not there for you to question," Zane snarls.

"No offense, there, Knox, but in a murder investigation, everyone is up for questioning."

"Murder?" I whisper, and all gazes shift to me, almost like they all forgot I was here in the first place. Man, if I could only go back to that.

"Tessa Lane, I presume? Or rather, Lisa Phillips. That's the name you were using, right?" Jack crosses over toward me, but Zane slides between us.

He and Jack remain rooted where they stand, each of them glaring at the other.

"This is ridiculous." Brenda rolls her eyes. "Both of you to your own corners. Let's not let your egos sink the boat."

Jack takes a step back. "I only need information."

"Then you're going to give us ten minutes."

"Sure," he replies.

"I'm assuming you can make your way back to my sister's place?"

"Sure, but it's closed."

"Exactly. She'll let you in when you get there." Zane doesn't move from his spot even as Brenda and Jack head toward the cabin door.

"I'll see you in ten," Jack says. "If you don't show, though, our next interaction won't be so friendly."

With that barely veiled threat, he turns to leave, with Brenda following on his heels.

As soon as the door is closed, Zane pulls his phone from his pocket and taps on the screen before pressing it to his ear. All while the blood is hammering so loud in mine that I can barely hear what he says.

CIA?

FBI?

Murder?

What's happening?

ZANE

"Thanks for this," I tell Anastasia, keeping my voice barely above a whisper so Brenda and Jack can't hear me from where they're seated at a café table near the front door of my sister's coffee shop. Tessa is standing just beside me, silent as she's been since they left the boat.

I can feel the nerves pouring off of her, and if I can't calm her down, I worry this conversation is going to go very poorly.

"Of course. Are you sure you don't want me to stay down here?" my sister asks, her gaze shifting from me to the table they're sitting at, then back to me.

"Nah. Head upstairs. Do me a favor, though, call the team and have them on standby should this go sideways."

"Consider it done." Anastasia reaches over and squeezes Tessa's hand gently. "You know where to find me." With one final glance at the corner table, she heads toward the back and up the stairs.

"You ready?" I ask Tessa.

"No. But let's go anyway."

I rest my hand on her lower back and guide her toward the table. The contact is as much for me as it is for her. We take our seats, and I cross my arms. "So the FBI is investigating self-defense these days? That's new."

"I'm not here for you," he says, then shifts his attention to Tessa. "I'm here for you."

"Me? What about? I didn't kill anyone!"

"That's to be determined." He reaches into his pocket and withdraws a photograph, then slides it on the table between us. "Do you recognize them?"

Tessa leans in and studies the photographs. A petite blonde woman smiles out of the image as she stands beside a dark-haired man with dark eyes and a wide smile of his own. I don't recognize them, and based on the look Tessa is giving, she doesn't either.

"No."

"No?" Jack confirms.

"No. I don't understand what this has to do with me."

"Start talking, Weathers," I snap. My patience is already wearing thin, thanks to Brenda springing this on me like a perfectly orchestrated trap, but until I start getting some real answers, I'm feeling rather volatile.

"You're looking at Karver and Alara Benson. The owners of Southeast Environmental Commission."

Tessa shakes her head. "No. I met Karver and Alara; this is not them." She slides the photo back.

"Dental, fingerprints, and DNA sampling confirm that these are the Bensons."

Tessa's quiet a moment. "Dental? Why would you need —" She pales. "They're dead?"

Jack nods.

"What exactly are you accusing Tessa of?" I ask, unease crawling up the back of my neck.

"Nothing yet. Their bodies were discovered in a remote campsite outside of Denver. They'd been dead three and a half months."

"Three and a half *months?*" Tessa chokes out. "I was hired three months ago."

"If that's true, then my best guess is that whoever hired you was pretending to be them. But I need to know *exactly* what they looked like and what they said."

"*If* that's true? Surely you're not accusing her of a double homicide."

"You don't even know this woman," Brenda says.

Anger surges to the surface, and I have to actively fight against exploding right here at this table. Somehow, I don't think Anastasia would appreciate it if I flipped her pretty café table.

"I didn't kill anyone," Tessa insists.

"But you did change your name. Multiple times," Brenda says. The way she watches me tells me that she'd been hoping I wasn't aware of it.

"That doesn't equal murder. Tessa was trying to hide from an abusive family situation."

"Sure. But she avoided taxes for nearly two decades and forged state documents for three different names. That's a crime that carries a hefty jail sentence."

"I can make all this go away." The first words Brenda ever spoke to me come rushing back with horrible clarity. Bile burns in my throat.

"You are *not* going to blackmail her," I snap, shooting up from my chair with such force that I send it flying backward. My muscles tremble with barely leashed rage. Whatever she's done to me, she will not put shackles on Tessa, too.

Tessa flinches.

Brenda grins at me, clearly ecstatic to have gotten a response.

"We don't care about the name changes," Jack says, clearly frustrated. "The only thing I want to know is who murdered the Bensons."

"Then you should talk to the other employees. I never even saw them again after that initial meeting. All contact was through email."

"None of their employees have seen them since they went missing. Their assistants received emails from them saying they were taking a last-minute trip and would be back in a few months. Then, they were told to onboard you as a new secretary."

"I don't understand why they would hire me then.

Nothing out of the ordinary happened while I was working there."

"That's the piece we can't figure out." He crosses his arms and studies her. "You sure you don't know them? Seems awfully handy that you were struggling and just so happened to catch a break like this. Surely it ended all your financial troubles."

Before I can even respond, Tessa pushes up from her chair. "I would *never* hurt another person. I would rather starve to death. I'm telling you the truth. The two people who hired me looked nothing like these two." She points to the picture. "I worked directly with Genevieve Logan during the time I *was* employed there. Up until my apartment was ransacked and someone attacked me when I tried to run."

Jack's gaze narrows. "Someone attacked you?"

"Yes."

"She showed up with a stab wound in her thigh, as well as multiple bruises and defensive markings." I cross my arms, trying to read his expression. Either he's a great actor, worthy of an Academy Award, or he's genuinely surprised.

"What was taken from your apartment?" he questions.

Slowly, Tessa takes her seat again. However, I remain standing, although I do pick up the chair. Anastasia will chew me up and spit me out if I damage the furniture she restored herself. "I never looked."

"You said you were escaping an abusive family situation?" Jack asks. "Care to elaborate?"

"I don't see what that has to do with anything."

"Is it possible that's who was after you then? Who tossed your apartment?" he presses.

"Given that he died two years ago, no." Tessa crosses her arms.

"It seems probable that they were after her because she could ID them," I offer.

"That's what I'm leaning toward, too," he replies.

"Add to that what happened right after she arrived, and what happened last week, I'd say it's more than probable," Brenda says.

Considering the fact that Jack doesn't ask for clarification on either event, I'm guessing Brenda took the liberty of filling him in.

"What is your involvement in this?" I ask her. Brenda Leroy does *nothing* without an ulterior motive.

"A member of my team has been at the receiving end of bullets twice since she came back to town. That makes this my business."

"I'm hardly a member of your team," I retort. "I thought your preferred term was 'asset.'"

She glares at me. "Either way. You're my business. And you've had nothing but trouble since Little Miss Small Town decided to return home."

"No," I reply, letting the bite of her words wash over me so I don't lose my head to the anger trying to root within me. "That's not it."

Brenda reaches into the briefcase on the ground beside

her and holds out a folder, so I cross and take it from her. "You're being activated," she says. "One of the employees, who was hired a few months before Tessa, has opened their own private company a few blocks away from the original building."

"And why isn't the FBI talking to them?" I question, shifting my gaze to Jack, who honestly looks about ready to explode. I imagine having Brenda come in and take over is not something he's overly thrilled about.

"Because the government has decided I'm only allowed to investigate the murders. Since that particular employee has an alibi, they are of no further interest to me," he replies.

If I weren't so frustrated, I'd laugh. Seems Brenda has her claws in his higher-ups, too. *At least it's not just me she's controlling.* "So explain to me why the government is interested in the murder of two do-gooders? Isn't that local PD's jurisdiction?"

"It's not the Karvers were interested in. However, Cal Markson has loose ties back to an environmental terrorist group known for targeting high-profile companies and staging elaborate attacks on and off US soil."

I look down at the mugshot in front of me. "This guy has a list as long as my arm. Why hasn't he been officially charged with anything?"

"We think he has someone covering for him; we just can't figure out who. Thing is, Markson is a small fish. I want the shark at the top of his food chain," Brenda says.

"Which is why you and your team are headed to Savannah, Georgia."

"If they're dangerous, though, why are you sending Zane?" Fear laces Tessa's voice, and Brenda grins, prepared to eat her alive at the first opportunity.

"Zane killed someone with his bare hands a week ago, and you still wonder why I keep him around? He and his team are good at what they do. And when things go sideways, they're the most brutal group of mercenaries I've had the pleasure of working with."

"Not at all how I would put it," I snap, fresh anger washing over me. Mercenaries? We're *not* mercenaries.

The back door opens, and I turn as Weston, Ryker, Sawyer, and Garrison all stroll in. Each of them is wearing an angry expression. They come to stand behind me and cross their arms.

Even Jack Weathers appears to be slightly intimidated. He stands, likely not wanting to be the only man sitting.

"Mercenaries?" Sawyer questions. "That's not a great way to talk about us. Tank, maybe, but me? Come on, I'm cute as a button."

"And deadly as a viper." Brenda pushes to her feet and takes her briefcase. "Call yourselves whatever you want, but what was the body count on that last mission? Seventeen? Eighteen? I can't remember." She taps a sharp nail to her chin. "Either way, violence seems to come as naturally to you as breathing," she adds with a grin in my direction.

I'm afraid to look at Tessa.

What if she's buying this act?

For a woman raised in such a violent home, the last thing she would want is to be tethered to someone capable of taking a life. How could I have been so foolish as to think otherwise?

"To be fair, most of those were mine," Weston adds coldly. It's not that he's cold about the deaths. Each and every one, even as necessary as they were, eats him alive. But he's trying to take the attention off of me.

Which means Tessa's expression is likely twisted in horror.

"Hmm. Well. Talk to your leader. He has your next orders." Brenda strolls out of the coffee shop without a second look back.

"Can't say I'm a fan of hers," Jack says. He turns to Tessa. "I'll be in contact with any other questions. Can I have a word?" he asks me.

"Sure." I glance back at Weston, who offers me a slight nod, letting me know he's watching. Then, I follow Agent Jack Weathers out onto the sidewalk in front of Anastasia's place.

"I don't believe Tessa killed anyone," he says.

"She didn't."

Jack nods. "You should know that Miss Button-up? She is coming for your girl—hard. I'm not sure why, or what the trouble is there, but if she could pin this entire thing on her, she would."

"Why are you telling me this?"

"Regardless of what you think of me, Mr. Knox, I'm not a fan of bullies. Government-issued or otherwise. Have a nice night." He heads down the dark sidewalk, and I cross my arms, trying to prepare myself for whatever waves Brenda just caused in the already brewing storm between Tessa and me.

CHAPTER 22

TESSA

Zane has been silent since we got back to the boat, and it's so hard for me to focus on anything but the look on his face when Brenda practically called him a murderer. I'm sorry, a *brutal mercenary*.

Brutal? Is she out of her mind? No, not out of her mind. I know what she was trying to do. I'm not stupid.

She was attempting to jam a wedge between us. And after how close we've been getting? I won't let her.

Not now. Not ever.

"How are you doing?" Zane questions as he finally takes a seat across from me in the booth. He slides over a mug of fresh tea since our last two were cold by the time we got back.

"I mean, I'm a bit shaken. To know that the people who hired me likely murdered the people they were pretending to be. And I know it's not logical, but I'm kicking myself for not seeing through it. Shouldn't I have sensed some-thing? Anything?"

"You couldn't have known. All of the employees went along with it; no one sensed anything was off."

"I know, but still." The warmth of the mug against my hands is soothing an ache in my chest. "I feel bad for them. I know that I didn't know them at all, but from everything everyone said about them at work, they were good people."

Zane starts to reach over and take my hand but hesitates.

Why? Because of what Brenda said? Or because he thinks I might have had more to do with this than he's letting on?

"The FBI agent knows you're not involved in their murders. If that helps at all."

"Really?"

He nods.

"Is that what he told you outside?"

"Among other things."

"Such as?"

Zane looks down at his mug as he holds onto it like a lifeline. "You know I don't ever want to hurt anyone, right? I take no joy in causing anyone pain, and I'll do anything to save a life."

"I know you're not a killer."

"I told you. I've killed before."

I swallow hard at the images of blood pouring out of the wound in my attacker's neck. A wound caused by the very hands holding onto a teacup right across from me. "I know that."

"Even before what happened last week. I've killed dictators no one will ever remember, taken out high-profile targets who were holding innocents hostage, and even those who were about to launch an attack that would have taken the lives of millions. Even with that, I tried to bring them to justice first. The only time I will pull a trigger is when it's their life or someone else's."

"Zane." I reach over to touch his hand now, and he stills beneath the contact. "I know that."

"It's important to me that you do. That you don't think of me as a..." He trails off, swallowing hard. "As a violent man."

And then it hits me.

He's upset because he's worried that I'm looking at him like I did my father. A man capable of horrific violence because it brought him pleasure to inflict harm on someone else.

"Zane, I know that."

"Tessa, I hate that I've done it. I've begged for forgiveness, I've fought to find my way to the light whenever it would have been so much easier to descend into darkness." He closes his eyes and shakes his head. "The others are the same. None of them takes any pleasure in causing harm, and I do believe—as twisted as it sounds—that we've made the world a better place." Because I sense he needs to be heard, I don't respond. "I killed three men running a sex trafficking ring last year. They'd captured a group of young girls from an overseas boarding school. One of them was the daughter of a politician here in the States. We got there, but we were too late for one of the girls. She was seventeen, and I still haven't forgiven myself for that."

His pain fills the space around us, and I squeeze his hand, hoping the contact will help him remain rooted in the present.

"I'm the one who found her. And when I did—I snapped. Sawyer pulled me off the man who killed her. He saved the monster's life —until that monster drew a knife I hadn't seen. He charged at me, and I took him down without a second thought."

"He would have killed you otherwise. He killed that young girl."

"Even then. Even knowing what he did to her. To countless others we'll never know about. I still felt guilty doing it." A tear rolls down his cheek as he's thrust back into that memory, and it's all I can do not to go to him now. To wrap my arms around him and hold him close.

"I've done bad things. And I won't go so far as to say I'm a good man. But I'm trying. And if Brenda hadn't sunk her claws into me, I might stand a chance at fully moving forward. Every mission, every set of orders, they put me back in that position of having to choose between life and death. Living life with your finger on the trigger is a terrible place to be."

Because I can't take it anymore, I release his hand and

slide out of the booth, then sink to my knees on the seat beside him so I can face him. Cupping his face with both hands, I run my thumbs over the stubble coating his jaw. "Zane. You are the absolute kindest man I've ever known. It was you who showed me that hands were for more than violence. That they could hold someone gently." Lifting his, I place it on my cheek. Partially because I need to feel it, and partially because I need him to remember. "From the time I was thirteen on, it was your smile that got me through each and every day. Even after I left, I'd go to sleep dreaming about you. You were the first person on my mind every morning, no matter how hard I tried to forget you."

Tears burn in the corners of my eyes as I stare into his.

"You are not a brutal mercenary. You *are* a good man. You showed me that I was loved beyond measure. That I was created by a loving God and not some accident or mistake like my dad wanted me to believe. And even though I strayed from that faith over the years, I'm trying to find my way back because *you* inspired me to do that. Because you've taught me that we are not our pasts."

Zane swallows hard and brushes his thumb over my cheek.

"Don't let someone like Brenda convince you that you're nothing but a killer. Don't make the same mistake I did by letting someone else dictate who you are. Because you, Zane Knox, are the man I fell in love with all those years ago, and the only man who has ever made me feel like I could be anyone I wanted."

Heart hammering against my ribs, I stare at him, trying to decide whether what I want to do is a terrible idea or the only thing that makes any actual sense.

"You're driving me wild, Tessa," Zane growls, his gaze dropping to my lips. "But I won't take that step. It has to be you."

I want to.

So badly.

But is it a mistake?

Will we love only to lose?

And even if that's a risk, isn't it one worth taking?

I lean in, my lips only a whisper from his. Zane's hand slips around to the back of my neck, and he buries it in my hair. Desire shoots through my body, coursing through my veins like a hurricane.

And when I can't take it anymore, I close the distance and press my lips to his. Lightning shoots through me as Zane comes to life in my hands. Before I can even fully comprehend what's happening, we're out of the booth and he's setting me on the counter, stepping up between my legs and kissing me like our lives depend on it.

Who knows? Right now, maybe they do.

He's oxygen, and I've been struggling to breathe since the day I left. He demolishes every wall I'd put up around my heart, devouring the distance I'd tried so hard to maintain because I was afraid of what it meant to truly let myself love Zane Knox.

I'd nearly died the last time I lost him.

This time? I know I won't survive.

I grip his shoulders now, giving back every ounce of ferocity he pours into the kiss. The boat rocks as though the ocean itself is drawn to what's between us.

With a growl, Zane releases me and steps back, his gaze wide and wild. "We have to stop," he says, breathless. "We—"

"I know." I can't help but smile because, *man,* Zane Knox can *kiss.* And oh, how I've missed it.

"I won't—" He trails off and runs a hand over the back of his neck. "I'm not suggesting anything, but you should know that I won't go to bed with a woman outside of marriage. I've done it before, but I won't do it again."

"I feel the same," I tell him.

"Good." He nods, then grins. "I've missed you, Tessa."

"I've missed you, too, Zane."

His smile spreads, and my stomach flips. "I do think we might need a chaperone, though. Because now that I've tasted what's between us, I desperately want more." He moves in close again, cupping my face and resting his forehead against mine.

"What do you have in mind?" I ask.

"I have a few ideas."

CHAPTER 23

ZANE

Since it was too late last night to go anywhere, I spent the entire night lying awake and staring up at the ceiling, almost hoping that Tessa was going to come out, and also terrified that she would.

She didn't. Which is definitely what was best for both of us. I meant what I told her. The next woman I take to bed will be my wife, but that doesn't mean that I feel like testing that particular temptation. Especially when it's been building for eighteen years.

Anastasia offered for us to stay with her, but with the risk to our lives right now, I thought it best to take Garrison up on his offer to have us stay in his apartment right next door to the community center where he works. Which is exactly where we went as soon as he texted that he was awake.

Tessa is currently reading in the guest room, while the

team and I have gathered in Garrison's office to discuss the orders Brenda dealt out last night.

"So, we're back on mission. Fantastic." Sarcasm drips from Sawyer's words as he takes the folder from me and studies the transcript. I know my team is just as tired as I am of being at Brenda's beck and call. "I'll get to work on prepping the bugs."

"It should be a quick one. Get in, place the bugs, keep watch, record, and leave. A week max." I cross my arms as I lean back against the cabin of my boat. My mind *should* be on formulating a plan to obtain the information Brenda has requested, but instead, it's on Tessa.

Is she reading the Bible?

Is she thinking about last night, too?

Of that kiss that incinerated me from the inside out and left me desperate for more?

"Do we know what kind of friction we're going to hit when we get there?" Ryker questions, pulling me back to the present.

"Unknown for now," I reply. "But we'll be setting up an OP and getting eyes on them as soon as we get there." Establishing the operational post is only one part of the puzzle. We have to get in and get out without being spotted. Something that we're good at—but considering this mission is on US soil, and if we're caught, there's no one coming to bail us out—it's a risk.

Add to that, whoever is running this show has ties to the

CIA; well, there's no telling how much trouble we could hit.

"I'll pack what we may need should things go sideways," Garrison says with a nod.

"Great, but—" I trail off as I prepare for his push back. "I need you to stay here and watch Tessa while I'm gone."

Garrison arches a brow. "You're grounding me?"

"No. I'm just assigning you to a different post. She's at risk, and I need someone I trust to watch her."

"Aww, poor Demo. He won't get to blow anything up," Sawyer says with a sarcastic pout.

"You sure about that?" Weston questions. "We've never done an op with one man down."

"I know that. And to be honest, no, I'm not sure. But we don't have a choice. I won't take Tessa on mission, and I don't have anyone else I can call in on such short notice. We need Sawyer for communications, and you and Ryker for a Plan B. We *shouldn't* need to blow anything up."

"Shouldn't and won't are two different things," Ryker comments.

"If you have a different suggestion, I'm all ears," I reply dryly.

"I don't mind," Garrison says quickly. "I'll pack you what you need just in case, then keep an eye on things here."

"Thank you."

He nods. Since Garrison's day job is as a counselor for high-risk teens at the community center, I know I can count on him to keep Tessa safe—and calm. The guy may set charges for us, but he diffuses for everyone else.

"If everything goes well, this is nothing more than an information gathering mission," I say.

"And if it goes sideways?" Weston asks.

"Then we'll be prepared for that, too." I take a deep breath. "Look, I don't like it either, but something that FBI agent said last night has me concerned that this isn't what it looks like." It was another reason I couldn't sleep. I kept running over everything he said in regards to Brenda and Tessa.

"When he had you go outside with him?" Weston questions.

I nod.

"What did he say?" Garrison asks.

"That Brenda has it out for Tessa. He said that Brenda is coming for her and that if she could find a way to pin all of this on her, she would."

Sawyer arches a brow. "So you think we might be getting sent off on a wild goose chase?"

"I can't rule it out."

"Do you really think Brenda is heartless enough to leave Tessa purposefully unprotected like that?" Garrison crosses his arms.

"There is no doubt in my mind she would. I don't believe she'd take matters into her own hands, but if she can set it up to get Tessa out of the way, she'll do it."

"But why?" Sawyer asks.

"Because Tessa is a distraction," Weston answers. "An obstacle standing in the way of the Cap following every single order Brenda throws his way. Tessa gives Zane a reason to not want this life." He crosses his arms.

"Ooh. You sure Garrison is enough then?" Sawyer jokes.

Garrison chuckles. "I'll keep her safe," he promises.

"Thanks. Keep an eye on Anastasia, too, please. If Jack drew parallels, then it's possible someone else might, too."

"You've got it, Cap."

"Do you really think Anastasia's at risk?" Sawyer's tone is lacking all humor. A rare thing for him. But when it comes to my sister's safety, there's little else he takes more seriously. Which, as an older brother, I can appreciate. As his friend, though? His teammate? I wish he'd just tell her how he feels already so we can all stop dancing around it.

"I don't think so. But I don't want to take the risk." I study them, feeling the weight of everything they've been through over the last six years. "Listen, I think this needs to be the last one."

"Excuse me?" Weston arches a brow.

"You know something we don't, Cap?" Sawyer questions.

I sigh. "I'm likely in this until they put me in the ground or I become too old to be useful. But you guys don't have to be. You can lead normal lives. Start families."

"We're a team," Garrison says.

"Besides. You wouldn't last ten minutes without us,"

Sawyer adds with a grin. "We both know you're useless with a computer."

Chuckling, I run a hand over the back of my head. "This isn't your fight, though. This was my mistake. You don't have to keep fighting."

"We're with you until the end," Ryker says.

"What about your lives? You gave up everything for this. Your lives, homes. And for what?" Frustration pulls at me, but it's not at my team. It's at the fact that I practically condemned us all to a life sentence over *one* decision.

A decision I can confidently say I'd make again, even knowing the outcome. We lost two lives, but we saved four others.

"Because we're brothers," Weston says. "Maybe not in blood, but we're family. And that kind of loyalty isn't something to abandon just because things get hard."

"We may not be behind bars, but we're all serving a prison sentence," I remind them. "But you guys don't have to."

"Only because you took the fall." Ryker stands and crosses his arms. "The truth is, each and every one of us would have made that same choice."

Weston, Garrison, and Sawyer all nod in agreement.

But it doesn't alleviate the guilt I carry. "I just want you all to live long, happy lives."

"That's not up for you to decide, Cap," Sawyer says. "The truth of it is, we're not going anywhere. Not unless you're out, too, or we're shipped home in a pine box. So suck it up, buttercup. You're stuck with us."

"When are we heading out?" Weston asks, shifting the subject so I can't protest any further. Not that it'll do any good. We've had this argument many times over the last six years, and it always ends the same way.

"We'll be wheels up at sundown."

Exhausted, I take a seat on Garrison's couch. After checking in with my mom and Anastasia, and ensuring the boat was prepared in case any storms roll in while I'm gone, I've completed all of my pre-mission tasks.

They've become second nature to me now, but it still doesn't make saying goodbye to Mom and Anastasia any easier.

I know all too well that, even when a mission seems like it'll be smooth, there are a million things that can go wrong.

Garrison headed over to the community center as soon as I got in, and the others are preparing to take off in two hours. The private plane Brenda sent for us is already at the small airstrip outside of town, fueled and ready to go when we are.

I sigh. Of all the missions I've been on, all the times I've had to say goodbye to my family, this one is the hardest. Glancing back at her door, I will it to open so I can see her before I leave. I could go knock. See if she's up, but I'd hate to wake her when I know she's been struggling to sleep.

So, I lean my head back and close my eyes. Not a minute later, though, I hear the faint squeak of the door behind me and turn to see Tessa step into the living room. Bathed in the soft light from outside, she's a sight to behold in blue leggings and one of my flannel shirts. It falls to just below her thighs, and the bright red plaid contrasts perfectly with the dark strands of her hair where it rests just past the collar.

"Hey. Sorry if I woke you."

"You didn't." I smile, and she returns it, then crosses over to sit beside me. "Did you get any rest?"

"Not really," she admits, then chews on her bottom lip. Her tell for having something on her chest that she wants to say but isn't sure she should.

"What is it?"

"That obvious?" she asks.

"I know you exceptionally well."

"I'm worried. And I know that I don't really have a right to be after what I did. But I—" I silence her when I slip a hand around the back of her neck and pull her in for a kiss.

Those soft lips move against mine, a friction that causes a hammering in my blood.

Pulling away, I rest my forehead against hers. "If you

have no right to be worried about me, then I have no right to be worried about you. And, I am."

"I'm not going anywhere, though."

I pull away. "That didn't keep someone from trying to take your life twice already."

Tessa takes my hand in hers. "Please come back to me. I want to know what's next for us. I want to see where this can go. My life has been incomplete without you, Zane."

Reaching up, I cup her cheek in my hand and run the pad of my thumb over her soft skin. "I just got you back, Tessa. I'm not going anywhere."

She smiles, then leans in to press her lips to mine. The simple gesture sends heat through my body with such force that it would have knocked me to my knees if I weren't already sitting. Tessa stirs desire in me unlike anything I've ever felt because it's coupled with love.

And the fact that, even after so many years apart, I can still clearly picture our future.

It's slightly different now, but still there.

Clear as crystal.

The front door opens, and Garrison walks in.

Tessa and I pull apart, but I drape an arm around her shoulders, and she leans against me.

"I can leave and come back," Garrison offers with a grin.

Tessa laughs, and I smile at my friend. "No need. Everything okay?"

His amused expression falters. "I have this kid I'm

working with who is really struggling with self-worth. It'll be okay, though. I'll get him there." He smiles. "You guys up for dinner? The diner is serving meatloaf tonight, and I'm starved."

I look over at Tessa. Aside from church service and Anastasia's café, she's been reluctant to go many places since she hasn't wanted to face anyone in town just yet.

"That actually sounds great," she says with a smile.

"Yeah?" Joy surges through me. Maybe, just maybe, she'll get used to being out and about in Stormwatch Landing again. And then, once all of this is over, maybe that future I've been dreaming of isn't too far out of reach.

"Let's do it. It's been a long time since I had one of Maddie's vanilla shakes."

CHAPTER 24

TESSA

Stormwatch Landing without Zane feels empty. Kind of like my life did until I found my way back here again. He's only been gone a handful of hours, but when I look out through the window of Garrison's apartment, I know he's not out there.

And that stings more than I thought it would.

Garrison is seated at the kitchen table, his gaze focused intently on the laptop in front of him. He's been there most of the morning, taking a handful of calls and responding to what looks like some pretty intense emails.

He's incredibly friendly, and not once has he treated me with anything but kindness. Not that I would expect anything else. I know Zane wouldn't have left me with him if he weren't safe.

And there I go, jumping right on in to blindly trusting

him all over again. I smile. Zane Knox has my heart in a chokehold, and I hope he never lets go.

Garrison pushes back from the table and stands to stretch. "I could use some coffee. How about you?"

"I can always use coffee," I reply.

He flashes a smile. "Great." He moves around the island that separates the kitchen from the dining room and turns on a large machine with way too many buttons for me. "Zane said you like lavender vanilla, right?"

My heart flips in my chest knowing that he thought of me. "I do."

"Great. Anastasia dropped off some lavender and vanilla syrups yesterday."

"That was thoughtful of her."

"She's like that." He goes to work prepping the coffee, so I head over toward the open balcony doors. It overlooks the ocean, and I smile as I close my eyes and let the salty sea breeze toy gently with my hair.

Home.

I've missed it dearly. And even though the danger hasn't passed yet, I can't help the peace that settles over me like a comfortable blanket. No matter what happens, I'm staying in Stormwatch Landing.

Because this is my place.

My home.

"Here you go." Garrison steps up beside me and offers me the mug.

"Thanks."

"No problem." He takes a sip of his coffee. "I've been a lot of places, and this is my absolute favorite."

"Is that why you settled down here?" I ask.

He nods. "After we were discharged from the military, I didn't really have anywhere else to go. I'd planned to do twenty years and then retire on a beach somewhere to live out the rest of my days."

"Alone?"

He shrugs. "My aunt raised me, and she passed away right before I enlisted. I didn't have anyone and didn't see that changing."

"Zane told me that he's the only one Brenda can control. That you guys joined in of your own volition."

"We did. All of us were there that day. And like we told him, there isn't a single one of us who would have made a different choice."

"He told me what happened. I think he's a hero."

Garrison smiles. "He'll never see himself that way."

"Trust me, I know." I laugh. "When I was a kid, I'd been so alone. Having friends meant having to explain bumps and bruises, or why I wasn't at school after I'd broken an arm or leg. Then Zane." I sigh and shake my head, the memory one I will never forget. "I'd gotten caught stealing food from the General Market and was hauled down to the police station to wait for my dad. Zane was there, waiting for his to get off his shift, and he just looked at me. I don't know how to explain it, but when his gaze locked on me, it was like I was being *seen* for the first time ever. That probably sounds crazy," I add with a laugh, then take a sip of coffee.

"Not crazy at all," Garrison replies.

"He was just—everything. I tried to push him aside so many times, but he wasn't having it. He'd just show up. Outside the school when I got out of class, whenever I went anywhere, he was there. And it was more than that. He'd actually talk to me. Or, try to, anyway. I wasn't overly social back then."

"What changed?"

I smile. "A vanilla shake at Maddie's place."

"Really?"

"Really. I was there, working part-time to try to get some money for food, and he came in. He ordered two vanilla shakes, then just sat in the corner. I was so frustrated at this point because he'd been coming in alone and ordering two shakes for weeks, so I went over to confront him. I yelled at him for following me and told him to leave me alone. You know what he did?"

"What?"

"He smiled at me. Said his name was Zane Knox, and we were going to be friends. Then, he scooted the vanilla shake toward me." I laugh. "I was so stunned that I just stood there, staring at it until Maddie came over and wrapped her arm around me, told me to take a break, then gently guided me into the booth. After that, we were inseparable."

"That's a great story."

I glance up at him. "Thanks. I think so, too."

"Choosing to leave the way you did must have been hard."

The all-too-familiar knot in my chest tightens, constricting my breathing. "It was."

"As a man, I can understand how angry Zane might have been that you didn't give him the chance to take care of you. But as his friend, I understand your desire to keep him safe."

"I wish I could go back and make a different choice."

"Would you?"

I consider. "I don't actually know. He would have killed my dad, Garrison. Or lost his life trying. Either way, I'd lose him. But maybe if I'd gone to the police sooner, it wouldn't have happened."

"Maybe. Maybe not. You're here now, and that's what really matters."

"I hope so."

"Zane is the best man I've ever known. He cares about people. About how they feel, their needs. He deserves someone who will do the same for him."

"I will."

He offers me another smile, then turns his attention to the water once more. There's a faint scar hidden beneath his short beard, and while I want to ask about it, I decide against it. There are plenty of scars of my own I'd rather never discuss, so poking at someone else's just isn't something I'm comfortable with.

"So, Demo, huh? Did you really get that nickname because you like to blow stuff up? Or was it something else that branded you with that?"

He barks out a laugh. "Kind of. Our first mission, I set the charges a little too close to where Ryker and Sawyer were set up. They were fine, but everyone started calling me Demo after that."

"And what about Ryker? You all call him Tank, right?"

"Yeah." He chuckles. "He's practically indestructible. A mission we were on six months ago, he had to be bound with chains because he snapped their ropes."

I gape at him, trying to imagine a scenario where *anyone* could break free of ropes. "Who chained him up?"

"It took three of them. And the only reason they were able to is because of the gun to Cap's head."

My stomach plummets, the imagery settling into my mind like a horrible nightmare. "Cap is Zane?"

He nods. "It all turned out okay, though."

I try to shove the image of Zane with a gun to his head out of my mind. *Lord, please protect him.* The prayer comes so easily to me that it nearly catches me off guard, but there's a warmth that settles in my chest. A familiarity that feels an awful lot like coming home.

"Why do you guys call him Cap? Was his rank Captain?" I ask.

"Nah. But we always said that, if anyone could get promoted to captain early, it was him. Captain is equivalent to an Army colonel," he explains. "He was a lieutenant commander, on track to be a commander."

"Wow. Lieutenant Commander Knox. Has a good ring to it."

He grins. "Yeah, we thought so, too. But everyone he trained with just called him Cap or Captain. Of course, only when no one higher up was around."

"I imagine they wouldn't have taken too kindly to you guys promoting him."

"Nah, not at all." He finishes the rest of his coffee. "I have to get back at it. You good with the diner for dinner? Or I can see if Anastasia minds bringing something over?"

"I don't mind at all. The diner sounds great."

"Awesome." He takes my now-empty cup and heads back inside, leaving me standing on the porch overlooking the ocean.

Lieutenant Commander Zane Knox.

He'd been advancing in the Navy before one choice ripped it all away from him. I can't help but draw similarities to the decision I made eighteen years ago, when one decision ripped my future away from me.

Then again, he'd been saving lives when he made his choice.

Was mine truly about anyone but me? About my own shame for going to that trailer and trusting my dad when I should have known better?

CHAPTER 25

ZANE

Silently, I breach the roof entrance of the building we were sent here to watch. The sign outside still reads *For Lease,* but over the last twenty-four hours of monitoring this place, we saw over a dozen different people carrying boxes in but leaving with nothing in their hands.

Since they don't look like movers or renovators, my best guess is this place is a staging facility for whatever they have planned next.

Sawyer comes forward with his tablet in hand. He sticks the long wand into the open doorway and watches the scan on his tablet. If anyone is talking on the floor just below us, we'll know about it.

When nothing pops, he sticks it back into his bag and offers me a nod.

Weapon in hand, I move in first, with Sawyer on my

heels, Weston behind him, and Ryker bringing up the rear of our breach party. Near soundlessly, we move down the steps and pause just outside the door. Even though Sawyer's mic should have picked up any noises, I crack the door, and he listens again, just in case.

Sweet, sweet silence.

As one unit, we step out onto the top floor. The concrete ground is covered in a thin layer of dust, and there are a few painter's tarps in one corner with some large buckets of paint beside them. Aside from that, though, the warehouse floor is completely empty.

We head toward the stairs. All the while, Sawyer is keeping an eye on the tablet in his hand. The third floor is completely vacant, too, lacking even the paint cans and painter's tarps. One more floor down, and we find a few empty crates, a table saw, and some boards set up on sawhorses.

Nothing overly suspicious. Honestly, the farther in we get, the more my stomach begins to churn. Surely, Brenda didn't send us off on a wild goose chase. Surely, she would have done at least some of her own research before sending us to an empty building—right?

The thought of Tessa momentarily pulls me out of the moment.

I'd checked in with Garrison right before we headed over here, and everything was fine. But this twisting in my gut says otherwise.

Focus, Knox.

We hit the doorway leading to the basement stairs, and as always, we pause a moment until Sawyer gives us the all clear. As soon as he has, I push through and move out onto the basement level.

The elevator shaft is directly to the right, and like the upper floors, this one is mostly barren. There are a few crates in the middle of the room, but no activity.

"We're clear," Sawyer says as he puts his tablet and mic away.

"What is this place?" Weston questions as we move farther into the room.

"I don't know. But let's get a look around so we can be gone before anyone shows up." I gesture off toward the right. "Cowboy, you and Tank go check out that side. Cable Guy and I will see what's in those crates."

"Sure thing, Cap," Weston says. Then he and Ryker move off toward the right to get a look around the corner.

Sawyer and I close the distance between us and the crates, and I withdraw my large knife to pry the lid off.

"I can't make sense of this, Cap," Sawyer comments. "Something feels off."

"I feel it, too." With one final movement, the crate pops open, and I shove the lid off.

My heart stops.

My stomach plummets.

Adrenaline surges through my veins as I try to process exactly what it is we're seeing.

"Tank! Cowboy!" I bellow. "Get back to the stairwell!"

"I can't diffuse this, Cap. I need Demo. We need Demo." Sawyer is panicking. And I certainly can't blame him.

"We don't have Demo." *And Brenda had to have known we wouldn't.* She would have known I wouldn't leave Tessa unprotected, and Garrison was the most logical choice to leave behind.

Is this really her, though? Is she truly trying to eliminate us?

Red numbers on a clock count down from thirty seconds.

Thirty seconds to get to safety from the basement level of an office building before the entire thing collapses on top of us.

It's not enough time.

It has to be enough time.

God, please let it be enough time.

Ryker and Weston race toward us and, together, the four of us sprint back toward the stairs. It's the strongest point of the building—and our only chance at survival. Even still, the chances we'll live to see the sunrise are slim to none.

Ryker reaches the stairwell first, and he rips the door open. Weston sprints inside, then Sawyer. I pause, and he moves without argument, knowing I won't go in before he does. I slam the door shut behind us right before a deafening *boom* robs me of a future I should have had.

And Tessa's smile is the last thing I see before the world goes dark.

CHAPTER 26

TESSA

With my Bible in hand, I sit curled up on Garrison's couch, a blanket on my lap, a hot cup of chamomile on the table in front of me. I can hear the shower going, and in this brief moment of silence, I can almost pretend Zane will be coming through the front door any minute.

The two minutes I had to talk to him earlier weren't nearly long enough. But he said that, as long as tonight went well, they could potentially be on their way back first thing in the morning. I smile.

I can't wait.

Shifting my attention back to the Bible, I continue reading through the book of Esther. I remember being so drawn to it when I was a teenager. The strength she must have had to prevail despite everything stacked against her has always been inspiring to me.

"Who knows if perhaps you were made queen for just such a time as this?" That singular verse from Esther 4 runs over and over in my mind. It's hard for me to believe I have any special purpose. Any genuine reason for being born. Perhaps that's why I struggled so much to keep my faith since leaving Stormwatch Landing.

I never felt worthy enough for anything.

Not for Zane.

Not for happiness.

And certainly not to be a mother, though secretly it's all I wanted. To show my child the love I never had.

Something moves in the shadow of the hall, so I glance over, expecting to see Garrison coming toward me. That expectation dies quickly, though, and my stomach plummets.

The teacup clatters out of my hand and hits the ground with a *thud* as the liquid saturates the fluffy rug beneath Garrison's coffee table. I set my Bible to the side and slowly get to my feet as I stare down the masked intruder coming toward me.

I don't scream, though. Not yet. Because if I can keep his focus long enough for him to pass the bathroom, then Garrison's arrival will be a surprise.

You've got this, Tessa.

Swallowing hard, I take a step back—and bump into a large frame.

"Garr—" I start to scream, but a large hand comes around to cover my mouth. As my attacker lifts me, I plant both feet on the arm of the couch and shove back, flinging him—and me—into the wall.

The bathroom door opens, and Garrison rushes out wearing only a pair of sweats, his hair still wet from the shower. He races forward and tackles the guy in the hallway, taking him to the ground. A sickening crack fills the apartment, and the first guy falls still on the floor.

My attacker snakes a meaty hand over my mouth, making it nearly impossible to breathe. Lungs burning, I continue to fight against his hold, but it's no use.

"Keep coming, and I'll pull the trigger," the man snarls as cool steel is pressed to my chin.

I swallow hard and fall still. *Come on, Garrison.*

But he hesitates—and that hesitation is just long enough that a third man I hadn't seen slips out from Garrison's slightly open bedroom door.

I try to scream. Try to warn him.

But with tears in my eyes, I watch in absolute horror when the blade of a knife is driven into Garrison's side. He cries out, then rips himself free of the blade before spinning and landing a kick on his attacker.

Blood pours from the nasty wound in his side, and he stumbles, falling forward onto his knees. I squirm, trying to get to him so I can help. Garrison's expression looks so defeated, so broken that it *crushes* me.

No. Please don't die. God, please!

My attacker laughs from behind me. I slam my foot

down onto his boot, but that only makes him laugh harder. "Steel toe, sweetheart," he mutters into my ear.

Bile burns in my gut, and I fight as hard as I can against his hold, twisting and turning, until something hard slams into the back of my head and I fall forward onto the tea-stained carpet. Vision blurry, I can barely focus on anything. But I can see Garrison.

Still on his knees, a hand pressed to the wound in his side, he tries to crawl to me. The man who stabbed him grips a handful of his hair and exposes his throat.

"No!" I scream. "No!"

He lowers the blade to Garrison's neck.

"Leave him," the man behind me says right as my vision begins to fade. "He'll be dead soon anyway. Just like the rest of them. We need to get going before someone shows up and we have another body to deal with."

The rest of them.

No, God. Please, no.

My throat burns, and I fight for consciousness. Fingers gripping the carpet, I try to crawl my way toward Garrison as the man who'd stabbed him releases his hair and shoves him to the carpet. If I can get the blood stopped, then maybe he'll stand a chance.

A hand closes around the back of my neck, and I'm ripped up from the ground and thrown over a shoulder. Regaining some of my strength, I thrash in his hold.

"Let me go! Help! Garrison!"

"Shut her up," the man who'd stabbed Garrison orders. "Now."

"We need her alive," the man carrying me orders as he rips open the front door.

"But not conscious," the other man says, then raises his fist and slams it into my jaw. My vision wavers, darkness closing in on my mind like smoke.

Zane.

Weston.

Ryker.

Sawyer.

Garrison.

Are they all dead because of me?

"Tessa, wake up."

Zane's voice is almost enough to pull me out of the fog, but the pain is so great that even thinking about opening my eyes is too much.

"Please, Tessa." He shakes me, and fresh agony shoots through every inch of my battered body. "I need you." His choked plea has me trying to move. I flex my fingers toward him, and his warm hand closes around mine. "I'm going to kill him for this." His fury is what reaches down and finally rips me out of the fog.

Because, no matter how angry he is, my dad is still

bigger. Meaner. And unlike Zane, he won't hesitate for fear of hurting someone.

"Please don't," I whisper as I open my eyes. "I'm okay, honestly."

"Then I'm calling Officer Leopold. Now." He gets up off the floor and reaches into his pocket for the cell phone his mom has him take whenever he leaves the house.

"You can't. Please. He's my dad."

"And you're my girlfriend," Zane says. "I won't let him keep doing this to you."

"He won't." I try to sit up. "Please, Zane. I just need you right now." Tears burn in my eyes as I remember hit after hit.

I'd come home too late.

I hadn't brought dinner.

I needed to be taught a lesson.

Zane kneels in front of me and cups my cheeks. "Then leave with me. Come with me, Tessa. I'll make sure he never hurts you again. Please, baby. Just come with me." His gorgeous green eyes are full of pain, and I know I must look rough.

I certainly feel it.

The closer we get to graduation, the worse it's getting.

"Leave with me, and I won't call Officer Leopold. But if you choose to stay, I will call. Even if it means you end up hating me. I won't let this happen anymore."

Zane brushes tears from my cheeks.

I've wanted to run away my entire life. But I could never bring myself to do it because I'm all my dad has. What if I leave and something happens to him?

What if I stay and something happens to me?

Don't I get to choose me?

"Please, Tessa," Zane pleads.

Fear pushes past the pain, and even though the idea terrifies me, I nod. "Okay, Zane. I'll go."

"Then let's go now. He's passed out, but we don't have long." He straightens and starts shoving things into my backpack. All I can do is sit there and watch him. Is this really it? The last time I will stand in this room?

I get to my feet and sway, but a hand on the dresser keeps me standing as I open the top drawer and reach to the bottom to pull out a small floral brooch. My grand-mother gave it to me just before she passed away.

She was the only family I ever knew who had a tender hand.

It was after she passed that my dad really lost himself in the liquor. He turned into the man who raised him, giving in to the pain of losing his mother and taking it out on me. That's the only reason I've struggled to stay. Because I thought that maybe, somewhere deep down inside the monster...was my dad.

But that was only the foolish dream of a child.

I shove the brooch into my pocket right as Zane finishes cramming what he can into my backpack.

"Okay, baby. Let's go." He takes my hand and tugs me toward the door. After peering out into the hallway, he steps out.

My dad's drunken snoring carries toward us from the living room, and as we step inside, the adrenaline surges through my veins.

What if he wakes up?

What will he do to Zane?

I keep my eyes on him the entire time, watching him like one might watch an approaching predator. When he doesn't wake even as we open the door and step out onto the rickety porch, the freedom I'd been so afraid to hope for surges through my veins.

Zane shoulders my backpack, then lifts me into his arms and rushes down the porch. He moves quickly even as he holds me, the only sound our mixed breathing and the gravel crunching beneath his boots.

About half a mile down, he sets me down beside his truck, then unlocks the door and helps me climb inside. It's not until he's behind the wheel and we're headed toward his house that I let out the breath I've been holding.

My body begins to tremble, the adrenaline leaving me in a rush.

"It's okay, baby." Zane reaches for me, so I slide into the center of his bench seat and curl against his body. He presses a kiss to the top of my head. "You're safe now. I'll always keep you safe, Tessa. Always."

"She's waking up." A putrid stench beneath my nose rips me from the dream. My vision hazy, I come awake in the main office space of Southeast Environmental Commission. "There you are, sweetheart. How nice to see you again."

He smiles, and even through the drowsiness of just coming to consciousness, his face isn't one I'll forget. Dark brows, short hair, a scar right on the tip of his chin, he's unmistakable. "You. You lied to me."

The man who hired me in that diner, what feels like lifetimes ago, leans back against the counter behind him and crosses his arms. "Don't beat yourself up. You were so desperate for any kind of attention; you would have fallen for anything." He looks past me. "Do we have confirmation yet?"

"Not yet," another man replies.

"Confirmation of what? Why am I here? What is happening?"

He shifts his attention back to me. "Oh, my bad. Here, you'll want to see this." He spins the office chair I'm bound to, my wrists zip-tied behind my back, until I'm facing a TV screen.

It takes me a moment to realize what it is I'm looking at. The news is on with coverage of a building collapse in Savannah on the screen. The thing looks nothing like a building anymore, just a pile of rubble. Concrete and steel beams alike. Dust is still settling, and emergency responders are moving through the rubble with search and rescue dogs.

"We're told that there were four men inside when the building came down. It's unknown if they worked there or were seeking shelter for the night." The footage transitions to a newsroom where a woman with curly blonde hair is sitting behind a desk, a mask of sadness on her face. *"No survivors have been recovered, and at this point, it's looking more like a recovery."*

Four bodies. Downtown Savannah.

No.

"What is this?" I demand, tears already in my eyes because I know enough to piece together what I'm looking at.

"I can see all over your face that you know." He grins. "You know what? People said it would be impossible to get rid of them, but I found that forty thousand tons of concrete will crush even the sturdiest bugs. It also happens to be exactly what you need to rid the world of four former Navy SEALs who should have died a long time ago. And the fifth? Well, you know what happened to him."

"What? No!" I scream and fight against the bindings holding me. I have to get free. Have to find Zane. He survived. He had to survive.

Horror twists in my gut as the TV screen shifts back to

the damage downtown. There's no way they survived that. If they were in there, they're gone.

And then my abductor's words hit me. *"He'll be dead soon. Just like the rest of them."* They killed them all.

No. No. God, please, no. Please, Lord. Don't let this be true.

"I don't understand why this is happening. What did they do to you? What do I have to do with any of this?"

"Aww, sweetheart. Unfortunately, you're collateral damage in this war. Though, to be honest, you're not really necessary anymore. Not now that Knox is dead." He reaches forward and strokes my chin. I look away, not wanting to give him the satisfaction of seeing the fear in my eyes, but he pinches my chin and moves me to look at him. "Boss isn't quite ready to let you go, though. Seems she's taken a dislike to you and has other plans."

"What does that—"

"Can you stop socializing and just get the job done?" A feminine voice orders as heels click on the tile floor.

Her voice isn't one I'll forget anytime soon, so when Brenda steps into my line of sight, I'm not at all surprised.

"You," I growl. "He trusted you! They all did!"

"Trust?" She arches a brow. "Hardly. Fear would be a more accurate term. Either way, they served their purpose and became liabilities. You saw to that."

"You killed them?" I choke on the words because, even as I see the collapsed building before me, even as I can still picture Garrison's blood pouring from his wound and pooling on the floor beneath him, speaking them out loud makes it real. "No. No. I won't believe it."

Brenda grips either side of my chair. "Well, believe it, Tessa Lane. But don't worry. You'll be joining them soon because we have big, big plans for you."

CHAPTER 27

ZANE

"How bad?" Doctor Lani Hunt, the youngest of the Hunt siblings, demands when the four of us reach the stairwell of the private plane they flew in on. Her dark hair is swept up into a ponytail that swings as she walks. Dark eyes that miss nothing travel over the four of us.

I imagine we all look rough. Crawling your way out of a collapsed building will do that. Still, we made it out. Something I send a silent thank You to the Lord for. He protected us and guided us toward what must be one of the last payphones in the city, then brought the Hunts here safely.

Without knowing who to trust, there was only one call I could make after what happened. And it was to Dylan, who sent his two brothers and sister out to rescue us.

We should all be dead. But when the building came

down, it left a gaping hole in the side of the stairwell. Just large enough for us to slip out before the news crews and first responders showed up. *Thank You, God.*

"Concussions would be my guess," I say as we all but collapse onto the floor of the plane. Weston, Ryker, and Sawyer all drop down into seats and close their eyes. Blood crusts on their faces and arms, and anywhere there's no blood, concrete dust clings to their skin.

I'm sure I'm not any better. But we're alive.

"We weren't followed. I'm going to tell him Lani wants to look you guys over before we can leave." Bradyn Hunt, the eldest Hunt sibling and the leader of Hunt Brothers Search and Rescue, heads for the cockpit of the plane while his brother, Riley, starts offering us water bottles.

Lani starts for me, but I shake my head and point to my team.

She purses her lips, but doesn't argue as she heads over and starts looking Sawyer over.

"They good?" Riley asks.

"Do I look like I know yet?" she snaps. "Sorry, just trying to listen."

He holds up his hands. "Yes, ma'am."

"We need to get to Brenda," Weston growls as soon as Lani finishes looking him over. "She set us up."

"We don't know that for sure," Sawyer replies.

"Don't we?" Ryker demands. "No way her intel was legitimate, and she's too smart to take someone's word without looking into it first. She had to have known we were walking into a trap. No one else knew we were going to be there."

Lani finishes with my team and crosses over to me. She presses her stethoscope to my back. "Deep breath."

I do as she says, coughing and sputtering when my lungs burn, thanks to the dust I inhaled.

"They're okay to travel," she says. "I'm going to start treating surface injuries." She retrieves her medical bag and crosses over to kneel in front of Sawyer, who has a nasty gash on his forehead. We'd slapped a field bandage on it, but blood has already seeped through the gauze.

"We're good to go," Riley calls out.

Bradyn offers a thumbs-up from the cockpit.

All while my mind is still on Weston. *"She set us up."* He's right. Ryker's right. All signs point to Brenda sending us in there to die. The question is, why? "Can I use your phone?" I ask Riley. We'd destroyed ours and left them in the rubble. That way, if someone tried to track them, they'd be right where they hoped to find us.

"Sure thing." He offers it to me, and I type in Garrison's phone number.

It rings once.

Twice.

Three times.

Then goes to voicemail.

Fear creeps up my spine. He *always* answers. Or, at the very least, sends a text saying he'll call back. I wait, holding my breath, but no message comes through. Even with this being an unknown number, he would answer.

Unsure what else to do, I call him again.

"Garrison's not answering?" Sawyer asks. His expression tells me he's thinking the same thing as I am: We weren't the only ones led into a trap.

"No. I'm calling Leopold." If it's not an emergency, Garrison will likely be annoyed that I sent the police over there, but if it is…

"This is Officer Leopold," he answers.

"It's Zane."

"Zane." His tone is sharp, laced with emotion. "Listen—"

"What happened?" I all but choke on the words. Is he okay? Is Tessa okay? Did I leave them to die by following the orders of a traitor?

"Garrison was attacked in his apartment. Stab wound to his side. The attacker used a serrated blade for maximum damage. He suffered a collapsed lung and lost a lot of blood."

No. No. No.

The lump in my throat makes breathing impossible. "Is he alive?" My gaze levels on my team. All of them are staring back at me, their expressions hard as they expect the worst news.

Even Lani and Riley stop what they're doing to focus on me. I pinch the bridge of my nose. *God, please don't let him be dead. Lord, please wrap us in Your light. Please, God, protect us. In Jesus' name, amen.*

I put the phone on speaker because repeating whatever he's about to say is likely going to be too hard. "He's in surgery right now. A neighbor found him. I was actually just about to call you because I don't think he has any family here. I wasn't sure who else to call."

"Tessa?" I choke out.

"I haven't had a chance to go check on her yet."

"She's okay, though?"

"I'm headed to the boat now just to check and see. I sent an officer there to wait outside and keep an eye on things."

The boat. What little hope I was clinging to that she wasn't involved is gone. "She's not on the boat."

"Where is she? I want to make sure she's okay."

"She was staying at Garrison's apartment."

He goes completely silent, processing what I just said. "You're sure she was there?"

"Positive." I choke on the word, my entire body rigid as I sit here.

"She's not there, Zane," he says, speaking the words I was terrified to hear.

There wasn't a body. That's good news for now, I try to remind myself, but all I can see is Tessa bloodied and broken as she fights for her life. "Then they've taken her."

"Who? Do you know who is doing this?"

"I'm not a hundred percent sure, but I need you to do me a favor."

"What is it?"

"Keep Garrison in the hospital under a false name. To anyone not on this call, he died right after surgery. I'm bringing a doctor with me; she'll treat him when we get there." I lock eyes with Lani, who offers me a single nod. "Send someone over to watch my mom's house, please. I'm going to call Anastasia and have her head over there, too."

"Why? What's going on, Zane?"

"Someone just tried to take all five of us out in one night. I want them to think they succeeded so they don't see me coming for them. We're on our way back. Call me with an update." I end the call and tighten my hand into a fist around the phone. If it were mine, I'd crush it just to have some control.

"They tried to kill Garrison?" Weston growls.

"And took Tessa," Sawyer adds.

I tap my sister's contact, then breathe a sigh of relief when she answers with a groggy, "Hello?"

"Listen, Anastasia. I need you to pack a bag and get to Mom's house. Now."

"What happened? What's going on?" A faint click in the background tells me she likely just turned her lamp on.

"Do not open the bakery. Do you hear me? Get to mom's house now, and you two stay put until I get there. Don't open the door for anyone. Don't answer the phone unless it's me. Do you understand what I'm saying? *No one.*" My voice trembles.

"Zane, what's going on? You're scaring me."

Fear finally sinks its sharp talons into me, momentarily robbing me of my ability to speak. They nearly killed Weston, Ryker, Sawyer, and Garrison. They took Tessa. If this is Brenda, she knows about my family—will they go for them, too?

"Zane?"

"Hey, Anastasia, it's Sawyer." He coughs. "We can't tell you everything right now, but please get to your mom's. Take your gun and get there now. Text this number when you do, okay?"

"Sawyer. Are you guys safe?" Her voice cracks beneath the weight of emotion, and Sawyer closes his eyes tightly, his expression tortured.

"We're okay. Just please get there now."

"Are you sending Garrison over? How is Tessa?"

"We'll tell you everything when we get there, okay?"

She doesn't answer for a few moments. "Okay. Zane?"

"I'm here." Tears slip from my eyes, and I pinch the bridge of my nose, hoping the pressure will keep me grounded and prevent me from completely losing it.

"I love you and stuff."

"I love you and stuff, too," I reply. It takes every bit of strength in me to keep my tone level when all I want to do is tear apart this entire world until I find who did this. Until I find who took Tessa…and make them pay.

Hospitals are not my favorite place to be, but they've never really bothered me before. Not until now, when I'm sitting here beside Garrison's bed, waiting for him to open his eyes.

Leopold is scouring Garrison's apartment, surveillance cameras, and anything else he can think of, looking for any sign of where Tessa might have been taken. Tucker Hunt is doing the same, though on a much larger scale, from his computer room back in Texas.

Bradyn and Riley have set up shop in my sister's apartment while she is staying with my mom. Sawyer is with them now, just in case whoever came for Tessa and us makes a move on them as well.

I'm betting they don't, though, because they already think we're dead.

"They took her." Garrison's voice cuts through my thoughts, and I quickly get to my feet, then cross to his bedside. His eyes are glassy, his expression slack. "They took her. I'm so sorry, Zane. I tried."

"It's okay. We'll get her back." I saw the blood stain in his apartment; it's a miracle he's even still here. Hearing his voice settles a bit of the gnawing fear that's been eating me alive ever since I got the news. "They're working on identifying the guy in your apartment," I tell him.

"They were so fast. I didn't even see the third guy." He sucks in a ragged breath, then closes his eyes and winces in pain. "I was just getting out of the shower when I heard her. I came out, and there were only two. The third guy was hiding."

I can imagine how terrified she must have been. Not just being taken, but did she see Garrison get stabbed? Does she think he's dead? "Just stay calm, okay? We'll get it figured out."

He nods, but the movement is slow. Then, he opens his eyes and narrows them on me as if he's seeing me for the first time. "What happened in Savannah?"

"They blew the building while we were in it. Set a thirty-second countdown on a crate that was rigged to blow the moment we opened it."

His eyes widen. "What kind of bomb?"

"I have no clue. Didn't get a good look at it, but it leveled the building. We were in the basement."

"How are you here?" he asks. "Are you here?"

"I'm here, brother. God brought us through." I gently clasp his shoulder. "We have you here under a fake name, but I'm going to get the doctor so she can look you over, okay?"

The door opens, and Lani steps in. "Hey there." She smiles brightly.

"This is Doctor Lani Hunt," I tell him.

"Or, as I'm referred to most often in circles like this, the youngest Hunt sibling," she adds with a laugh. "Anyway, I'm treating you since technically you're dead."

He turns to me. "What?"

"We're letting them think they succeeded in taking us all out."

He nods and closes his eyes. "So how bad is the damage, doc?"

"Collapsed lung, some muscle and tissue damage from the serrated blade. But your worst enemy was the loss of blood. They gave you a transfusion, but—medically—you really shouldn't have survived."

"Thank God above that I did," he says, then tries to sit up. "So what's the first step in finding her?"

"You're not going to find anyone," Lani says as she steps forward and places a hand on his shoulder to keep him from getting out of bed. I do the same, wanting to ensure he rests long enough to heal. "Seriously, any overexertion and you'll collapse that lung again."

"I have to help." There's so much guilt on his face. So much brokenness. But even though I know he wants to see this through, I can't risk losing him, too.

"Lani is right, Garrison. We need you to stay put."

He shakes his head. "The last time you went anywhere without me, you all nearly died. I nearly died. We have to stick together."

"You have to heal, brother. Otherwise, they will have succeeded in destroying us." I reach forward and cover his hand with mine. "It wasn't your fault."

His eyes fill, and he takes a deep breath. "Make them pay."

"Even if it's the last thing I do, brother, they will."

Chapter 28

Tessa

The zip ties bite into my wrists as I continue trying to work myself free from the bindings. I've seen countless videos of people escaping them, but I'm definitely not having the luck they did. Even still, I won't quit. I twist my wrists, moving them opposite each other in an attempt to find some leverage so I can get free.

Warm blood trickles from the wounds, but I'm hoping it'll help me slip free. If I can, then I can get help. Maybe I can call Zane and—my throat constricts. And what? If they're right and he's buried in that rubble…I shove it aside, redirecting my thoughts to the things I can control.

I have to get to a phone. Then I can call the police.

You've got this, Tessa. So instead of focusing on the pain in my heart over all I might have lost, I focus only on getting free.

Pain shoots up through my right arm when I accidentally tweak it, and I hiss through clenched teeth.

Lord, please. Please help me.

I've been praying all night, leaning on Him, trying to drown out the voices telling me that I'm all alone. That, if God loved me, then I wouldn't be here right now. But I know that's not true. I know now that God may not deliver us from our pain, but He will always bring us through it.

I don't just know it, either.

I *believe* it.

Because otherwise, I'd have been dead a long time ago.

The sand dollar pops into my mind. Those five beautiful doves born of death and brokenness. *I'm not alone.* Closing my eyes, I pause, trying to escape for a moment and just listen to the silence of the room.

I sit in this space, and as the anxiety closes in, I send up a thank you.

Thank You, Lord, for bringing me back to Zane.

Thank You for giving us the time we had.

If this is the end, I still thank You. Because You've been with me my entire life, even on the days where the darkness was so thick I couldn't see You. I pray these things in the name of Jesus Christ, amen.

Opening my eyes, I'm filled with an unexplainable peace.

No matter how this plays out, I'll keep my eyes focused on Him.

I won't turn away again.

"You say that you feel like you can't stay on your feet? Then remain on your knees, Tessa, and pray." Pastor Reeves' words have come to me more than once over the past few hours. They've been my comfort while I've been trying to escape, my hope when everything feels so completely hopeless.

Faith is strength.

And for the first time in my life, I'm jumping into it without hesitation. Without doubt. I *know* my God is there. I *know* He loves me.

My wrist slips free with such force that I nearly topple out of my chair. I stare at my bloodied hand, momentarily shocked. *Thank You, God!*

Without wasting another moment, I tug my other hand free, then get to my feet. Heart racing, I peek out through the small sliver window in the office door. When I don't see anyone, I check the handle. *Unlocked. Yes!*

Adrenaline surging through my veins, I step out into the hall. My bare feet move soundlessly on the thin carpet, and I continue forward as quickly as I can while also paying attention to any noises.

A room to my right is partially open, so I peer inside. It's empty.

I continue down the hall until I reach a stairwell. After opening the doorway slowly, I descend the stairs until I reach the first floor. Pulling the door open, I peer outside into the empty office space. There are cubicles and a secretary's desk, but it's otherwise empty.

However, I know exactly where I am.

Back at the beginning.

Southeast Environmental Commission.

I rush out of the staircase and sprint toward the nearest cubicle. Every one of them had an office line and a computer. If I can reach someone, then I can hide until I get help.

Hope surges through my system when I see the phone sitting there. I kneel down, trying to keep my head below the top of the cubicle divider, then hover a hand over the top of the phone. *Lord, please let there be a dial tone.*

After taking a deep breath, I lift the phone and nearly weep with relief when I hear the familiar tone.

"9-1-1, what's your emergency?"

"Help. I'm being held against my will at the Southeast Environmental Commission."

"Can you give me your name?"

"Tessa Lane. Please, they—"

A door slams, and tears spring to my eyes. I take the phone and pull it beneath the desk as footsteps echo through the empty room.

"Ma'am, are you still there?"

"Send help, please," I whisper. "Zane Knox. Stormwatch Landing, South Carolina." And then, because I'm not sure he can come, I add, "Or Agent Jack Weathers with the FBI. They'll know what to—" The line goes dead. "Hello?" *No, please, no.* Risking being seen, I sit up and check the dial tone.

"She's around here somewhere," someone says. The voice is deep and masculine, and I recall it instantly. *"Keep coming and I'll pull the trigger."* He'd held a gun to my head as Garrison tried to save me.

It all comes flooding back to me, the sight of him killing that first man.

Of the blade being driven into his body.

Of him falling.

Of the blood pouring from his wound.

No. I won't focus on that now. I shove those thoughts aside, wishing more than anything that I'd memorized any scripture at all for this moment. Something to give me strength.

Something I plan to remedy the moment I'm safe.

Quickly, I replace the phone and use the bottom of my shirt to clean the blood as best I can. Then I crawl out and move to another cubicle. Making myself as small as I can, I close my eyes and wait for them to leave so I can find somewhere else to hide until help arrives.

That is, if help is coming at all.

"What do you mean you *lost her?*" Brenda demands as she enters the room. From the volume of her voice, she's not too far from me, and that thought sends my pulse skyrocketing.

"We cut all the phone lines just in case she tries to make a call. We'll find her."

"You'd better, Markson. I'm going to do what I can to

head this off, but we have forty-eight hours to pull this off. Find her. Get her under control."

A door closes, and I close my eyes.

Markson. As in Cal Markson? The guy she sent Zane after? Anger burns hot in my veins, momentarily obliterating the fear. Brenda will pay for her part in this. Somehow, someway, I will make sure of it.

"You heard her. Find the woman." The door slams again.

With a deep breath, I peek out and start crawling along the carpet as soon as I see that the immediate coast is clear. I need to keep moving. Otherwise, I'll lose this twisted game of hide and seek.

The pain in my hands and wrists intensifies with every movement, but I breathe through it, shoving the pain into a box in my mind just like I did while growing up. Hide it, and you won't feel it.

That was my motto. And right now, it may be the only thing that will keep me alive.

I reach the edge of the cubicle row, so I pause to figure out where to go next. I can turn back around and hide or make a run for the kitchen. It's straight ahead, right on the other side of this big, gaping hallway.

"She's going to hang us out to dry if we mess this up," Cal says somewhere behind me. His voice makes my decision for me, so I crouch down and move as fast as I can toward the kitchen. The door is propped open, giving me a chance to get inside without anyone noticing me.

As soon as I'm safely hidden, I straighten and start looking for a weapon. That's what Zane would do, right? Find a way to protect himself?

As quietly as I can, I open drawer after drawer until I find an old set of steak knives. I palm one, then note the fire extinguisher hanging on the wall. *Perfect.* Keeping the knife in my hand, I take it off the wall and tuck myself into the small pantry to wait.

If I'm lucky, they've already looked here, and help will arrive before they decide to come in again. If I'm not lucky, well, I'm not going down without a fight.

"Did you check in here?" The kitchen door creaks as it's shoved open the rest of the way. Footsteps have me holding my breath.

Lord, be with me. Please. I need strength. Help me.

A hand closes around the handle of the door, and he pulls it open. A man I recognize from the mugshot of Cal Markson stands before me. His eyes widen in shock, but I don't give him the chance to alert the others before I slam the fire extinguisher into his face. He stumbles backward, and the kitchen table splinters beneath his weight as he lands on top of it.

I sprint out, extinguisher still in hand.

The second man—a bald man with a terrifying neck tattoo—rushes toward me, a snarl on his lips. I sprint to the side, adrenaline surging through my body as I make a mad dash toward the front of the office building. It's a busy street, so as long as I can get to the door, I can find help.

Right?

A large arm bands around my waist.

I scream and thrash, but the fire extinguisher tumbles from my grip. Armed with just the knife, I stab backward into my attacker. His grip loosens on me, and I manage to slip free, but I don't look back to see where the blade hit him. It doesn't matter. Getting free does.

Getting help does.

My entire body goes rigid as sharp, sudden burning shoots through every one of my muscles. I fall forward, hitting the ground with enough force that it knocks the wind from my lungs.

"Keep fighting and I'll happily tase you again," Brenda says.

I grunt, the doorway within sight.

Until it's not.

A hand closes around my ankle and drags me away from the light.

Away from safety.

My arms are tied behind my back again, and I'm pulled up against a hard chest.

"Get her out of sight," Brenda snarls. "You, deal with him. He knows my face."

Him? Who's here?

A piece of duct tape is slapped over my mouth as the man holding me carries me just out of sight of the door. Brenda is with us, a firearm in her hand.

"Can I help you?" I hear a man ask, his tone friendly.

Monster. He's a monster! Help me! I want to kick and scream, but it's useless.

"Agent Jack Weathers, FBI." Hope floods my system at the sound of his familiar voice.

"What can I do for you, Agent Weathers?"

"We received a 9-1-1 call from this location. A woman who's been missing since yesterday identified herself and said she was being held here."

"Really?" The other man laughs. "There's no one here," he assures Jack.

I am! I'm here! Help!

"Do you mind if my team and I take a look around? I'd like to see for myself."

"Stall for three minutes," Brenda whispers, likely into an earpiece the guy currently talking to Jack is wearing.

"Agent Weathers, I'm not sure what kind of prankster you're dealing with, but we're in the process of clearing things out since we were shut down. I'm sure you heard that our owners were murdered."

"And see, I'm the one working that case. I actually interviewed everyone who works here, and I don't recognize you."

Yes! Because it's all fake! Help!

I try to scream against the duct tape, but no audible sound comes out as I'm thrown over a shoulder and carted up a set of back stairs.

Brenda moves up behind me. I can't see her face, but her tall heels click on each step, all while my stomach rolls.

So close. I was so close.

We enter a dark room, and I'm tossed down into the chair. The man secures my wrists, and I glare up at Brenda as she steps into my line of sight.

With sharp, red nails, she reaches up and brushes the hair from my face. "Did you really think you would get anywhere, Tessa?" she asks. "If Zane couldn't escape, what makes you think you could?" She clicks her tongue. "Less than a day from now, this will all be over, and you'll be little more than a headline."

As she turns away and leaves the room, followed by the guy who brought me here, I'm plunged into complete darkness. There's not even a sliver of light beneath the doorway to allow me any chance of finding something around me to help. That is, if I could even get up off the chair.

My muscles scream in agony, and my head pounds like an anvil has just been dropped onto it. And as I sit here in the dark, it's all I can do *not* to spiral.

So I go to that place in my mind again.

Not the one where I store my pain, but the place where I hide when things get hard.

My happy place.

Sitting with Zane on his dad's boat, two young teenagers with their entire lives ahead of them.

Here, real life can't touch me.

Here, I'll be forever safe.

ZANE

"Zane!" Anastasia rushes forward and throws her arms around me. I'd sent Sawyer, Weston, and Ryker ahead to get showered, changed, and to check in on my mom and sister, while I'd remained at the hospital.

Riley Hunt came and relieved me, though, offering to stay and keep an eye on Garrison until I can get back. Bradyn is with his service dog, Bravo, back at Garrison's apartment. They're trying to pick up on Tessa's scent to see if we can get a direction she was taken out.

My mom comes out of the kitchen and wraps both arms around Anastasia and me. "Honey, I am so glad you're okay. Come on, get a shower, and I'll get you some food." She and my sister pull away.

Weston and Ryker are sitting at the dining room table,

barely-touched sandwiches sitting in front of them. Sawyer is on the couch, seated in front of his open laptop.

"I will, Mom, thanks."

"Are you okay?" she asks.

"I will be once we find Tessa."

"Sawyer told us what happened." Anastasia's eyes fill as she crosses her arms. "I can't believe it. Garrison—" She trails off and covers her mouth with a shaking hand.

"He'll be okay, Anastasia." Aside from us, the Hunts, and Leopold, Anastasia and my mom are the only ones who know Garrison is alive. Even when the neighbor who found them came to check on him, she was given the news that he hadn't survived his injuries.

It has to be this way until we get Tessa back and figure out who is trying to kill us. Though my money is on Brenda. That's where all signs are pointing. I just can't figure out what her motives would be.

Was this truly triggered by Tessa's arrival?

Or was this the plan all along?

Someone knocks on the door, and everyone stills. The room falls completely silent until my mom looks up at me. "Do I answer it?" she whispers.

Withdrawing my handgun, I peer out through the peep-hole. *Agent Weathers. What are you doing here?* Because I don't think he'd have warned me about Brenda having it out for Tessa if he were a part of this, I take a risk and open the door myself.

He arches a brow and looks me up and down. "You look rough."

"A building fell on me earlier today."

"So you *were* in that Savannah mess?" I nod. "Everyone thinks you're dead," he adds.

"Because, to everyone else, I am. Question is, can I trust you with the truth?"

He doesn't look the least bit offended, which speaks volumes. "A 9-1-1 call was received yesterday morning. A woman claiming to be Tessa Lane said she was being held at the Southeast Environmental Commission."

Hope floods my system, and I pull the door all the way open so he can come in. "You found her?" I close the door behind him, and he crosses his arms.

"We searched the building and found no sign of her. As soon as I finished, I hopped on a plane here because none of you were answering your phones."

"We've been a little busy," Weston quips.

"I see that. I'm assuming she's not here?"

"No. Someone gutted Garrison to get to her," Ryker growls.

Jack's expression turns furious. "Is he—"

"You said she wasn't there?" I quickly change the subject. I may trust him with the knowledge that we're alive, but Garrison can't defend himself. And that makes him a different story.

"Not that I saw. But that doesn't mean she wasn't there. Or—"

"That she isn't still there, just hidden."

He pinches the bridge of his nose. "We scoured that place, but it's a big building. They saw us coming, and that means they could have hidden her."

"She's alive. That's what matters," Anastasia says.

"She was alive yesterday," Weston says.

"No, she's alive. I can feel it." It's the same feeling I had over the last eighteen years she was missing. Despite what everyone said, what the police said, I *knew* she was out there somewhere. This time, I won't stop looking until I find her.

"Then maybe you can—" His cell rings, so he pulls it out of his pocket and groans when he sees the readout. He turns it to face me, and I see Brenda's name on the screen.

"She can't know we're alive."

"Yeah, I got that." He answers it, then puts it on speakerphone. "Weathers."

"What are you doing in Stormwatch Landing?" she demands.

"Excuse me? I didn't realize our relationship warranted location tracking. Did you chip me?" he jokes, but there's no humor on his face.

"I make it a point to know where people are."

Jack arches a brow. "To what do I owe the honor of this call?"

"Have you heard from my team?"

"I have not. Was I supposed to?"

"They're not answering their phones. The building they

were watching is nothing but rubble, and I received a troubling update this morning about one of them. Garrison Holt was murdered last night."

"Well, I'm sorry to hear that," he replies.

Anger burns in my gut. She wouldn't have known that any other way because *no one* reported it.

"I assumed that was why you were there."

"Actually, no. I'm here to check in on Tessa Lane."

Brenda goes quiet. "Oh?"

"Yeah. I recently had a troubling phone call myself. That Ms. Lane was being held against her will at the Southeast Environmental Commission office. You wouldn't happen to know anything about that, would you? I know your contacts are much more adept at finding sensitive information than mine."

She's silent for a few moments. "I'll look into it. But as far as I know, Tessa was staying on Knox's boat."

"Looked there. She was nowhere in sight."

"Where are you now? I'm in town, but I only have about twenty minutes before I need to make my flight."

She's here?

"Actually, it doesn't matter. I'm headed to Zane's mother's house to ask her some questions. Meet me there."

Without waiting for Jack's response, she ends the call. Before I can even open my mouth to speak, a black SUV pulls up outside of my mom's house. "Get in the back," I tell everyone.

"She's going to expect me to be here," my mom insists.

I shake my head. My gut is screaming at me that Brenda is behind this, and the last thing I'm willing to do is put my mom and sister right in her crosshairs. "It's too risky."

"If you don't want Brenda to know you're alive, you all need to go. Now." Jack unholsters his pistol and checks it before sliding it back into his shoulder holster.

"I'm not leaving my mother and sister unprotected," I say, hands clenching into fists.

"I will keep them safe. You have my word. But if you don't get back there now, she's going to know you are all alive. Something you said you didn't want, right?" When I don't move, he continues, "Look, we need to know where Tessa is. Let me distract her, and you and your team come back around the front. We'll flank her. Then I'll leave the room so you can do whatever it is you do to extract information."

I arch a brow. "Whatever it is?"

He shrugs. "I imagine there's a good reason you were brought on to do whatever it is you do for her. I told you, I'm here to solve a murder. Now I can add another body and a disappearance to that. You help me do that, and I'll go to bat for you."

Garrison and Tessa. That's who he's talking about. "Thanks."

"No problem. Go."

"Give me your cell," I tell Anastasia. She reaches into her pocket and hands it to me without argument. After shoving it into my own, I give her and my mother hugs, then slip down the back hall and prop the window open. "We're heading out, and we're going to circle back around front. It's well past time Brenda starts answering some of our questions," I tell the team.

I withdraw the cell phone and text Bradyn.

Me: Brenda is here. Backup may be needed.

As soon as the text is sent, I shove the phone back into my pocket and wait.

A series of rapid knocks, loud enough to be heard even from back here, sends my heart racing. If I'm wrong about Brenda and she's not involved, what we're about to do will land us in the type of prison no one knows exists.

I know I'm not wrong.

A few moments later, I can hear the door open. "Can I help you?" Anastasia asks.

"I'm Brenda Leroy, your brother's boss? I was wondering if—what are you doing here?"

"You knew I was in Stormwatch Landing," Jack replies smoothly. "And you asked me to meet you here."

"How are you here already?" All of the friendliness is gone from Brenda's voice. Replaced only with stern anger and clear suspicion.

"Jack and I are dating," Anastasia blurts. "He was here when you called."

Beside me, Sawyer stiffens. It's subtle but there.

"Oh?" Brenda questions.

"Yeah, it's new," Jack says smoothly. "But Anastasia

told me she hadn't heard from Zane, and since the call at Southeast Environmental Commission was a bust, I hopped on the first plane out here."

"You flew four hours to console your new girlfriend?"

"I did."

I gesture toward the window. Since I've been working with her for over six years now, I can read Brenda without even being in the same room as her. And the tone of her voice screams disbelief. She smells something else going on, and we need to make our move before she makes hers.

Quietly, we slip from the spare bedroom and out onto the back porch. One by one, we move around the house. I peer out over the small fence toward the front of the house. Two armed security guards are keeping watch.

If Brenda hears us coming, she'll likely engage to save herself.

But how are we supposed to distract them without being caught?

Even as I think it, Bradyn's rental truck pulls up.

Thank You, Lord.

He climbs out, Bravo off his leash at his side. The dog's ears are pointed straight up, his focus intently on the men standing at the front door.

"Who are you?" One of the guards asks.

I prepare to make my move as soon as they're fully distracted.

"A friend of the family. Who are you?"

"Same," the guard replies. "I'm afraid you can't go inside."

"And I'm afraid you can't stop me," he replies. *"Fahs, Bravo."*

I don't even have to speak German to know what he just commanded his dog to do because the animal goes into attack mode. I lunge forward, weapon drawn, but by the time I'm up on the porch, both men are on the ground. Ryker quickly zip ties the hands of the man Bravo has a hold of, while Sawyer does the same with the other man, who is currently unconscious, thanks to Bradyn.

"Perfect timing," I tell him.

"God's timing always is. I had a feeling you may need me, and I was on my way when the text came through." Weapon in hand, he remains near the door. "I'm betting she heard that."

"Let's hope we can—"

Anastasia's piercing scream has Sawyer kicking the door in without so much as a heartbeat of hesitation. We move in behind him. Jack has his weapon drawn and trained on Brenda, who somehow managed to get a hold of my little sister.

The blood pounds in my ears when I see the gun pressed to her temple.

Brenda's eyes, wide and wild, are staring straight at me. "I knew you were alive."

"You're outnumbered, Brenda. Drop it," I growl.

"Nah, I'm going to walk out of here, and you're not

going to stop me. We both know you won't risk your sister. Or will you put a bullet in her like you did that teenage girl six months ago?"

I swallow hard.

"What's the move, Cap?" Sawyer demands, his tone urgent.

Brenda ducks down behind Anastasia, keeping herself completely shielded.

"It's okay, Zane," Anastasia says. Her eyes are shimmering with tears, but she doesn't look afraid. More determined. Her eyes quickly glance down then back up at me, signaling that she's about to make a move.

I offer one single nod to let her know I'm ready.

Anastasia drives her elbow backward. The hit jolts Brenda just enough that the gun drops slightly. It goes off, and Anastasia screams. My heart races as I sprint forward, tackling Brenda to the ground. She thrashes, but I throw the gun to the side and flip her over onto her stomach.

Ryker is right there with a zip tie, securing her hands.

As soon as I know she's not going anywhere, I rush over toward Anastasia. Sawyer, Jack, and my mother are all hovering over her. Sawyer has his shirt off and is pressing it to the side of her face.

My heart plummets. "How bad?"

She pulls the shirt away just enough for me to see a nasty gash on her cheek. Similar to the one still healing on my cheek. Tears stream down her face, and her body is trembling.

"Sawyer, get her to the hospital for stitches."

"Take my truck," Bradyn says as he hands him the keys.

"I'll drive," my mother says, taking the keys as Sawyer lifts Anastasia into his arms. She pauses next to me. "You make her pay for hurting my girls." It warms my heart knowing she's not just talking about Anastasia but about Tessa as well.

"She won't get away with it," I promise.

Ryker and Bradyn step out onto the porch first, each of them grabbing a hold of one of the men on the porch and dragging them into the house.

As soon as they're propped up against the wall feet away from each other, Bradyn and Ryker cross their arms and stand watch, Bravo sitting happily at his owner's feet. Sawyer steps out with my sister, my mom closing the door right behind them.

I turn toward Brenda. Jack and Weston have her seated in a chair. There is no emotion on her face. No anger, no fear—just an expressionless mask.

"Where is Tessa?" I ask, keeping my voice level. Interrogation happens to be a specialty of mine. Not because I go out of my way to cause pain but because I don't allow the subject to believe I won't.

Brenda knows my reputation, though. She knows my limits. Which means she knows what I'm willing and not willing to do for answers.

Fortunately, she also knows that Ryker has his own

reputation. And if need be, I'll pass it over to him.

"Where is she?" I ask again.

Brenda grins at me. "Do you know why I chose you?"

"I'm not interested in that."

"I chose you because of how predictable you are. It's sad, really. I can look at any situation and know exactly how you're going to behave. It's how I knew you'd leave Garrison here when you went to Savannah. How I knew you'd go to the basement, and how I knew you'd come back here after you survived."

With a grin of my own, I drag one of my mom's kitchen chairs over toward her, then slide it right in front of her. "That's all well and good. But you crossed into uncharted waters when you got Tessa involved."

"Me?" She rolls her eyes. "I wanted nothing to do with bringing that trash in."

I ignore the insult and focus only on getting answers. Brenda wants to rile me up, but it'll be too late for her when she realizes she won't. "Then how is she involved?"

"You've made a lot of enemies, Zane. People who want to see you hurt."

"Who?"

She grins at me, clearly thinking she's won. "You really haven't pieced any of it together, have you? What a shame. Either way, you won't make it in time. Tessa will be dead in five hours, and there's *nothing* you can do about it."

"Do you really think I don't already have a team headed straight for the Southeast Environmental Commission's building?" I ask with a laugh. It's a total bluff, but I'm running out of time.

The slight shift of Brenda's expression tells me everything I need to know.

"She's there." I shove the chair aside and push to my feet.

"Five hours is not a lot of time," Ryker comments.

"I'll call my team." Jack is already on the phone.

"You're going to fail," Brenda sneers. "You'll never make it in time."

"You made a mistake when you went after what was mine," I growl.

"I've been pulling your strings for longer than you can even imagine, Knox," she snaps back. "And when they find out what you did to me, you'll never see the sunlight again. I'll make sure of it."

"Murder, attempted murder, kidnapping, assault—I wouldn't count on it," Jack says. "Get a tactical team over to Southeast Environmental Commission. Tear that building apart brick by brick if you have to, but find Tessa Lane."

As soon as he hangs up, I turn to Bradyn. "Can we get there in time?" I ask, almost afraid to hear the answer.

"Pilot is fueled up and ready to go," he replies.

Brenda laughs. "You're going to be treated to one unforgettable show, Knox. I hope you enjoy it."

CHAPTER 30

TESSA

The man pacing back and forth in front of me might as well be a deranged animal. He stares at the door with such anger, such frustration, that I can feel it even as his gaze is trained away from me.

My mouth is still duct-taped, my hands tied to the chair. But it's not my bindings that have my heart racing or sweat beading along my skin.

It's the vest strapped with explosives, weighing heavily on my chest.

I'm afraid to so much as take a deep breath but can do nothing except sit here and pray.

Pray for God to forgive me.

For Him to be with me.

For Him to save me.

And if that's not His plan? I've made peace with it. But I do pray He saved Zane, Garrison, Weston, Ryker, and

Sawyer. That they're somehow not buried beneath tons of rubble or currently lying in a morgue.

"This is taking too long," the man growls, then reaches into his pocket to withdraw his cell phone. After tapping on the screen, the phone begins to ring. The ringing stops… and it's silence. "Where are you? You were supposed to be back over an hour ago. We need to get this moving."

"Brenda can't come to the phone right now," a deep voice says. My heart leaps in my chest as the recognition is instant. *Zane. He's alive!*

I try to make noises, but I don't risk moving out of fear it'll set off the bomb.

"Lieutenant Commander Zane Knox. Have to say, I expected you to sound a bit more muffled. Being buried under forty thousand tons of rubble and all that."

"I should have known you were behind this, Martin," he growls. "I'm honestly surprised to hear your voice, though. Since you should be living out the rest of your days in a windowless prison. Tell me, how's the shoulder?"

"A lot better than your girlfriend's is going to be when she's blown to smithereens."

Zane is quiet.

Tears stream down my cheeks.

"Let her go, and you'll walk away from this a free man. I'll see to it."

"Now that's quite a generous offer, Lieutenant Commander. Let me think on it. Ummm, no. Not interested."

"You're making a mistake," Zane snarls through the phone. I can picture his expression, the anger…and the fear. Emotions I know are mirrored on my own.

Still, I close my eyes. *Thank You, Lord. Thank You for saving him.*

"No. You made the mistake. You never should have gotten involved. All of this could have been over six months ago. But, no, Zane Knox had to ride in as the White Knight prepared to save the innocent damsel. It would have been one life, and now it'll be many. Their blood is on your hands. *Tessa's* blood is on your hands." He ends the call, then taps the screen again.

Seconds later, another voice comes on. "Markson."

"Watch the perimeter. Zane Knox knows where we are. Brenda has been compromised." The call ends, and he shoves his phone back into his pocket before turning toward me and withdrawing a knife. "Well, it looks like we're going to have an audience for this one." He grins, a sadistic smile that promises pain in the very near future. "It's go time, Tessa Lane. I am sorry that you were dragged into this, but there really was no other way. Someone had to wear the vest, and given who you are to him, I figured it might as well be you." He slices through my bindings, pockets the knife, then tugs me to my feet. I cry out, utterly terrified about what's coming.

Will Zane get here in time?

Or is this it?

God, please grant me strength. I know You have a plan,

even if I can't see it. But, God, I'm so scared. If this is it, if my time has come, I understand, but please don't let anyone else die.

The man Zane called Martin hauls me toward the door and pulls it open. Bright sunlight assaults my eyes, and I squint in an attempt to figure out where we are. Wind whips at my hair, and he pushes me forward. I stumble out, barely managing to right myself before falling forward.

"Steady feet, Tessa. You don't want to fall while you're wearing that." His tone is light, happy, and it reminds me all too well of my dad whenever he'd been about to do something terrible.

It's not anger that truly scares me anymore.

But this cool, detached attitude in the face of such evil? That's terrifying.

"Don't even think about running," he says, then shows me a black remote in his hand. "You make a single move that I don't approve and I'll blow it now. I've started over before, and I have no problem doing it again. There will be another chance to get this right. Another six months. A year. Five. One way or another, what must be done will be done."

I lower a hand near the clip on the side. Could I get it off fast enough?

"If you think about unclipping that, you should know it's pressure sensitive. You undo that and it's going to go off."

My heart sinks as all hope vanishes.

Lord, please be with me. I don't want to be alone.

"Brenda is missing out, but I'll make sure she hears all about it." He shoves me forward, guiding me around a vent pipe. My stomach turns into a pit when I see what's waiting for me on the other side. A thin, makeshift bridge that will take me over to the adjoining building…if I can move across it, four stories up.

Wind whips at my hair and dries the tears as they fall from my eyes.

"Your job is simple, Tessa. Walk across that bridge, and take the stairs down one floor. Then, it'll all be over. You can do that, right? It's so simple." He reaches up and rips the duct tape from my mouth. "You won't feel a thing."

Pain shoots through my face. "You're insane."

"No, sweetheart. I'm a visionary."

"Who's over there? Who are you trying to hurt?" *Stall, Tessa. Stall.*

"Do you really think I'm an idiot?" he questions. "Zane won't get here in time, if that's what you're thinking. And even if he does, my guys will terminate him before he so much as reaches for the door handle." He laughs. "He won't be here to save the day. Not this time."

"I wouldn't count on that." That wonderful, familiar, masculine voice is music to my ears. Martin turns, taking me with him. Zane, dressed in some sort of black tactical uniform, is standing just behind him, his gun aimed straight at Martin.

"Kill me and we all go boom," Martin says, holding up

the remote with one hand and banding the other around my waist, pressing me against his chest. "Take a step and we all go boom."

"You okay, Tessa?" Zane asks, but he doesn't take his gaze off Martin.

"I'm okay," I reply, voice quivering. "Garrison—"

"Don't worry about him right now, okay?" Zane says softly.

The ache in my heart spreads. Did he not make it?

"She won't have much of anything to worry about soon." Martin takes a step back, then freezes in place.

"I wouldn't move any farther if I were you." Weston's voice is familiar and a major relief.

And when I see Sawyer and Ryker both come into view behind Zane? Tears begin to flow. They're alive. They're okay.

Thank You, Lord.

The relief is so overwhelming I nearly sink to my knees. Would have if it weren't for Martin's hand gripping the back of my neck.

"It's getting a little crowded. Should I go ahead and make some space?" He raises the remote.

"It's over, Martin. The FBI has this building completely surrounded. They also managed to piece together the rest of your plan, thanks to one of Brenda's guards, who started singing like a canary the moment he was offered a deal. Fifteen minutes from the time he was asked to the time we knew everything. The conference next door has been evacuated. No one is over there."

"Is that so?" Martin growls.

"It is. So let Tessa go. The fight is between you and me, not her."

"You're wrong. It has everything to do with her because she's the easiest route to hurting you. Do you know how excited I was to stumble across her in that diner? It was truly an accident but such perfect timing. We needed a patsy, and what better than the daughter of a drunk? How angry she must be at the world." He leans in and presses his lips to my ear. "I recognized you instantly because Zane could never shut up about you. He flashed around a photograph like you were the sole reason he got up in the morning." He laughs. "Brenda hated the idea, but she'd already royally messed up in France when she couldn't keep you on a leash."

Zane takes a cautious step forward. "And what leash is that?"

Martin laughs. "What do you think this is? Some action movie where I tell you my entire plan? Nah. Because even though today failed, there's always tomorrow. I'm nothing if not patient." He shoves me forward, and Zane lunges to catch me.

My hands and knees scrape against the rooftop, but Zane is right there before my body hits the ground, his strong arms coming around me.

Weston, Ryker, and Sawyer all sprint past us, heading straight for Martin.

"Tessa. Are you okay?" Zane cups my cheeks with gentle hands, and I stare up into his eyes as my body begins to tremble.

"I am now."

A soft *beep* draws my attention from him to the countdown clock on my vest. "No, no, no! You have to go!" I shove myself backward and frantically move away from him.

Zane stares at me, his eyes wide. "Let me help! We need to get it off."

"We can't! He said it'll go off instantly if I take it off." I'm frantic as the numbers count down from two minutes. Two minutes. That's how long I have.

Martin laughs, and I turn to where Ryker has him pinned to the ground.

"Tell us how to diffuse it," Ryker orders, his large hand around the back of Martin's neck.

"Nope. I promised Zane a show. I intend to give him one even if it kills me, too."

"Get Garrison on the phone," Zane orders.

Sawyer rushes forward with a cell phone in hand.

"Garrison?" I ask. "He's alive?"

"He is." Zane moves in closer, but I take a step back.

"Go, Zane. Please. All of you have to go. Now."

"Tessa, you have to let me try," Zane pleads. "Please don't make me watch you die."

"If you come closer and it blows—"

"It won't."

"Show me the connections," Garrison says from the phone. Sawyer steps forward, but Zane takes the phone from his hand.

"You, Tank, and Cowboy get him downstairs to Jack."

"Cap—" Sawyer starts.

"Go," he orders. The strain in his voice tells me everything I need to know—we may not be walking away from this, and he won't let his team go down, too.

Because he won't let me die alone.

Sawyer clenches his jaw but offers a single nod to Zane, then a soft smile my direction. "We'll see you soon, Tessa."

"I know," I say despite the burning lump in my throat.

Ryker moves past me. "See you soon, Tessa," he says, mirroring what Sawyer said.

I pray he's right.

"I'm not going," Weston says.

"Please, go," Zane tells him. "Someone has to watch out for Anastasia, and if something happens, that's up to you, brother."

Weston's jaw clenches. He doesn't respond, just marches past us and heads for the exit.

Zane is already walking around me in slow circles, showing Garrison the vest currently counting down to my last breath.

"Lean in to the wire plate near the clock," Garrison says.

"Come on, Demo. Give me something, even if it's wrong—"

"It won't be. Okay. You know those compressed air cans I make you guys carry? Do you have one?"

"Yeah." Velcro tears as Zane reaches into a pouch on his tactical vest and withdraws a small aerosol can.

"Good. You need to locate the clips to rip that vest free the moment that clock freezes. They've buried the wires between her and the vest, so there's no way to diffuse it while it's on her."

"She said, if I take it off, it's going to detonate."

"It will. Which is where the can comes into play. You're only going to have seconds—fifteen max—to get it off of her. Toss it and run as fast as you can. The blast zone on that won't be large enough to take the building down completely, so if you can get far enough, you stand a chance at not being buried in the rubble of the top floor."

"Okay." Zane moves around me, his hands tracing the vest until he finds the buckles on either side of my waist. "Tessa, I need you to undo this one, okay? When I say go, unclip it."

"Zane," I choke out, tears blurring my vision.

"It's going to be okay. We have a future now, remember? Things to do." Tears shimmer in his eyes, too, and he leans in to press his lips to mine. The kiss is soft, gentle, a somber goodbye should this all go sideways.

Then he pulls back. Takes a deep breath.

"Ready?" he asks.

I nod.

Zane bows his head and closes his eyes. "Lord, please be with us. Please grant us more time. In Jesus' Mighty Name we pray, amen."

"Amen," I whisper.

Cold air hits the side of my neck.

"Go!" he orders.

I close my eyes tightly and unclip the vest. He rips it free from my head and flings it to the side. We sprint in the opposite direction, and Zane throws his body over mine as we dive behind an air conditioning unit.

The blast shakes the very air around us, and I scream when the rooftop caves in. Zane wraps an arm around my waist and pulls me against his body as we slide down into the darkness.

CHAPTER 31

ZANE

Standing on the other side of observation glass while Brenda sits just inside, her hands cuffed to the table, feels surreal. For six years, she's been the shadow living over my life. Ready to swoop in and remind me of my greatest failure, all in an effort to control me.

And now, she's headed to jail for a long, long time.

What this means for my team, I'm not sure, but I know that, no matter what it is, I can face it head-on with Tessa beside me.

I wrap an arm around her shoulders, and she leans against me.

After being treated for multiple cuts and scrapes, we'd received a police escort here to the Savannah FBI Field Office. Though we've yet to see Jack because, the moment we got here, we were ushered into this room and left staring at the woman who tried to kill the both of us and everyone we cared for.

According to the team member who cracked, she and Martin had been working together for a long time. The French diplomat's daughter was the first in a long string of coordinated attacks on members of an environmental agency trying to stop the destruction of protected land for the drilling of oil.

She and Martin worked with Karver and Alara Benson to open Southeast Environmental Commission, a front for their movements. After all, who's going to look at an environmental agency for terrorists pushing back against a movement they should have stood for?

Things went sideways, however, when the Bensons decided they didn't want any part in harming the daughter of the French diplomat who was spearheading the movement. A man who was in town for one day, attending a conference at the building right *beside* the Southeast Environmental Commission's building. An event that was moved because the original building went down due to what they're calling a gas explosion—with me and my team inside.

Tessa told us what Martin had told her. That she was merely an opportunity to get back at me. It boils my blood knowing how close she got to losing her life, all because Martin wanted vengeance against me.

Maybe I should have killed him six months ago when I had the chance. Except I couldn't have known this would happen, and if I had, I would have been taking a life just to take it.

"You okay?" I ask Tessa.

"I can't believe it's over. I mean, I'm so glad, but it feels like I'm sitting here, waiting for someone else to come after us."

I nod because that's a feeling I know quite well. "I'm sorry you got pulled into this."

"I'm not," she replies, tipping her face up to look at me. "Because it brought me back to you."

I grin, unable to help myself. "Maybe next time, you can just send me a postcard."

"There won't be a next time because I can't live a day without you, Zane Knox. And I hope you feel the same."

"More than." Warmth spreads through my chest as my heart practically grows three sizes just hearing her declaration. Before I can say anything else, though, the door opens, and a middle-aged man wearing a black suit and bold yellow tie strolls in, carrying a manila folder.

"Lieutenant Commander Knox. I have to say, it's quite a pleasure to meet you face-to-face. Though I am sorry it's under such vile circumstances." He offers his hand, so I take it.

"Not in the Navy anymore. Who are you?"

"Richard Caldwell," he says. "Brenda worked for me."

"So, you're the guy behind the strings."

He chuckles. "No, not quite. Brenda had an opinion all her own when it came to how things should be. We just hadn't realized how far she was willing to go to get things done."

"What does that mean?"

He offers me the folder he carried in. I open it and am greeted with images taken by drone on that day six years ago. The day that changed the entire course of my life and those of my team. "You should know that Brenda orchestrated that entire event. She fed information to the enemy in an attempt to get you right where she wanted you."

Rage burns hot and fast through me, and my hands tighten on the folder. "People died that day. Good people. Innocent people."

"I know. I was unaware of her involvement until only a few hours ago. Just as I was unaware of the arrangement she had for you. In our systems, you were listed as an independent contractor, but according to Jack Weathers, the arrangement was more forced than that. Is that true?"

"She told me prison was waiting if I didn't accept."

Anger flashes over Richard's face, and he crosses his arms. "That's not how we do business."

I lift the images and see a DD214 with my name on it. An official proof of the time I spent in the military.

Beneath it, there's also one for Weston, Ryker, Sawyer, and Garrison.

All with honorable discharge listed for each of us.

Emotion fills me because I never thought I'd see one of these. As far as Brenda was concerned, as far as she told me, at least, our records had been completely wiped. No mention of our service remaining.

"You and your men deserve honors for the work you've done over the last six years. And the time before that. You've saved countless lives. Unfortunately, since we technically don't exist—"

"Neither do we."

"You didn't. But you do now." He taps the folder. "I apologize for my negligence. Everything she did on our end was above board, but it seems there was a whole lot more than we ever knew."

"I—thank you."

"Of course. You are hereby relieved of duty, Lieutenant Commander Knox. You and your team can return home to your normal lives. Whatever that may look like."

"What will happen to Brenda?"

"She and Martin Shaw will be going away. You won't need to worry about them anymore. We also apprehended Cal Markson and a dozen others. None of them will see the light of day as free men again. You have my word."

"And the men who tried to kill Garrison Holt back in Stormwatch Landing?"

"Being interrogated as we speak. It's funny how much someone will talk when they know they're facing life in prison."

"It's really over?" Tessa questions.

Richard turns to her. "It is, Miss Lane. You should

know, we've wiped the records of your aliases. As far as the world knows, they never existed."

"No charges will be pressed for falsifying the records in the first place?" I ask. It's one of the things I've been worried about. While I may understand why Tessa changed her name, she did technically break the law.

"Not a single one. As far as the government is concerned, you have always been Tessa Lane." He smiles, then claps his hands together. "Okay, well, I need to get this show on the road. Take care, Lieutenant Commander. I hope you and your team can find some peace now." Richard shakes my hand, then Tessa's.

"Thank you, Mr. Caldwell."

"You're welcome," he replies. "Take care." With a final smile in our direction, he closes the door behind me.

"Zane, this is—what are you going to do now?" Tessa asks. "You have your freedom. Your chance at a normal life."

I stare down at the DD214s in my hand.

What *does* this mean? I always assumed I'd die before I got a taste of the freedom that comes from not having someone else call the shots.

So what will I do now?

I set the folder aside and slide one arm around Tessa's waist, then cup her cheek with the other as I draw her closer. "I know exactly what I'm going to do now."

"Oh? What's that?" she asks, tilting her face up to look at me.

When I stare into her dark brown eyes, I can see the future. Marriage. A home. Children. Laughter. Joy.

It's all right there—just within reach.

"Well, I have a wedding to get to, if the bride will have me."

Tessa's smile is blinding, and she winds both arms around my neck. "Is that a proposal, Zane?"

"Nah, I already proposed. That's my promise to you. Tessa Lane, I will love you until the very last breath in my chest. I will do what I can to make you the happiest woman in the world. God brought you back to me, and I don't plan to waste a single moment."

"Then this isn't me accepting your proposal—because I already did. I never stopped loving you, Zane. I've made a lot of mistakes, but you're the only one who's ever truly made me feel like I'm *not* those mistakes. Like I can be something more."

I lean down and capture her mouth with mine. The kiss is meant to seal a promise, but desire thrums in my veins as I hold her against me, tasting forever on her lips.

"Feel like sailing around the world with me?" I whisper against her mouth.

"I'll go anywhere with you, Zane. Until the last beat of my heart."

"Good. Then I have a plot of land to show you."

"What?" She pulls back and stares up at me.

"Didn't I tell you? I own an acre right on the water."

Her eyes fill with tears. "You do?"

"It was my wedding present to you. I bought it the week before we were supposed to get married."

"Zane—how?"

"I'll tell you everything, but right now, I want to get back home so I can marry you, Tessa. Whatever you want, I'll give it to you. But I don't want to wait to be your husband."

"I don't want to wait, either." She grips the front of my shirt and pulls me in to press her lips to mine. "Let's go home and see Pastor Reeves about a wedding."

Thank you so much for reading! I hope you enjoyed Zane & Tessa's story just as much as I enjoyed writing it. If you feel inclined to do so, please consider leaving a review! They help so much!

Turn the page for a brief look at SEAL of Bravery, the second book in the Iron Tide Brotherhood series!

Bonus Chapter:
SEAL of Bravery

Katelyn

By the time I've reached the last flight of stairs leading toward my apartment, the double shift I just pulled at the diner hits me like a tidal wave. My feet throb with every step, and I know they'll likely be swollen by the time I do manage to get my shoes off.

If only I could get away from my fear of elevators, then I could have saved myself a lot of pain. Unfortunately, that fear outweighs any desire I have to be off my feet right away. Besides, it only takes a few extra minutes to make the climb.

And, stairs are good for you, right? Isn't that what the experts say?

My final text from Thomas came in two hours ago, so I know he's already home and in bed, sleeping in preparation for school tomorrow. Though, I suspect he made it a point to be in bed before I got home to avoid the conversation we are absolutely going to have about his struggling grades.

Stormwatch Landing was supposed to be a fresh start for us. In a lot of ways it has been. But moving constantly has caught up to my boy and his grades are suffering for it.

No more. It's the promise I made to myself when we moved to this small South Carolina town. We will be here until he graduates—no matter what.

I sigh as I step onto my floor, then head down. Unease trickles up my spine when I notice the door to my neighbor's apartment cracked open. He seems like a kind man, though I don't have much to go off of since we've only shared a wave here and there.

Mainly because whenever I see him, my entire nervous system goes into straight overdrive. The guy is attractive with a capital "A". As in, should be on the cover of every magazine everywhere.

Given my luck with handsome men I've done everything I can to avoid him. Including hiding out whenever I hear his door open or close. Even if I'm already on my way out. Because in my experience, they have heavy hands and very little internal substance. Thomas's father ensured I understood that.

Still…why is his door open? I cautiously approach, trying to look through the crack in the door without actually peering inside.

And then a knocked over teacup catches my attention. I move in a bit closer, and my gaze lands on what I can see of a Bible laying open, halfway dangling off the coffee table as though it had been tossed there.

More unease slices through me and I know without a doubt, *something* is wrong.

"Hello?" I ask as I knock on the ajar door. "Are you—" The door swings open, revealing a battlefield inside.

Adrenaline surges through my system as I race inside, looking for my neighbor. What if he's hurt?

What if the person who made this mess is still here?

I pause long enough to withdraw my phone and preemptively dial 9-1, just in case. "Hello?" I move further into his living room, then come around to the side of the couch. As I turn toward the hallway, and spot the bare-chested man face-down in a pool of his own blood, that adrenaline kicks into overdrive.

Right behind my neighbor is a man in a mask, the only thing visible are his yes, frozen open and staring at the ceiling.

My stomach twists and panic pulses through me as I fall to my knees beside my neighbor, while dialing the last 1 and hitting call. I put it on speaker and set it on the floor next to me as the nurse I've tried so hard to bury surfaces.

"9-1-1 what's your emergency?"

"My neighbor has been attacked. Male, mid-thirties," I trail off as I feel for a pulse, then breathe a sigh of relief when I feel the faint thump against my fingers. "Faint pulse, thank God."

"What is your location?"

I rattle off my address. "I'm going to roll him over to see where the blood is coming from." Both of my hands are already slick with his blood as I slide them beneath his muscled chest and waist. With great effort, I manage to roll him over.

It takes me all of a heartbeat to find his injury. A massive, jagged wound is in his side, and the blood has begin to slow, which means he doesn't have long.

"Nasty stab wound," I tell the dispatcher.

"We have help on the way."

"Thanks." I rip the sweater over my head and press it to his side, then glance over at the other man. "There's another man here, but—" Maintaining pressure with one hand, I reach over and feel for a pulse on the other man.

There is none.

"The other man is dead."

"There's another man?"

I nod, then realize she can't actually see me. "He's wearing a mask. I just found them this way. My neighbor is breathing, but—" I scream when a large hand grips my wrist. My gaze locks on my neighbor's, his dark eyes wide and pleading.

"Help. Her," he chokes out.

I scan the room. "I don't see anyone else. I can't leave you to look or you'll bleed out. Help is coming, okay?"

Her. Who is her?

His eyes roll back in his head and I press firmly onto his injury as the blood continues to pound in my ears.

"No, stay with me. Are you there?" I try to wake him, but his head lolls to the side.

"Ma'am, are you still there?" the dispatcher asks.

"Yes, sorry. I'm here." My throat tightens. Is there someone else here? Someone else who needs help?

"Did I hear that right, is there someone else there?"

"I don't see anyone else," I say. "And I don't want to risk leaving him to check. He's going to die if I release pressure." Tears swim in my eyes. *Please don't die.* There's so much blood.

So. Much. Blood.

Panic begins to push through my rational mind and even though I know I'm safe, my body's fight or flight kicks into gear and I want to run away.

Far and fast.

"Stay right there. Help is on the way."

"Okay. Please hurry."

My gaze drops to where his hand has gone limp on my wrist. His chest is slick with his own blood, and it saturates the diner uniform I'm wearing, staining the rust-colored skirt a shade darker.

Those eyes flutter open again, but they're glazed over and staring straight up at me as though he can't really see me.

"I'm here," I tell him. "You're going to be okay." *Please be okay.*

"I—" he starts, but his eyes roll back into his head and he falls silent again.

"Stay with me, okay?" I say again. "Please stay with me."

But he doesn't stir again. In the distance, sirens grow closer, but his breathing grows more shallow.

Because I don't know what else to do, and he'll need a miracle to survive, I lower my head and pray, even though I can't remember the last time I talked to the Lord.

"Our Father, who art in Heaven, Hallowed be Thy name."

Pre-order SEAL of Bravery today and get ready for another thrilling adventure featuring your favorite SEALs.

Did you know? If you pre-order directly from my site you save a few bucks AND get to read every new release early? Check it out at https://jessicaashleybooks.com/

**Demolition is his specialty. But nothing prepared him
for the single mom next door.**

Former Navy SEAL Garrison "Demo" Holt came to South
Carolina to rebuild his life after his military career went up
in smoke. Now, as a counselor for troubled teens, his
mission is to guide the next generation out of chaos and
into the light.

Katelyn Ellis has one goal: to keep her son safe. That
means staying off the radar and far away from the man who
vowed to take him from her. The last thing she needs is her
protective, former military neighbor stepping into the line
of fire.

But when Garrison reaches her son in ways no one else can, Katelyn's walls start to crumble. And when a fierce coastal storm knocks out the power and shatters her apartment windows, she has no choice but to accept Garrison's offer to stay close—just until the danger passes.

Only the storm isn't the worst of it. Her enemy has found them. And the only thing standing between Katelyn and deadly revenge is the one man she swore she wouldn't trust with her heart.

A swoony small town romantic suspense with a protective hero, a mother willing to risk it all for her son, and an epic story of faith in the fire.

Continue the Iron Tide Brotherhood series with SEAL of Bravery today!

About the Author

Jessica Ashley started her career in 2016 writing romance novels for the secular world, before feeling the Lord pulling her in a different direction.

She is now a three-time award winning author of Christian romance, and has published nearly twenty novels and novellas since 2024.

She is an Army veteran, who resides in New Hampshire with her husband and their three children.

You can find out more about her and her books by joining her newsletter via her website: https://jessicaashley books.com/ or by joining her Facebook group, Romance, Redemption, & Rescue: Jessica Ashley Books.

Member of the ACFW.

Awards won:

- *First-place in the Romantic Suspense category of the Firebird Q1 2025 Book Awards. (Pages of Promise)*
- *Readers' Favorite Gold Medal Winner for excellence in writing. (Bravo)*
- *Literary Titan Gold Book Award Winner. (Echo)*

<u>Coastal Hope Series</u>

Pages of Promise: Lance Knight

Searching for Peace: Elijah Pierce

Second Chance Serenity: Michael Anderson

Tactical Revival: Jaxson Payne

Perilous Healing: Silas Williamson

<u>Coastal Hope Short Novels</u> (*Website Exclusives*)

Badge of Hope: Alaric Simmons

<u>Coastal Hope Novellas</u> (*Website Exclusives*)

Pictures of Hope (*Coastal Hope Prequel Novella*): Alex & Lilly

A Coastal Holiday Short: Caleb & Carmen

A Coastal Valentines: Lance & Eliza

A Coastal St. Patrick's Day: Elijah & Andie

A Coastal Easter: Michael & Reyna

A Coastal Thanksgiving: Jaxson & Margot

A Coastal Christmas: Silas & Bianca

<u>The Hunt Brothers Search & Rescue</u>

Bravo: Bradyn Hunt

Echo: Elliot Hunt

Romeo: Riley Hunt

Tango: Tucker Hunt

Delta: Dylan Hunt

<u>Hunt Brothers Short Novels</u> *(Website Exclusives)*

Lima: Lani Hunt

<u>Hunt Brothers Holiday Novellas</u> *(Website Exclusives)*

A Hunt Brothers Valentines: Bradyn & Kennedy

A Hunt Brothers St. Patrick's Day: Elliot & Nova

A Hunt Brothers Easter: Riley & Jules

A Hunt Brothers Thanksgiving: Tucker & Alice

A Hunt Brothers Christmas: Dylan & Emma

<u>Iron Tide Brotherhood</u>

SEAL of Honor: Zane Knox

SEAL of Bravery: Garrison Holt

<u>Other Standalone Novels</u>

Critical Velocity: Beckett Wallace